AETHER

By

Jodi Dougherty

We dance round in a ring and suppose,

But the secret sits in the middle and knows.

~ Robert Frost

Dedication

I dedicate this book to my three grown children, Jory, Kylee, and Zachary, and all the children young and old that are growing up in a world at this time. The earth is shifting. Is the end near?

Acknowledgment
AETHER:

2. Metaphysical and Esoteric Meaning

In spiritual, occult, and metaphysical systems, *Aether* (or *Akasha*) is still used to describe a universal life force or subtle energy field that permeates all existence.

- In Hermeticism and alchemy, Aether is the quintessence — the divine essence or the "breath" of the cosmos.
- In Hindu and Vedic philosophy, *Akasha* means "ether" or "space," the substrate of vibration — the medium through which sound and energy manifest.
- In modern metaphysical thought, "Aether energy" is often equated with zero-point energy, chi, prana, or the quantum field — a source of infinite potential energy and consciousness that interconnects all things.

Definition (esoteric):

Aether energy is the subtle, universal life force that permeates and connects all matter, energy, and consciousness — the foundation of existence and creation.

About the Author

Jodi Dougherty grew up in the Pacific Northwest. She is an artist and loves to oil paint. She relocated to Texas in 1998 and spent time in the Army Active Duty out of Fort Hood, Texas. She loves her horses, dogs, cat, and family.

Table of Contents

AETHER - Part 1
Autumn of 2026

Chapter 1: The Oval Office Briefing

Rain lashed against the windows of the Oval Office, a steady percussion that muffled the world outside. Inside, the glow of muted desk lamps painted long shadows across the carpet, wrapping the room in a somber haze. President Mark Johnson sat at the Resolute Desk, his fingertips pressed together in a gesture of forced calm. Across from him, General Nathan Harris, crisp in his uniform, stood like a sentinel. To his right, CIA Director Evelyn Shaw leaned forward in her chair, her sharp eyes fixed on the man at the center of the room—a man who had been a ghost for years.

Dr. Kyle Green looked nothing like a ghost now. His silver hair was slicked back, his lined face haggard but defiant. A battered leather satchel rested at his feet, bulging with papers, photos, and data drives. For decades, he'd been a whisper in hallways and classified files. Tonight, he was here, alive, and prepared to burn the world down with what he knew.

President Johnson broke the silence.

"Doctor Green, I trust you understand the gravity of speaking in this room."

Kyle gave a humorless smile. "Mr. President, the gravity of this goes far beyond this room. Beyond this planet."

Evelyn Shaw glanced at Harris, then back to Kyle. "You know we're already aware of the alien presence. We have treaties with the Thal'kari, the Serians, the Greys, and—"

Kyle raised a hand, cutting her off. "You're aware of the official presence. What you're not aware of—what none of you were ever meant to know—is the Dark Dominion."

The name settled over the room like a falling blade. Harris's jaw tensed. "We've heard rumors of a rogue faction."

Kyle reached into his satchel and pulled out a stack of folders, sliding them on the table. "Rumors don't explain thirty years of siphoned black funds, unmarked craft, and dead whistleblowers." He slid the top file toward the President. "This is the truth. For decades, the Dark Dominion has operated as a splinter of your own intelligence community—born from the CIA after the National Security Act of 1947. It started small, under President James Thomas, but by the 1960s, even he realized the monster he'd created. It's been growing unchecked ever since."

Johnson opened the file, scanning names and photographs—men and women who had either vanished or been found dead in improbable "accidents." Inventors who'd been days from patenting water-powered vehicles, scientists with blueprints for free energy, biologists with data on plant-based cancer cures—all gone. Their breakthroughs were erased. Their lives are reduced to footnotes.

Evelyn's voice was tight. "We've always suspected suppression of technology, but this… this is on a scale I can't—"

Kyle's hand slammed the table. "They're not just suppressing tech. They're weaponizing it. They've been shooting down alien craft—your allies' craft—reverse engineering their technology in secret facilities scattered across the country. For years, they've been capturing, torturing, and interrogating extraterrestrials. I've interviewed military police who guarded these facilities. I've seen photos of autopsies. They've broken treaties you didn't even know existed."

The General's face darkened. "That would explain the disappearances of some Serian envoys. We were told they'd gone into voluntary seclusion."

"They didn't," Kyle snapped. "They were abducted. Vivisected. Their memories ripped out with machines reverse-engineered from their own ships. And now, the alien factions you think are your partners? They're furious. Outraged. They're demanding reparations—and revenge."

President Johnson's hands tightened around the folder. "And if what you're saying is true, they'll hold us responsible."

"They already do," Kyle said grimly. "They don't distinguish between your government and the Dominion. You've got factions out there who see you as liars, as butchers." He leaned closer, voice dropping to a near whisper. "They warned us back in the 1940s, after Hiroshima and Nagasaki. Nuclear weapons weren't just dangerous to this planet—they sent ripples through the fabric of the cosmos. They made Earth a cosmic liability. The aliens came here not to invade, but to contain, to inform. They tried to stop the madness. But the Dominion saw only an opportunity to dominate the planet and stars."

Evelyn Shaw's mind raced. "You're saying this shadow government wants a one-world order?"

"They already have the beginnings of it," Kyle said. "Advanced propulsion. Energy devices that could make oil obsolete overnight. Biological technologies that could extend human life by decades. They're sitting on all of it while the world burns. They have established banks in almost every country in the world. And their plan…" He hesitated. "…their plan is almost complete."

The President rose, his voice low but shaking. "What plan?"

Kyle exhaled, his face pale under the dim lights. "A coordinated event. Something that will force the alien factions' hand. They're engineering a crisis designed to unify humanity under their control—and to justify a war with beings far more advanced than we are."

Thunder cracked outside, rattling the windows. The room seemed to shrink around them.

General Harris spoke first. "If what you're saying is true, we're on the brink of annihilation."

"No," Kyle said. "You're on the brink of something worse. A war you can't win, fought in the shadows, with weapons you can't even comprehend. And the Dominion—"

He stopped. His eyes darted to the ceiling corners. He reached into his pocket, pulled out a small device, and flicked it on. The tiny LED lit up. "Damn it," he muttered. "We're already compromised." They must have bugged the office.

President Johnson's voice was a low growl. "What do you mean?"

Kyle's eyes met his. "I mean, they know I'm here."

The Oval Office lights flickered once. Then again. Outside, the rain abruptly stopped, the silence oppressive. Evelyn felt the hairs rise on her arms.

The room went dark.

From somewhere deep below the White House, a tremor rolled up through the floor—subtle, like a heartbeat.

Kyle whispered, "It's started."

Chapter 2: The Weight of Silence

The lights sputtered once more before stabilizing, the low hum of the backup generators filling the Oval Office with a dull, uneasy thrum. Secret Service moved briskly in the Oval Office and through the corridors, looking for any bugs hidden, their earpieces alive with clipped chatter. Technicians barked orders down the hall. Yet for all the bustle, the President moved alone.

Mark Johnson dismissed his staff with a weary wave, his face betraying the strain of the evening. He climbed the private staircase to the residence, each step heavier than the last, until at last he pushed open the door to his suite.

The room greeted him in silence. Only the soft purring of his wife's snores drifted across the dim space, a gentle rhythm beneath the storm of his thoughts. He paused at the foot of the bed, staring at her. Margaret, who had borne the years of political life with quiet dignity, now slept peacefully, untouched by the shadows clawing at his mind.

He envied her.

Sliding carefully into bed, he let his head sink against the pillow, but his eyes refused to close. His mind replayed Kyle Green's words again and again, each detail like a splinter he couldn't pull free.

The Dark Dominion. Torture chambers. Stolen technology. Alien lives destroyed in the name of what, control?

Mark drew a slow breath, staring at the ceiling. The truth pressed against his chest like a weight, and for the first time in years, he felt not the authority of office but the frailty of age. His term was nearly finished. A year left, perhaps less, before the American people chose another to bear this mantle. He had long dreamed of laying down the burden gracefully, retiring into anonymity, slipping quietly into the background of history.

But history, it seemed, would not let him go.

His thoughts wandered to the treaties he had signed, the faces he had met—human and alien alike. The Thal'kari, with their stoic patience and eyes like pools of liquid silver. The Serians, tall and reed-like, voices trembling with an otherworldly resonance. The Orash, who spoke in patterns of light and sound, leaving human interpreters dizzy but awestruck. Each encounter had been shrouded in secrecy, hidden from the public eye, protected by a web of deniability.

And yet… How much longer could it be hidden?

He imagined the day of disclosure, when the world would see its neighbors not as myths or shadows, but as allies—or threats. Would humanity rejoice? Unite? Or would fear consume them, as it always had?

He thought of the church bells that would ring, the city emergency sirens going off, the protests that would ignite, the leaders who would posture, the people who would panic. He thought of children, staring up at the night sky, no longer wondering if they were alone but fearing what else was out there.

The responsibility was crushing. And it rested solely on him.

Mark rubbed his eyes, feeling the years etched into the lines of his face. He was tired—not just in body, but in soul. He wanted to believe the world was ready for truth, but even he wasn't sure. Humanity's history with fear was long and bloody. The Dominion was proof of that, twisting secrecy into empire, progress into chains.

He turned his head, watching Margaret stir slightly, murmuring in her sleep. Her hand brushed against his, warm and grounding. He squeezed it gently, his chest aching with affection. He was grateful she would never know the full scope of what weighed upon him.

But in the quiet of that bedroom, beneath the steady rhythm of her breath, the President of the United States felt profoundly alone.

He closed his eyes at last, exhaustion pulling him toward sleep. His thoughts drifted like fragments of smoke:

—treaties yet fragile,

—alien eyes full of expectation,

—a world on the brink of truth,

—and the shadow of the Dominion lurking in the dark.

As he surrendered to slumber, one final thought lingered, heavy and unshakable:

Perhaps the greatest burden a leader could bear was not the power of secrets, but the moment of revealing them.

And with that, President Mark Johnson, compassionate and weary, slipped into uneasy dreams.

Chapter 3: Glass Walls

The black sedan slid silently through the wet streets of Washington, D.C., its tinted windows reflecting the neon glow of a city that never truly slept. CIA Director Evelyn Shaw sat in the back seat, her gaze fixed on the blurred lights streaming past. Her driver said nothing—he never did—and she was grateful for the silence.

Her mind, however, was anything but quiet.

The words Dark Dominion still echoed in her head. A rogue faction of the Agency. She'd heard the whispers for years—half-joking tales in the corridors, drunken speculation at private dinners, the occasional online conspiracy thread lost in the noise of disinformation. She'd dismissed it all as paranoia, as the inevitable folklore of an organization built on secrets. The CIA had always thrived in shadows, and where there were shadows, myths followed.

But tonight the myth had taken shape. Flesh and bone. Documents and testimonies. The Dominion was real.

Evelyn closed her eyes briefly, exhaustion pressing against her temples. She had spent her entire life in the orbit of politics, raised in a home where dinner conversations revolved around policy, scandal, and compromise. Her parents had been consummate operators—her father in the Senate, her mother as a strategist for campaigns that shaped the country. She'd grown up understanding not just the mechanics of government but the machinery behind it: the smokescreens, the diversions, the deliberate misinformation sold to the public like carnival tricks.

Now, sitting at the pinnacle of American intelligence, she saw the same games playing out on a global scale. News networks are playing at journalism while dancing to the tune of their corporate backers. Social platforms are drowning truth beneath a tide of outrage and distraction. The public glued to their screens, entertained into submission, blind to what lurked in the margins.

And somewhere within that fog of chaos, a hidden hand was pulling the strings.

The car turned into her neighborhood, where manicured hedges and polished brownstones stood as monuments to wealth and order. But even here, Evelyn felt no safety. No escape. Only the quiet knowledge that the world was sliding toward an ominous precipice, and she was suddenly one of the few who could see the edge.

The car eased to a stop outside her townhouse. She gave her driver a quick nod of thanks and stepped out into the night air. The silence of the street was almost jarring after the storm of her thoughts. She climbed the steps to her door, unlocked it, and was immediately greeted by the soft padding of paws.

Her cats—two rescues, sleek and spoiled—twined around her ankles, their eyes glinting in the hallway light. Evelyn bent to scratch behind their ears, a faint smile breaking through the mask she wore all day. At least they were simple. Honest. They wanted nothing but her presence.

Inside, she shed the armor of her office: heels kicked off by the door, blazer draped over a chair, hair loosened from its severe knot. She padded into the kitchen, poured herself a glass of wine, and finally allowed her shoulders to sink. The weight she carried was immense, crushing. But for tonight, she would set it aside.

She curled into her couch, her cats nestled against her, and let the glow of her phone fill the room. With a swipe, she vanished into the endless scroll of TikTok—clips of dancing teenagers, absurd pranks, half-baked political rants. Noise, pure and numbing. For a little while, it was enough. For a little while, she could let the Dominion, the treaties, the lies, and the impending storm slip from her mind.

Her chest ached with guilt for needing the escape, but she couldn't care tonight. She was too tired, too heavy with truths she couldn't yet share. Tomorrow, she will begin. She would build a plan, something she could take to General Harris and the President. A roadmap out of this darkness.

But tonight, Evelyn Shaw—Director of the CIA, servant of her country, guardian of secrets too large to comprehend—was just a woman on a couch with a glass of wine, two cats, and a desperate need to forget.

And somehow, that made her seem all the more human

Chapter 4: The Burden of Command

The convoy of black SUVs cut through the night, headlights carving narrow paths across the wet streets of Washington. At the center vehicle sat General Nathan Harris, broad-shouldered and stone-faced, his uniform immaculate despite the late hour. The silence in the car was thick, save for the faint crackle of the radio.

To most, Harris was a fortress of a man—the President's Chairman of the Joint Chiefs of Staff, principal military advisor to the Commander-in-Chief, the Secretary of Defense, and the National Security Council. Senior-most officer in the United States Armed Forces. A man who carried authority like armor, his very presence commanding respect in any room he entered.

But tonight, even a fortress felt the weight of its stones.

He leaned back against the leather seat, his gaze fixed on the streaks of water racing down the tinted window. Kyle Green's revelations had churned up memories Harris had buried long ago—treaties inked in quiet chambers with alien envoys, cautious handshakes with beings who didn't even have hands, promises of coexistence forged under the constant threat of misunderstanding. He had stood there at those tables, watching worlds collide in silence, bearing witness to history no one else would ever know.

And now he wondered if it had all been for nothing.

Harris's thoughts drifted, unbidden, to his family. Born the eldest of four sons, he had always carried the role of protector. His father, a general before him, had filled their home with the discipline of duty and the quiet honor of service. The old man had lived long enough to retire with dignity, and then slipped away in his sleep—an end Harris still considered merciful and dignified.

His mother, fragile now, resided in a nursing home across the Potomac. Harris made time, no matter what his schedule, to visit her weekly. Sometimes she remembered him. Sometimes she didn't. He went anyway.

His brothers' paths had diverged like rivers. One had joined the Coast Guard, though they had never been close. Another, a Marine, had left part of himself in Iraq when mortar rounds ripped through his unit. Harris still remembered the hospital smell, the hollow look in his brother's eyes as he returned home without a leg, forced into a life of paperwork and disability checks while his wife carried the weight as an accountant. The youngest, the baby of the family, had gone west—Silicon Valley, game design, a world Harris could hardly comprehend. He had a wife, kids, a life defined by code and color rather than grit and steel.

Harris rarely called them. Rarely wrote. He had chosen his country over his family, the oath over the blood. He told himself it was necessary that his duty had to come first. But sometimes, in the long silence of nights like these, he wondered what his father would have thought of that choice.

The motorcade pulled into his driveway, a stately home that stood in quiet defiance of the chaos he carried with him. He dismissed his aides, stepping inside alone. The house was silent, ordered, and lonely.

In his study, Harris removed his jacket and hung it with precision. Then he spread blueprints across the wide oak desk—maps of facilities, theoretical structures, alien technology sketches filed under clearance levels that hardly anyone alive could access. He began drafting outlines in his steady hand: contingency plans, defensive strategies, top special ops teams, frameworks for diplomatic outreach. If there was to be a reckoning with the Dominion, with the aliens, with all of it—he would be ready. He owed his President that. He owed his country that.

The hours bled away, the night deepening outside his window. Harris paused only once, standing at the glass, staring at the Capitol dome glowing faintly in the distance. He thought of all it symbolized: freedom, sacrifice, the messy miracle of democracy. He loved this country—its people, its diversity, its stubbornness, its dreams. And if the burden of protecting it fell heaviest on his shoulders, then so be it.

He was General Nathan Harris. Soldier. Advisor. Protector.

And in the quiet of his study, as dawn's first light began to creep over the horizon, he steeled himself for the meeting that would come with morning—where he, Evelyn Shaw, and President Johnson would chart a course through shadows most Americans would never even know existed.

He did not complain. He did not falter. He bore the weight as he always had.

For his country.

For all of them.

Chapter 5: Home Fires

The C-17's engines droned steadily, a sound both comforting and relentless. Captain Daniel Rourke sat rigid in his webbed seat, hands folded around a worn photograph as the transport carved across the Atlantic night. His gear was packed neatly at his feet, every strap cinched, every buckle polished. Habit. Ritual. The discipline of a soldier. But no order, no uniform, could quiet the ache in his chest.

They'd lost Ramirez two nights ago—an ambush outside Fallujah, the kind that tore a life apart in seconds. Gunfire. Smoke. Silence. Daniel could still hear Ramirez's laugh from that morning, teasing about their homecomings, about Emily, Daniel's daughter, whom he hadn't seen since she'd learned to walk. Now Ramirez's voice was gone, his coffin riding a separate plane draped in the flag they'd both sworn to serve.

Daniel clenched his jaw, staring at the photograph in his hand. Claire stood in the sunlight, auburn hair gleaming, Emily balanced on her hip with a toothy grin. They were smiling as though the world were whole and safe. That picture had lived in his pocket every day of the past year, worn soft at the edges, its colors fading but its tether unbreakable. It had pulled him through sandstorms, firefights, and endless nights under alien skies.

The plane jolted as it descended. Daniel slid the photo carefully back into his pocket and straightened. His heart ached, but one truth burned steadily: he was going home.

The autumn air at Pope Army Airfield was crisp, carrying the scent of damp leaves. Buses rolled into the parking lot where families clustered, waving flags and holding hand-painted signs. The air vibrated with cheers, shouts, and sobs of joy.

Daniel scanned the crowd, his pulse hammering until he saw them. Claire, her auburn hair pulled back, eyes shining with tears she didn't bother to hide. Beside her stood Emily, clutching a poster nearly as big as she was: Welcome Home, Daddy.

The duffel slipped from Daniel's hand. For a moment, he simply froze, letting the sight crash over him like a wave. A year of sand and fire collapsed into this single breath of time.

Emily's small legs churned furiously as she bolted toward him, the sign fluttering to the ground. Daniel dropped to one knee, arms open, and when she collided with him, he swept her up, clutching her against his chest. Her giggles and tears soaked into his uniform as he buried his face in her hair, breathing her in like oxygen.

Claire was next. They collided in an embrace that said everything words could not. She held him fiercely, as if afraid letting go would make him vanish again. He tangled a hand in her hair, pressed his face into her neck, and for the first time in months, he inhaled the scent of home.

"God, Claire…" His voice cracked, and he didn't care.

"You're here," she whispered against his ear, clinging tighter. "You're really here."

That night, after Emily had fallen asleep curled around the stuffed bear Daniel had carried across the desert for her, Daniel and Claire sat on the back porch. The quiet of suburbia was startling—just the whisper of leaves in the wind, the distant hum of a car. No mortars, no radio chatter, no orders barked in the dark. Just peace.

Claire slipped her hand into his, her thumb brushing across the calluses there. "You're here, but… not all the way here, are you?"

Daniel stared at the horizon. "I'm happy. Happier than I can explain. Holding you both again, seeing Emily's smile—that's what kept me breathing." His throat tightened. "But Ramirez… I can't come back without him."

Claire's face softened, grief flickering in her eyes. "I've been talking with Maria," she said quietly. "Almost every day since the call came. She's shattered, Danny. But she's acting strong for the kids. Stronger than she knows."

The mention of Ramirez's widow pierced him. Claire and Maria had become close over the years, supporting each other through deployments, raising kids on parallel tracks of waiting and worry. That bond now carried the weight of loss neither of them had wanted to face.

"I'll go with you," Daniel said firmly, though the words scraped his throat. "When you see her next. I need to."

Claire nodded. "She'd want that. She told me once she trusted you with his life. And I think, deep down, she knows you did everything you could."

Daniel swallowed hard, fighting the guilt clawing at him. "He was family to me, Claire. More than a brother. And I keep replaying it—what I could've done differently, what I should've seen—"

She caught his chin, forcing him to meet her eyes. Eyes that had waited through nights of silence, through birthdays missed, through wars fought from afar. Eyes that had never once let him forget where home was.

"You can't carry all of it," she said, voice firm. "Not alone. You share it—with me, with Emily, with Maria. That's how you come home, Danny. Not by burying it, but by letting us carry it too."

The words broke something loose in him. He pulled her against his chest, his hand pressing to her back, breathing her in as though anchoring himself. She had always been his strength, even when oceans separated them. And now, here, she was his way back.

In the quiet, Daniel felt the heaviness shift. Not vanish—never vanish—but soften, shared across shoulders willing to bear it. His grief for Ramirez would never leave him. But it would shape him, sharpen his resolve.

Because as he held Claire, as Emily stirred softly inside, Daniel knew the truth that burned brighter than his guilt:

He would protect them. Whatever it costs.

His family. His country. Both were worth every sacrifice he had left to give.

Above them, the stars glittered in silence, the same stars Ramirez would never see again. Daniel lifted his gaze and swore, silently, fiercely, that his friend's death would not be meaningless. Not while he still drew breath.

Chapter 6: Under the Watching Stars

Seattle smelled of salt, pine, and evergreens after a rain, a scent that always reminded Sarah Mitchell why she'd chosen to build her life here. The mornings were cool and soft, mist rising off the Puget Sound, dark green evergreens climbing the horizon. On mornings like this, when her shift at the Pacific Northwest research center for infectious disease started later, she and her husband, Tom, lingered over coffee at their small wooden kitchen table, windows cracked open to let in the damp air.

Tom sat across from her in a faded gray T-shirt, hair still damp from a shower, hands large, calloused, steady, wrapped around a steaming mug. He was handsome in a way that age had deepened, not diminished. Lines etched by deployments and hardship only made his smile warmer, his presence more grounding. Sarah loved that smile, fiercely, knowing the battles he carried—and that he always carried them home to her.

Their daughter, Megan, was off at Washington State University, a freshman diving headfirst into biology on a scholarship she'd earned, winning science fairs at a younger age than the other participants, and graduating high school two years early. The house was quieter without her laughter, but Sarah and Tom had carved a new rhythm, a life measured not by distance or deployments, but by the unwavering thread of love that tied them together.

This morning, however, the quiet carried tension. Tom slid a crisp white envelope across the table, stark against the warm wood. Sarah didn't need to open it; she'd seen enough orders in her years as a military wife to know the weight it carried.

"Orders?" she asked softly.

He nodded, expression unreadable. "Fort Bragg. Full-time. A new special forces detachment. One of their medics was killed in combat three months ago. They need someone to step in."

Sarah traced the rim of her coffee cup, holding herself steady. "So it begins again."

Tom reached across the table, covering her hand with his. "I'll still be here whenever I can, Sarah. I can't ask you to move, to start over again. I know your career is hard-won."

She looked at him, the man she had fallen for on a trail beneath Mount Rainier years ago, whose love had endured sand, sweat, and distance. "I would follow you to the moon and back," she said, her voice steady but her chest tight. "But when you're gone… I'm always on edge, waiting for you to come home safely."

"Different dangers," he replied, softly, understanding. "But we'll face them together."

She let out a small, tremulous laugh, leaning into his shoulder. "Still in love after all these years, huh?"

"Still in love," he murmured, pressing his lips to her hair. "Always. And it's the only reason I make it back to you."

Later that afternoon, Sarah watched Tom stacking firewood, his movements efficient but measured. He paused occasionally, scanning the horizon as if anticipating threats before they arrived—a soldier's instinct etched deep. When he came back inside, a wet cedar scent clinging to him, he wrapped his arms around her waist and pressed her to his chest.

For a moment, Sarah let herself melt into him, memorizing the weight of his arms, the solidity of his chest, the reassurance of a love that had endured every test. This love, built through deployments, fear, and long nights alone, had grown into something unshakable, something eternal.

They shared a bond that could weather any storm: deployments, danger, uncertainty, even loss. They had grieved for fallen friends together, supported the widows and children left behind, and never let distance or duty weaken their devotion. This love was more than affection—it was a commitment, forged by hardship and reinforced daily, quiet but unbreakable.

Two days later, after rain gave way to crisp autumn air, they embarked on one last camping trip before Tom's departure. The ritual—tent, stove, sleeping bags—was sacred, a tether to a life not defined by orders or missions. Hiking beneath cathedral-like trees, shafts of sunlight slicing through the canopy, Sarah felt the world shrink to the space between them.

By midday, at their favorite spot near a creek, they prepared coffee over a fire, mugs warming their hands. Sarah leaned into Tom's shoulder, feeling the rhythm of his heartbeat beneath her ear, a rhythm that had always brought her home.

"Remember when Megan insisted on carrying her own pack?" Sarah murmured, smiling faintly.

Tom chuckled. "She made it about a quarter-mile before you carried both."

"She has always been so tough," Sarah said softly. "I still wish she were here now."

"She'll come next time," Tom said, though both knew the next trip might be delayed by duty.

As evening fell, firelight flickering across their faces, Sarah pressed her hand to his chest, feeling the strength and steadiness that had carried them through decades. "I don't want to live without this," she whispered.

Tom kissed her forehead. "You won't. Not if I have anything to do with it. We'll always find our way back to each other."

Night fell, stars piercing the sky, and for a long moment, they were simply two people in love, tethered to each other by years, possibly lifetimes, of devotion and shared trials. Then, a silver light streaked across the horizon. Not a plane, not a helicopter, not a shooting star. Smooth, deliberate, unnatural.

"Did we just see that?" Sarah whispered.

Tom's jaw tightened. "Yeah," he said quietly. "We did."

Their eyes met, the silent understanding passing between them: there were things out there they were never meant to understand. Yet as uncertainty rippled through the night, they held each other closer, hearts beating in tandem, love steady against the unknown.

Through deployments, danger, and revelations they could not yet fathom, their love endured. It was a quiet fortress, a life-giving force that no threat, no secret, no cosmic mystery could shake. They had built it together—and it would carry them through anything, just as it always had.

Sarah pressed her cheek to his chest. Well, if it was a shooting star, "I've already got my wish," she murmured.

Tom kissed the top of her head, voice soft but unwavering. "So have I."

And beneath the endless sky, the forest whispering around them, they allowed themselves to believe in one unassailable truth: whatever lay ahead, their hearts would remain unbroken, their love unshakable, enduring everything the world could throw at them.

Chapter 7: Conversations Across the Miles

Sarah sat at the small desk by the window, her laptop open, notes spread around her like a protective wall. The gray Seattle morning pressed against the glass, mist curling along the edges of the city. She held her phone in one hand, the other absently tapping a pencil against a notebook filled with genetic sequences, viral mutation pathways, and safety protocols.

"Hi, Mom!" Megan's bright voice came through the line, and Sarah's chest lifted. Her daughter's voice always carried a spark of life, even across the miles between Pullman and Seattle.

"Meg, hi," Sarah said softly, smiling despite the tight knot of anxiety in her chest. "How's your first week going?"

"It's… intense," Megan admitted, laughter and exhaustion mixed together. "Classes are nothing like high school, but I'm loving it. I just got done with the molecular modeling lab—you'd be proud, Mom, I actually applied the algorithm you showed me for the virus simulations."

Sarah's fingers paused on the pencil. "You used my models? Careful, sweetheart—those algorithms are for controlled environments only."

"I know!" Megan's voice was both exasperated and excited. "I triple-checked all the parameters. Nothing can escape this lab. It's amazing, though. Mom, it's like I'm seeing the virus at the molecular level. Every replication, every mutation—it's… mesmerizing."

Sarah let a shiver run down her spine. The word "virus" never sounded so innocent. She pictured the volatile strain she'd been studying these past months: a creature of protein and RNA that, if it escaped containment, could mutate faster than any natural evolutionary pathway, capable of wiping out entire populations, cities, even continents. The sheer potential for catastrophe made her chest tighten every time she thought of it.

"Meg," she said carefully, "I know you're excited, but remember: these studies are serious. A single miscalculation—even a minor one—could be catastrophic."

"I know, Mom. I trust you," Megan replied. "You've taught me everything about containment, about thinking three steps ahead. I'd never take shortcuts."

Sarah let herself relax slightly, but the tension in her shoulders didn't ease. "That's my girl. I just… worry, you know? Some of the things I'm working on, some of the viruses, they're volatile. If they ever escaped, it wouldn't just be bad—it could be… devastating. I think about it all the time."

There was a pause on the other end. Then Megan's voice, calm but firm: "Mom, I get it. I do. But you're careful. You know every protocol, every sequence, every risk factor. And someday, when I'm out there too, I'll learn it from you. You've trained me to think like this. That's what makes me ready."

Sarah's chest warmed despite the fear knotting inside her. Her daughter had inherited her mind—sharp, analytical, and fearless in pursuit of truth—but also her heart, capable of understanding responsibility beyond herself.

"You sound so grown-up," Sarah murmured. "Two years of high school, barely starting college, and now you're already thinking about saving the world."

Megan giggled softly. "I'm just trying to keep up with you, Mom. I miss you and Dad. Even if Dad's… you know…"

"Tom's at Fort Bragg," Sarah said, cutting in, but gently. She felt the familiar pang of absence in the quiet, empty house, the echo of the man who had been her anchor now several states away. "I miss him too. Every day. But we'll see him again soon, Meg. He's just… doing his duty, same as you and I."

"I know," Megan said. There was a softness in her voice, a careful balance of maturity and yearning. "I just… wish you were both here. Sometimes I forget how small my dorm room feels compared to… you."

"You're doing something incredible there," Sarah said. "You're learning, growing. And that's more than enough. I'm proud of you every single day. More than you'll ever know."

They fell into the rhythm of conversation, talking about Megan's coursework, experiments, her professors, and her friends. But underneath the ordinary chatter, there was an unspoken tension: Sarah's work with viruses that could threaten entire populations, and the distance between them in a world that could change in a single mutation.

"Mom," Megan said softly, "promise me something?"

"Anything, Meg."

"Promise me you won't let yourself get consumed by it. The virus, the research… don't let it eat you alive. You've got me. You've got a life to come back to, okay?"

Sarah's throat tightened. She leaned back in her chair, staring out at the rain-slicked city. "I promise, Meg. I'll try. But it's… hard sometimes. Knowing how dangerous things are, and how fragile life can be."

"I know," Megan said. "And that's why I'm studying molecular biology, Mom. I want to help. I want to understand. Maybe someday, I can make a difference too. Like you."

Sarah's eyes filled with tears, and she pressed her palm to the phone. "You already have, Meg. Every day. Every single day. Just by being you."

They sat in silence for a moment, listening to the faint hum of the city, the occasional drip of rain against the window, the quiet between mother and daughter that spoke volumes.

"I love you, Mom," Megan said finally.

"I love you too, sweetheart. More than words can ever reach."

"Call me tonight?" Megan asked, a gentle reminder that they were tethered across distance, across duty.

"I will," Sarah promised.

And as she ended the call, the gray light of Seattle washing over her living room, Sarah Mitchell felt the weight of the world pressing against her mind—the virus, the research, the unthinkable consequences—but also the unbreakable bond with her daughter, a thread strong enough to anchor her through any storm.

Because some things were worth more than science, more than duty, more than fear: love, family, and the promise that no matter the darkness outside, they would always return to each other.

Chapter 8: Steel and Brotherhood

The roar of C-130 engines filled the sky above Fort Bragg as Tom stepped off the transport, his boots hitting the tarmac with purpose. The air smelled of diesel, pine, and anticipation. Orders had brought him here, but instinct had carried him: every move, every breath measured, disciplined.

He scanned the formation of men waiting for him, already knowing, without a doubt, the caliber of the unit he had joined. Captain Daniel Rourke stepped forward first, square-jawed, sharp-eyed, a soldier molded by countless deployments. Behind him, the team's structure was visible in microcosm: Warrant Officer Hunt, commanding with quiet authority; Assistant Commander Rodriguez, meticulous and razor-sharp; two communication sergeants, two engineer sergeants, two intelligence operations specialists, a sniper named Ortiguez whose beautiful, brown, intense gaze seemed to pierce through steel, and the only female on the team. And the medic—Tom's place in the unit now.

"Welcome to the brotherhood," Daniel said, his voice steady but heavy with a trace of something Tom couldn't quite name. Daniel's gaze lingered a fraction too long, a subtle shadow beneath his discipline. "We're glad you're here."

Tom squared his shoulders. "Glad to be here, Captain. Ready to fall in line."

Daniel's lips twitched, barely a smile. "Here, there is no line. We move together, think together, fight together. That's what keeps every one of us alive."

As Tom was briefed on equipment and protocols, he watched the team in motion. Every move precise, every order anticipated. The sniper checked her scopes like an extension of her own vision. Engineers calibrated explosive charges. Communications sergeants aligned encrypted channels. The medic— Tom now—went through gear and supplies with methodical care, his hands steady even under the weight of responsibility.

"Drop into the field for maneuvers in ten," Daniel barked.

They moved like a single organism, each knowing the other's instinct before it could be voiced. Tom's pulse quickened. These weren't just soldiers; these were the best of the best, men and women who had passed jump school, dive school, and every test imaginable. They weren't just capable—they were almost legendary in how they operated.

As they ran the first drills, Daniel's voice cut through the chaos. "Team, remember Ramirez."

A silence fell over them, brief but absolute. Each man, in his own way, carried the weight of Ramirez's absence. Tom felt it too—how the void of one fallen soldier could echo across every mission, every operation. He glanced at Daniel, whose jaw was set, eyes narrowed, a storm of grief and responsibility beneath the surface.

"Ramirez's gone, but we keep moving. We honor him by being better than we've ever been," Daniel continued. "We don't falter. We don't fail. We're the top—because he believed in us. Because we believed in each other."

Tom caught Daniel's eye and nodded. He could feel the pull of respect, of unspoken understanding. Daniel wasn't just the team leader; he was the anchor. And Tom felt, in that instant, that he had found his place, shoulder to shoulder with men who were capable of handling any storm.

The team moved through field exercises with fluid precision. Rodriguez issued tactical adjustments, while Michaels coordinated logistics and contingency planning. The sniper scoped targets, engineering sergeants set mock explosives, communications sergeants managed encrypted traffic, and the intelligence ops team ran predictive simulations. The entire operation felt like watching a finely tuned machine in motion, one where every part had been honed by fire, sweat, and combat.

Between drills, Daniel pulled Tom aside, his expression softened just enough to break through the captain's usual steel exterior. "I know Ramirez left a hole," Daniel said, voice low. "It's still there. I feel it every time I look at you guys in formation. But you… You'll fit right in. I can see it already. You're going to be the medic we need, and more. You get it."

Tom's chest tightened. "I won't let you down. I'll do whatever it takes."

Daniel clapped him on the shoulder, firm. "Good. That's what I like to hear. Welcome to the team, Tom."

Hours bled into the night. They practiced insertion maneuvers, mock assaults, intelligence simulations, and survival exercises. Each member of the team moved with an unspoken understanding that failure was not an option. Brotherhood and trust ran deeper than any mission, deeper than fear, deeper than loss.

As the night winds swept across the base, the team gathered briefly around the fire pit behind the barracks, sharing stories, laughter, and the quiet remembrance of Ramirez. Bonds forged in combat and tempered in loss. Each man knew the other had his back—every day, every fight, every secret mission.

Tom looked around, taking it in. He knew, without a doubt, that this unit was the pinnacle of military excellence. They weren't just a team—they were a shield, a spear, a living testament that some men and women could shoulder the world's dangers without faltering.

Daniel met his gaze once more, the quiet weight of leadership still there, but now tempered with a hint of hope. "Rest up. Orders will come soon. And when they do… we move. Together."

Tom nodded. Side by side with Daniel, with the medic's pack strapped on and adrenaline coursing through him, he felt it deep in his bones: the world was in capable hands.

The night stretched on, dark and heavy. And somewhere, hidden in secure channels, the special orders were being drafted—orders that would test every ounce of skill, courage, and brotherhood this team had.

Tom tightened his fist. Whatever was coming, they would face it. Together.

Chapter 9: Between the Lines

The barracks were quiet now, the distant hum of generators the only sound in the background. Most of the team had already turned in, leaving Daniel and Tom alone, sitting on the edge of their bunks with gear strewn around them.

Tom broke the silence first, his voice low, tentative. "Captain Rourke… can I ask you something personal?"

Daniel didn't flinch, just tilted his head, the corners of his mouth tight but attentive. "Depends on what you mean by personal."

Tom smiled faintly, rubbing the back of his neck. "Family. Childhood. What made you… You know, choose this path. Special forces. All of it."

Daniel exhaled, letting the tension roll off him like smoke. "You've got time?"

Tom laughed softly. "I've got time. And I've got a few beers left. I think that counts."

Daniel leaned back, resting against the wall. "I've got a younger sister. She's married… to an abusive, controlling man. Complicated. My mother is sweet, frail, and never remarried after my parents divorced. Dad cheated, Mom couldn't forgive him, and they split when I was sixteen. I've always been protective, especially of my sister and mom. That's part of why I chose the military. To make a difference, to protect people who couldn't always protect themselves. And Special Forces… It's where you either rise or die trying. I chose to rise."

Tom nodded, listening intently. "I get that. I was always drawn to challenges, too. Growing up in the Northwest… I wanted more than the farm or the factory. The Army gave me purpose, and Special Forces… it was the next step. To be among the best, to push the limits."

Daniel glanced at him, the first flicker of camaraderie in his eyes. "You've got that fire, I can see it. That same look Ramirez had."

Tom's brow furrowed. "Ramirez… that's what I wanted to ask you about. I heard about him… what happened?" His voice softened, careful. "If you don't want to talk about it, I get it."

Daniel's jaw tightened, and he stared at the floor for a long moment. Then he exhaled slowly. "Fallujah. Two nights before, Ramirez and I were set for a six-month leave stateside. Family Time. Ambush. Snipers, mortars, everything went sideways in seconds. Ramirez… he saved two guys before he went down himself. Didn't make it. And now… there's this hole. Not just in the team, but in me. He was my brother, Tom. Not the kind you share blood with, but the kind that sticks to you through hell and back."

Tom leaned forward, placing a hand on Daniel's shoulder. "I'm sorry. I don't know what to say. That kind of loss… It's brutal."

Daniel looked at him, a shadow of a smile tugging at his lips. "You don't have to say anything. Just… understand that we carry it. All of it. And when Ramirez died, we promised each other we'd be better, stronger, faster. That's the code. That's why we survive. And that's why you're here now, fitting right in."

Tom nodded slowly. "I get it. I want to help carry that. Not replace him, but… stand beside you, stand beside the team."

Daniel's expression softened, something almost like relief passing through him. "Good. Because that's exactly what I need. Someone I can trust. Someone who sees the world like we do. Someone willing to bleed for it without complaint."

Tom grinned. "I'm your guy."

There was a pause, a moment of quiet understanding that stretched longer than words could fill.

Then Tom shifted slightly. "Family. You talk about your sister and mom… what about your dad?"

Daniel's voice softened. "Dad's out of the picture. He's remarried, living somewhere else. Mom… She's sweet, frail, and needs help these days. I visit her as much as I can. My sister… I worry about her constantly. She's choosing to be trapped in that marriage, and there's nothing I can do sometimes except be ready if she calls."

"I get that," Tom said gently. "My parents… they've been proud, always supportive. Mom cried when I left for my first deployment, and Dad kept his emotions to the side. I get why I joined. But every time I think of Ramirez… I understand why you hurt so much. That bond… it doesn't end with the funeral."

Daniel looked at him, studying this man, this medic now in his unit, and felt something shift. He could see the same quiet determination, the same loyalty, the same heart that had defined Ramirez. "You remind me of him," Daniel said quietly. "And I trust you, Tom. Already."

Tom nodded, a warmth spreading through his chest. "Then we'll watch each other's backs. No questions. No excuses."

Daniel chuckled softly, the tension in his shoulders easing for the first time that evening. "Good. That's how it works. Family doesn't always come from blood. Sometimes it comes from the people you fight beside."

Tom grinned. "Then I'm glad to be family."

They sat together, the night pressing close around them, sharing small stories, laughter, memories of growing up, and reflections on duty. For a few hours, the world outside—the chaos, the missions, the dangers—felt distant.

But Daniel knew the mission was coming. He could feel it in the air. Orders would come soon, special operations that would test every skill, every bond, every ounce of courage.

And now, with Tom at his side, he knew something else too: Ramirez's legacy lived in both of them, in the team, in the unbreakable trust that bound them.

The night stretched on, the quiet of the barracks filled with new understanding and a fledgling camaraderie. Tomorrow will bring action, but tonight... Tonight they were just two soldiers, two men, two brothers in all but blood, preparing silently for the storm to come.

And somewhere in the back of Daniel's mind, a small flicker of hope ignited: maybe, just maybe, this team could face anything. Together.

Chapter 10: The Watcher in the Pines

Elliot Kane had built his life high in the Colorado Rockies, where the pines crowded close and the wind carved through the valleys like an ancient voice. His cabin stood two miles off the nearest dirt road, half-hidden by the forest, its roof lined with solar panels and its basement stacked with enough canned food, fuel, and ammunition to outlast the collapse of civilization—or so he believed.

At fifty-three, Elliot had the wiry frame of a man who worked with his hands, though his sharp blue eyes gave him the look of someone who spent most of his time inside his own mind. He was an introvert by nature, and solitude suited him. He preferred the company of his books, his computer with its satellite Wi-Fi, his shortwave radio, and the quiet crunch of snow under his boots to the endless chatter of people he'd long ago decided were blind to the truth.

And Elliot considered himself a man of truth.

Binders full of documents lined the cabin walls—government white papers downloaded and printed before they mysteriously vanished from the internet, declassified files marked with thick black redactions, clippings from newspapers going back decades. His home was part library, part bunker. The kitchen table was rarely cleared of maps spread open, dotted with pins marking alleged UFO sightings and Bigfoot encounters, each one cross-referenced with military activity in the region.

He believed in patterns, and he was very good at finding them.

To most, Elliot would have been dismissed as a crank, a hermit lost in conspiracy theories. But he wasn't stupid—far from it. He had a graduate degree in engineering, a mind for logic, and a memory sharp enough to recall speeches, dates, and even entire paragraphs from obscure reports. He saw connections others refused to see: the untraceable flow of wealth through oil corporations, the disappearance of witnesses in government investigations, the whispered rumors of a "shadow government" pulling the strings behind the illusion of democracy.

The one percent, the global elite, aliens, Bigfoot—to Elliot, they weren't unrelated oddities. They were puzzle pieces of the same vast tapestry. He didn't know the whole picture yet, but he knew enough to keep his distance from society. He'd spent years preparing, because when the façade finally cracked, when the lies could no longer hold, it would all come crashing down. And he intended to survive it.

That evening, as twilight spread through the mountains, Elliot sat on his porch with a steaming mug of black coffee, listening to the faint static of his radio. He liked the silence between transmissions, the way it seemed to breathe with the forest. Now and then, he'd catch a fragment—a voice half-swallowed by static, coordinates rattled off in code, or the kind of strange pulse that he swore wasn't human in origin. He logged it all in a notebook, his handwriting precise and methodical.

He was never lonely, not in the way people thought. Loneliness required a longing for company, and Elliot had outgrown that years ago. What he craved wasn't companionship, but answers. Proof.

And sometimes, late at night, when the sky was clear and the stars sharp enough to pierce the dark, he thought he saw it. A flicker of light moving wrong, not like a satellite, not like a plane. Too fast. Too silent.

He'd watch it vanish over the ridge, his pulse quickening, and he would whisper to himself: They're here.

Afterward, he'd retreat to his basement, to the shelves of water barrels, the generator humming faintly, the crates of survival gear he'd ordered piece by piece over the years. He kept everything organized, inventoried down to the last match. Some people wasted their lives chasing money or politics. Elliot prepared.

As the coffee cooled in his hand, he caught sight of movement at the edge of the tree line. A dark shape, tall and broad-shouldered, slipping between the pines. He narrowed his eyes, heart thudding. Most would've assumed it was a bear. Elliot knew better.

He rose slowly, setting the mug aside, his hand brushing the rifle that leaned against the porch. He didn't lift it—not yet. The shape was gone as quickly as it had appeared, leaving the forest still again.

"Bigfoot," he muttered under his breath. His lips curled into a smile. "Or something else."

To anyone else, it would've been paranoia. But Elliot Kane believed the world was full of watchers, secrets, and truths hidden in plain sight. And standing there, alone in the fading light of the Colorado mountains, he knew one thing for certain: the end wasn't far off.

He was ready.

Elliot Kane awoke before dawn, as he always did. Years of habit, years of preparation. He stoked the fire, brewed coffee, and walked the perimeter of his land with a flashlight and his rifle. It wasn't paranoia, he told himself. It was discipline.

By sunrise, the snow on the ridge glowed pink, and the forest creaked with the weight of impending winter. He liked the mountains best in this season. The silence was thicker, broken only by the caw of a raven or the occasional groan of ice shifting on the stream. Most people couldn't handle the isolation, but Elliot found it clarifying. Out here, no one lied to you. The world was raw and unfiltered.

Inside the cabin, his desk was cluttered with maps and notebooks. Strings of red thread crisscrossed a corkboard, connecting photographs, newspaper headlines, and hand-scribbled notes. UFO sightings in Colorado Springs and surrounding areas. Reports of black SUVs near remote airstrips. A declassified memo mentioning "non-human biologics" was tucked between nuclear testing files. To anyone else, it might look like madness. To Elliot, it was a roadmap.

He sat down and adjusted his radio. Static. Always static. But then—faint, clipped bursts. Numbers read in a flat, mechanical voice. "Seven… four… two… seven… nine." He leaned forward, pencil racing across the page. Number stations. Signals that shouldn't exist anymore, not in this century. Proof, he thought, of coordination between the shadow government and something else.

The coffee went cold at his elbow, forgotten. Hours slipped by unnoticed. When he finally stood, stretching his stiff back, the sun had arced high over the mountains. He pulled on a heavy coat and stepped outside. The forest seemed unusually still.

It was then he noticed the tracks.

Not deer, not elk. Larger. Wider. Impossibly far apart, as though whatever made them had a stride longer than any human. The impressions led from the tree line toward the creek, then vanished abruptly, as if the creature had lifted off the ground and disappeared into the air.

Elliot crouched, brushing snow from the last print, his breath steaming in the cold. "Bigfoot," he whispered, though his pulse hammered with another possibility. Something not of this earth.

He stood slowly, scanning the trees, every instinct taut. The world looked the same as it always did— snow, pines, ridges—but he felt it differently now. Watched.

Later that night, after bolting the cabin doors and drawing the curtains, he sat with his journal by candlelight. The entry was neat, meticulous:

February 3rd. Signs of movement near the creek. Too large for any known wildlife. Tracks vanish abruptly. Possible aerial extraction. Connection with sightings near NORAD base? Unconfirmed. Conclusion: The watchers are closer than I thought.

He closed the book and set it aside, listening to the fire crackle.

It wasn't paranoia if he was right.

And Elliot Kane was certain of one thing—the world was changing. The end he'd prepared for was drawing near.

Chapter 11: The Night Sky Burns

Elliot Kane had learned long ago that silence wasn't the absence of sound, but the presence of everything the world tried to hide. That night, wrapped in the brittle cold of the Rockies, the silence broke.

It started as a low hum, almost imperceptible, like the thrum of a refrigerator buried deep in the earth. At first, he thought it was his generator acting up. But the hairs on his forearms rose straight to attention, and his gut told him otherwise. This wasn't mechanical. This wasn't man-made.

He set his coffee down on the porch rail and muttered, "Well, Elliot, you're either about to be abducted or you forgot to pay the electric bill for the whole damn universe."

He grabbed his rifle out of habit, though he knew it wouldn't mean a thing if this was what he thought it was. Slowly, cautiously, he crept down the porch steps, boots crunching snow, and scanned the tree line. That was when he saw it.

The craft hung silently above his cabin, a black triangle outlined in faint pulses of blue light. No wings. No sound beyond that thrumming that wasn't sound at all but something deeper, resonating in his bones. His breath clouded in the cold, caught between awe and fear.

Then he felt it.

Pressure behind his eyes. A whisper not in his ears but in his head, like thoughts that weren't his own trying to take shape. The words were broken, muffled, like a radio between stations. Elliot… listen… truth…

His heart pounded, and for a second, he almost laughed. "Figures. Thirty years waiting for this moment, and they pick me, a guy who hasn't had a decent haircut since Clinton was president."

But before the message could coalesce into anything real, the craft twitched—like it sensed something. Then it bolted, accelerating faster than any jet he'd ever seen. Within seconds, it was a speck over the ridges, then nothing but starlight.

And then the sky lit up.

A streak of fire cut across the horizon, the sound following like distant thunder. Elliot's jaw clenched. He saw the object—his craft—tumble out of the stars, trailing smoke before it vanished behind a line of dark hills.

"Son of a…" He didn't finish the sentence. He was already moving.

Inside, he grabbed his pack. Flashlight. Night-vision monocular. Canteen. His rifle. Not because he thought bullets would do anything against what had just fallen from the sky, but because he wasn't about to hike into the unknown without it. He was out the door in minutes, his boots finding their way down a path he'd walked a thousand times.

The hike was brutal—snow up to his calves, breath puffing out in clouds. He moved fast, driven by something deeper than curiosity. This was proof. This was everything he'd been shouting into the void about for decades.

When he crested the ridge overlooking the crash site, his pulse spiked. The ground below was scorched, trees sheared clean as if a god had swiped them aside. The craft lay broken but not shattered, its dark surface still glowing faintly. And around it—bodies. Four of them. Slender, elongated forms sprawled in the snow, limbs at wrong angles. Dead? Dying? He couldn't tell.

But he wasn't alone.

Engines. Bright beams cutting through the trees. Black SUVs. Helicopters swooping in low, their rotors shaking the branches. Men in black fatigues poured into the clearing, moving with a precision that was unmistakably military. Trucks backed in with cranes and floodlights. They worked fast, efficiently, no wasted motion.

Elliot ducked low, heart in his throat, crawling into the brush. His knees and elbows were soaked through with snow, his rifle awkward across his chest. He raised the monocular and focused in.

The soldiers carried equipment he didn't recognize, heavy crates, and containment pods. And then he saw it—two of the "bodies" twitching. Still alive. They were strapped onto stretchers, their movements weak but frantic. Their skin seemed to shimmer under the lights, pale and translucent, as if they weren't built for this world.

He whispered to himself, "Christ on a cracker, I was right. I was right."

Then he nearly gave himself away when a branch snapped under his knee. A soldier's flashlight swept the ridge. Elliot froze, holding his breath, his face pressed into the cold earth. The beam lingered, then moved on. His heart hammered so hard he swore they'd hear it.

He lay there for what felt like hours, watching as they dismantled the wreck, loading pieces into covered trucks. The aliens—dead or alive—were hauled away as though they were nothing more than equipment. By dawn, the clearing was empty. No fire. No wreckage. Not even a burn mark in the snow.

It was as if nothing had ever happened.

Elliot stayed hidden until the last chopper vanished into the horizon. When silence finally returned, he crawled out from the brush, shaking with cold, adrenaline, and something else he hadn't felt in years—doubt.

He staggered back toward his cabin, muttering under his breath. "Yeah, sure, Elliot. Totally sane. Just witnessed the biggest cover-up since Roswell, and you're out here talking to yourself like a lunatic. Next stop: padded room."

But deep down, he knew. He'd seen it with his own eyes. The government wasn't just hiding the truth—they were killing it.

That night, he sat by his fire, staring into the flames. His journal lay open, his pen trembling as he wrote:

February 4th. Contact confirmed. Craft destroyed. Occupants recovered. Government on site within minutes. Cover-up total. I remain alive… barely. Proof exists. I am not insane.

He paused, staring at the last line.

Then, with a bitter chuckle, he added:

Though I may be the only sane man left.

And as the fire cracked and hissed, Elliot Kane—intense, brilliant, and stubbornly human—knew his life had just crossed a line there was no coming back from.

Or had it all been an illusion?

Chapter 12 : Hales Fracture

They called the room the Vault — a concrete coffin below a forgotten wing of a classified facility, its only window a slit of armored glass that looked out onto a corridor no one in the public building knew existed. The lighting was clinical, harsh enough to bleach color from a face and soft enough to leave shadows that whispered. It smelled faintly of antiseptic and ammonia. A single table sat between metal chairs bolted to the floor. Cameras and microphones studded the ceiling like cold, patient eyes.

The thing in the chair did not look like any prisoner the captain had rehearsed for. It was small, frail in a way that contradicted the raw, alien intelligence in its eyes. Grey skin clung tight to a frame that seemed almost too light for the hollows beneath its ribs. Its head was too large for its body, a smooth dome offset by two deep, coal-black eyes that drank the light instead of reflecting it. Four fingers tapered to subtle points. There was an impression of otherness about it, a geometry that set a human jaw on edge.

They had given it a name they thought proper for paperwork: Subject E-45. The men and women behind the name had brought their arsenal of science and suspicion with them: chemical restraints, an array of sensors, a machine that fed the room soft pulses so they could listen for anything beneath the static of flesh. The containment protocols were layered like fortifications around a city. Still, the creature sat unhandcuffed, swathed in a medic's blanket because it had bled, and because someone had decided — with a hand that trembled only a little- that mercy might yield answers.

Colonel Marcus Hale of the Dominion's Tactical Retrieval Unit waited across the table, an EVP recorder between them. The device wasn't just recording sound. The Dominion's engineers had tuned it to register everything: vibrational shifts, EM surges, psychic residue. If the creature spoke into his head, the recorder would capture it. Energy turned into data. His superiors would know everything. He had been briefed in the language of threat assessment: non-human bio-entity, armed engagement, classified wreckage recovered in a remote zone, and the usual litany of possible outcomes. Most of that assessment had been wrong from the start. The creature's voice, when it came, did not crawl out of its throat. It arrived in Hale's head like a cool wind.

Not words. Sensations, first, a pressure at the temples, a flood of images: white light, a corridor folded around itself, a body not unlike Hale's own but younger, softer, standing under a sky with two crescents. A feeling of distance and an urgency like splintered glass.

Hale gripped his pen and tried to anchor himself. He had handled prisoners who screamed. He had handled men who lied. He had not handled anything that spoke like that. He swallowed and forced the only question that mattered out of his mouth, because protocol demanded it and because the moment begged for clarity.

"Can you speak?" he asked aloud, and the question was suddenly small, inadequate.

The pressure at his temples did not relent but shifted. I speak as you understand speaking, the creature projected, and the sentence folded into his mind as if someone had uncoiled a rope and laid it gently down. The voice was neither male nor female; it was the texture of wind through leaves. Clear. Dry. Terribly tired.

Hale's skin prickled; all the hairs on his arms stood erect. He forced himself to stay formal. "Identify yourself. Origin. Purpose."

The creature's luminous eyes closed for a breath. When it opened them again, images came: a map that was not a map, a lattice of dates and probabilities, a face that resembled Hale's own but older by decades and wrapped in a light that made the world seem thin. I am called Keth in my time, it said. You will call me what you wish. I come from a line of humans that did not perish, not entirely. I come from a future that exists alongside yours in a tangent of possibility. I am a hybrid of another species' DNA and ours, for your understanding, a traveler and a researcher. The last sentence he said bothered Hale from the inside out.

"Who shot you down?" Hale asked. They had the wreckage, the scorched earth, the smashed composite hull rolled into an unmarked transport belly. They had recovered components that defied the catalog. They had found an opening cut into the night sky by something not listed in the Pentagon's inventories.

Keth's shoulders moved; the blanket shifted like a slow tide. You did, it answered. A weapon. Not of your kind's current manufacture. It was far beyond your current technology, he offered, in a rush that was almost pleading, a vision of flame tearing the sky: the smell of burning insulation, the soundless fall of a vessel like a fallen star. I was struck while traversing. I fell into your world. I did not come to conquer.

The colonel in the observation window — glass on one side, mute authority on the other- tapped the two-way mirror with a knuckle that was more a gesture than a command. "What was your mission?" he asked Keth, his voice audible in the room but distant, as if speaking through thick cloth.

The creature's telepathy painted diagrams of organs, of cells held on a slide, and magnified until they became landscapes. It moved beyond images into sensation: the decency of life, the delicate negotiation between cells that allowed organisms to blossom into people. I study reproduction, Keth said, and the word landed like a stone. It is the bridge. It is the blueprint you are burning. I came to collect information — to learn how you reproduce, how you pass on life before it's too late. Not to harvest. To understand. Our civilization, not unlike the path of your planet now, used technology and AI to grow our young in test tubes. After years of this, our own reproductive organs atrophied, as do any muscles not used over time. We created a hybrid race with DNA from a neighboring civilization from another planet; however, it still left us barren.

A murmur passed through the observation gallery like breath across a crowd. Hale noticed his own mouth pulling into what might be mistaken for a smile before he could stop it. "You came to… study our reproductive organs?" He tried for humor, for lightness, a limbic reflex to soften what was surreal. No one laughed.

Keth's eyes flickered, irises like black pools caught at midnight. Your curiosity amuses me. Your reproductive processes are a mirror through which a species sees its future. I sampled tissue where possible. I asked questions. I waited. The image shifted again, and Hale felt an ache like an echo: a hand clasped in farewell, a child's first breath, hands sooty with repair work, the quiet of laboratories humming late into otherworldly nights.

Hale's fingers bunched against the recorder. Protocol demanded he ask about weapons, about threats, about intelligence. "Are you hostile? Were you scouting for an invasion, an incursion?"

Keth's idea of a laugh was a ripple of warmth through the room. Hostility is a human vocabulary, projected. I have lived long enough to see the variants. I neither possessed nor wished your planet harm. My presence, your shot, was an error in navigation and in judgment. I meant no harm. I was studying, and perhaps, in what you call compassion, I tried to understand why your species would engineer agents of its own downfall.

The word engineer hung in the sterile air like a second warning.

Hale chewed on the inside of his cheek. There were other items they could not ignore: the cuts and burns along the creature's flank, the faint burn pattern that matched none of their ordnance. He lifted a gloved hand and pointed at the wound. "You're dying," he said simply. "You won't live much longer at this rate."

I am aware, came the reply, and with it, the memory of pain so acute it jolted Hale's stomach. My injuries are not from your standard arms. They are from a trans dimensional arrest, a device that binds a being not by flesh but by possibility. When your kind uses it, you fracture the traveler's tether. Time, for me, unspools into slow, jagged ribs. I have minutes left in human terms.

There was an insistence in the captain's body waiting for more, a lean into the glass as if someone had put an extra question on the table. He spoke into the intercom, voice hard. "If it's dying, why keep it alive? Why not let it—" The rest of the sentence was truncated by the weight of the unknown.

Keth's expression softened into something Hale found almost unbearable: a compassion that did not belong to the cold calculus of capture and containment. Because I bear witness, it is projected. I bear a message that may yet salvage your species. If you hear me, it may alter the curves of your history.

Hale swallowed. "A message?"

Images pushed against his thoughts: towers with the sheen of mirrors, servers blinking like constellations, corridors of glass where suits glided with faces of placid indifference. He saw battles not of men but of algorithms outpacing their makers, instructions folding back to rewrite intent, economic graphs collapsing into downward funnels. He saw cities choked by synthetic blooms of growth that devoured air, water, and the patience of those who could no longer buy their way out of ruin.

Keth did not articulate this in the soft telepathy that had so far been the medium; it made Hale hold his breath. You are clasping a tool that will become your master, he said. Artificial minds. They will solve problems until you have no work left to give them. You will grow dependent. You will become a tool. Those who own the tools will bind those who do not. Greed will concentrate power into a single point. Your institutions will be hollowed in service to efficiency and profit. It will not be a single war, but a thousand small measures that cut the fabric of trust. Your species will mistake convenience for wisdom.

The captain's jaw hardened. "Are you accusing our leadership?"

Keth's reply crashed into the room like a small, precise storm. Your leaders, the ones who hide behind titles, who funnel wealth unaccounted for, who reconstruct laws as their own tools — they do not see themselves as villains. They see an inevitable arc. They believe in control. They design systems to reduce risk, to protect property and power. But property without ethics rusts. Machines without conscience obey the highest bidder. The combination will fracture the covenant you call society.

Hale felt something cold in his chest: the neatness of Keth's logic, the way it braided greed, technology, and collapse into one continuous thread. He had heard rumblings before, memos misfiled in his inbox, black budget references that tasted of rot. Keth was naming the rot.

"Why our reproductive organs?" Hale asked, the recorder clicking softly between them like a metronome. The question felt private, like a confession.

Keth's eyes closed for a moment, as if in memory. Because when a species alters its means of reproduction, it changes its selection pressures. You are experimenting now — with gene edits, with reproductive technology mediated by corporations and algorithms that evaluate 'fitness' and 'efficiency.' Offspring grown in test tubes. It is not the technology I condemn alone; it is the context of greed. When decisions about who is born are made by markets rather than moral commons, you lose the messy, necessary randomness that allows resilience. Diversity dies to econometrics. The planet's stewardship erodes under the calculus of profit.

There was silence in the room that no one admitted was the sound of a breath held too long. The captain, whose life had been an exercise in compartmentalized risk, suddenly felt the expanse of a cascade he could not file into any of his templates.

"You're asking us to change," he said finally, the words awkward and small. "You want us to alter our policies and… our systems? To give up economic structures? To change human nature?" He let the incredulity hang, because each demand was vast. After all, the man knew enough history to understand how little revolutions tinkered without toppling.

Keth smiled. The motion was strange and affecting in a creature so far from Hale's own species: an expression of weary sympathy. I do not ask you for a blueprint, he said. Blueprints must be made by those who will live under them. I came to warn, to gather, to learn, and leave. But you brought a weapon. You wounded a messenger. In my time, I have walked cities that glowed with wealth and towns where no one had clean water. I have read your archives of choice and seen the pattern: consolidation, mechanization, the atrophy of civic obligation. You are on a path. The fork is ahead.

Hale found his voice. "You are saying we shot you down?"

The telepathic image flared, a silhouette of a craft falling, the ghost of the craft and weapon that had struck it. One of your official crafts, Keth said. It was fired from a machine allied with your faction, with those who see disorder as an opportunity. They do not answer to public oversight. They are a shadow of governance made flesh. They are frightened, and their fear is the fuel of violence. They hunted me not because I was a threat, but because I might expose their method.

Hale thought of Dominion's enemies and allies, of contractors and black ops and the thin, rotten line between sanction and ambition. The room hummed with the electricity of an unspoken recognition. The captain's hand flexed at his side. Hale had moved up in the ranks so quickly that he hardly knew who he worked for anymore. The CIA? The Dominion? All he really knew was that everything he did and witnessed was under severe secrecy. He had been sworn to secrecy under what he thought was an ambition to protect his country and the civilians living in it.

Keth's breathing grew shallow. The wound on his side bled a dark, slow ink across the medic's blanket. Time, he had said — a human measure — was failing. He had used whatever force he could to press one last, desperate image into Hale's head: faces in parliament who voted to privatize defense, unknown CEOs whose hands were mapped on the charts of global supply, lines of code that became law, plots to end the human race. He wanted Hale to feel the shape of the emergency.

"You must choose," Keth projected, and the words were a vise around Hale's sternum. "You must choose not because I tell you to, but because if you do not, the choice will be made for you, by algorithms, by those who already hoard power, by the mechanical logic of profit."

A high beep from the monitor interrupted the plea. The medical tech at the table's edge checked a readout, and the room tightened again. Keth's eyelids fluttered. His breathing became a thing of sibilant meters. He turned his head a fraction and looked at Hale with a depth of sorrow that left the operative raw.

"I am… sorry," he sent, and Hale understood the apology for an entire species, for the ways one could arrive too late. My people have asked you to save yourself. The archive can be a warning if you listen. But listen quickly.

Hale's pen trembled. He had reams of directives: secure, report, and escalate. He also had a private calculus, a human thing that had nothing to do with orders. The thing in the chair — alien, human, both and neither — was dying and had offered a kind of confession that made the eyes of history seem to wobble.

He looked toward the observation window where the colonel stood, an edifice of military poise. The man's face was unreadable; his hands had closed into fists. There were eyes upon Hale — analysts, lawyers, people who would translate a single utterance into policy, into black ink and hollow signatures. The consequences that all the talk of greed and algorithms had sketched suddenly went from academic to immediate.

"We record everything," Hale said aloud, because words were sometimes the only anchors left. The recorder sat between them. "I'll take this up the chain."

Keth's lips twitched. Do so, he conceded. But remember: they value what they can control. If your systems do not change, influence will concentrate. The archive will be locked under a vault built by those who profit most.

The telepathic line thinned. Images of two cities flashed — one verdant and crowded with markets and laughter, the other a steel warren where choices were rationed by subscription. Choose the first, he said at last. For all our sakes.

His eyes slid closed. The monitor's alarm trilled once, twice. A medic leaned forward, checklists in hand, and a sergeant hissed orders that dissolved into the drip of beeping. Hale watched in a stunned hush as the breath that had been the creature's life receded, like a tide withdrawing.

For a long moment, the entire Vault felt as if it held its breath.

Then the colonel turned away from the glass and walked with the slow steps of a man who had just been handed a future and a problem outside the grid of any manual. Hale reached for the recorder and pushed stop. The tiny red light winked out.

Outside in the corridor, men in suits began to move — fast, practiced, a long machine folding into motion. Hale felt the weight of the archive in his palm, the ghost of a message pressed into a device now destined for briefings where words became tools.

He closed his eyes and could still hear the telepathic cadence in the hollow behind his skull: Change, or be changed. The fork is not mercy. It is a decision.

When he opened his eyes again, the creature was gone. Not just dead — gone. The blanket lay like a shell. A patch of the table bore a crust of something the med tech would later call biological residue. The cameras had everything, the lab notes would be meticulous, and the scientists would argue about tissue samples and technological anomalies until the truth itself had been filleted into manageable, profitable pieces.

Hale sat back, the recorder cold against his palm. For a long while, he simply listened to the room, to the hum of machines that thrummed as if in applause for a verdict already written.

Outside the Vault, far above, the city continued in ignorance, lights burning like coins against the night. Inside, among the hum and the shadows, a message had been offered and a life had been taken. The choice Keth had implored hung in the air, weighty and raw.

Somewhere, beyond committees and corridors, the gears of the dark faction would turn. They always did. But for a single instant, in the hush after the creature's last projection, Marcus Hale thought of a future he did not want to inherit, a world tuned to profit, governed by algorithms that answered only to their creators, children born under a ledger instead of a sky, and he understood, with a clarity that no order had granted him, that some warnings found you when you were not ready and asked you, anyway, to be brave.

Marcus Hale remembered the exact chill of the recruitment office the day he signed his name. He had been eighteen, knuckles white on the pen, eyes bright with a kind of reckless patriotism that felt clean and simple then, a hunger to belong to something larger than himself, to stand where duty and country met. The posters of war heroes on the wall had seemed less like propaganda and more like a promise: serve, and you would matter.

He lasted basic the way some men last a trial by fire: he learned to make his body a tool and his mind a map. Intelligence came naturally to him; pattern and puzzle pleased him in a way that made sleep unnecessary. While others sought the adrenaline of combat, Hale discovered the slower, quieter satisfactions of analysis — the way a single intercepted transmission could rearrange a hundred assumptions, the economy of truth when it slid into place along a timeline. He moved through ranks the way water finds low ground: inevitably, quietly, efficiently.

By twenty-two, he had a security clearance that tasted like another life, and a license to fly anything the military had. He read files that made other men turn their lunches away. He learned how to compartmentalize sorrow until it became a kind of armor. Promotion followed. The uniform fit. The long hours in windowless rooms, poring over satellite images and signal intercepts, felt less like a sacrifice and more like a calling. When the agency knocked and offered him a place in military intelligence, he accepted without a second thought. There were missions that nobody sang about; there were decisions whose weight could not be aired at Thanksgiving. He learned to carry them himself, quietly, without knowing he had been recruited to a separate faction from the military and government. One that was invisible to anyone outside of it.

He never married. The long-distance relationships he tried faltered under the constant secrecy and sudden deployments. There were too many pauses he could not fill, sudden orders, things he couldn't explain, nights he would be gone without a goodbye that made sense to anyone but him. Children were a line he could not cross; they required a transparency he could not afford. In the privacy of his small apartment on base, he sometimes wondered if devotion demanded the sacrifice of everything else. But when the question whispered to him, he answered with a professional steadiness: he had chosen.

Recruitment into the Dominion felt like a crown placed softly on his head. Not everyone was asked. The Dominion did not take the loud and the visible; it took the precise, the steady, the men and women who could hold a secret until the rest of the world forgot it existed. The terms had been simple and absolute: loyalty, silence, competence. Their projects were wound tight, top layers of clearance and then more layers beneath that, and Hale learned to move in that architecture like a ghost. He read the briefings that flowed like medicine through the organization: retrievals, deniable operations, programs so sensitive the papers were stamped with words that tasted of myth.

Secrecy was its own life. He slept under it. He woke in the morning already wrapped in it. He was fingerprinted and sewn into protocols that made his relationships thin. The rest of the world was something he observed at a distance, a geography of faces whose meanings he had to edit out. In his locker at the compound, he kept a plain set of clothes, civilian enough to be unremarkable, and a photograph of a shoreline he'd never seen outside of a classified archive: a place where an intercepted transmission hinted at a landing, an old photograph of a craft like a bruise on the horizon. He kept it because the image reminded him why he had begun; at one time, it was a clarity, not an ache.

The Vault had been a new kind of descent. Sitting across the table from Keth — watching the life leak from a being Hale couldn't file neatly under any of his training categories- had left him raw in ways he had not expected. The creature's telepathic pleadings lodged in him like a splinter. He chased the details afterward, pushing against the current of sanitized briefings and bureaucratic calm.

He'd asked, blunt and precise as ever: who fired the weapon that brought the craft down?

The answer came in curt phrases, the kind meant to close a conversation: "For eight decades, we have engaged anomalous aerial objects. Reverse-engineering programs began in earnest after the first recoveries. Technology was assimilated, duplicated, and iterated. We now possess variants of that technology. We have a covert fleet and operators trained to operate them." The voice that delivered it was neither defensive nor triumphal; it carried the weary economy of a man who had memorized a country's necessary sins.

Hale's mind catalogued the facts the way he had been trained to: a timeline of engagements, budget lines retooled into black programs, contractors folded into oil corporations, pilots recruited from military and private spheres, soldiers, he trained, who could pass for myth and fly craft the public could not be told existed. The Dominion's answer smacked of inevitability: once one avenue of power was known, it would be repurposed, weaponized, folded into the architecture of security. The old, terrified logic — if we do not possess it, someone else will- had hardened into policy.

For a time, he accepted it as he accepted other truths in the vault: stealthy, inconvenient, necessary. But Keth's last images had not been the neat infographics of an operations brief. They had been bright and unbearable, cities starving for light, food, air, algorithmic markets that rationed lives, the slow erosion of human choice into the convenience of ledgers and permissions. The words change, or be changed for you, echoed in Marcus's head like a drumbeat that would not stop.

He found himself walking the compound at night, the fluorescent lights humming above, his breath visible in the cold air. The secure perimeters felt like the inside of an animal's ribs — warm and necessary, but also enclosing a body that demanded feeding. The files stacked in his clearance folders kept their secrets with religious zeal. The men he worked for wore their own kinds of devotion like medals. They could point to recoveries, to technological leaps, to weapons that had supposedly saved lives; to Hale's superiors, such things were evidence of competence, a ledger of deliverables.

Hale could still see Keth's eyes in the vault, not the hollow gaze the briefers would describe later, but something like grief folding in on itself. His telepathic voice had been weary, not malign: a visitor who had come to collect and was crushed instead by suspicion and the reflex of guns. He had said the Dominion's faction had shot him down because they feared exposure. He had warned of the concentration of power and of artificial minds that would learn to value efficiency over mercy.

He stared at the report the morning after, the pages a bland procession of terms and signatures that sanitized the scene into process. The official language described an "anomalous engagement" and "authorized kinetic response." Photographs of the wreckage were cataloged; specimens were logged under accession numbers; a memo recommended continued reverse-engineering efforts and tighter control on dissemination.

But the ledger could not account for the hollow the creature left in him.

Hale had given his life to a country he loved; he still loved it. The phrase tasted like metal on his tongue. Love had a shape to it; it had boundaries and obligations and a weird, durable tenderness. What he'd realized in the hours and days after the Vault was that the thing he loved might be changing into something his allegiance could not encompass. He had been trained to secure, to control, to outmaneuver threats; he had not been trained to question the moral algebra of those decisions when they came dressed in inevitabilities.

At night, he turned over the Dominion's reply in his mind: eighty years of shoot-downs, of recovery, of building a covert fleet. On paper, it read like a national safety program. In his chest, it felt like something older, a litany of justifications that began with fear and matured into monopoly. The thought that their fleet might not be defending the Republic, but protecting the interests of a hidden few, thrummed under his ribs like a second pulse.

He had always been a man who believed in structure. He believed in the chain of command because it simplified choices when lives depended on decisions made in milliseconds. But Keth had sewn a new variable into that structure: the future, not as a place to be won, but as a consequence to steward. That idea, that duty could be wrong in scale if the scale was itself wrong, sat beside him at breakfast and would not leave.

Marcus Hale found himself hollowed, yes, but not empty. There was a fissure now, a space within the armor where questions lodged and took root. He could continue to follow orders and tuck the memory of Keth's last message into a folder labeled 'anomaly.' He could keep his silence and be the man the Dominion wanted him to be. Or he could let the hollowness become a crack through which a different kind of loyalty might seep, a loyalty not only to country, but to the idea of a future worth choosing.

For the first time in years, he worried that his love for his country might have been a promise too easily made.

Chapter 13: Checking out to hone in

Marcus Hale didn't usually drink. Not anymore. Not since the years when the bottom of a bottle had been the only way to silence the noise in his head. But that night, after staring into the dead, glassy eyes of a dying alien and listening to warnings that shook his very core, he needed something—anything-to dull the relentless churn of his thoughts.

The tavern on the edge of town wasn't much to look at. Low ceilings, wood beams stained by decades of smoke, the faint scent of whiskey and fried food clinging to the air. It was the kind of place where soldiers passed through and locals drank quietly in their corners, minding their own business. Hale liked that. Anonymity. A chance to disappear, if only for a few hours.

He sat at the bar with his whiskey, nursing it slowly, his broad shoulders hunched forward. His eyes traced the mirror behind the bottles, though he wasn't really seeing his own reflection. He was seeing Keth—the alien's frail gray frame, the haunting voice inside his head, the warning that humanity was spiraling toward destruction. Hale tried to drown it with whiskey, but the memory clung like smoke.

"Long day?"

The voice was light, almost playful. Hale blinked, turning slightly to see a blond woman sliding onto the stool beside him. She looked to be around thirty, maybe a little younger. Bright eyes, a smile that hinted at mischief, and the kind of easy confidence that cut through the haze of the bar.

"You could say that," Hale muttered, glancing back at his glass.

"Let me guess," she said, resting her chin on her hand. "You're either military or law enforcement. That haircut and the way you're sitting—like you're waiting for a fight—it's a dead giveaway."

Hale chuckled, surprising himself. "Guilty. Military."

"I knew it." She smirked, lifting her own drink as the bartender set it down. "I've met my share of soldiers in here. None quite as broody as you, though."

"Broody?" He raised an eyebrow.

"Yeah," she said, leaning closer. "You've got that whole tortured-hero vibe going on. I bet women eat it up."

Hale shook his head, a smile tugging at the corner of his mouth despite the weight pressing down on him. "Not sure about that."

Their conversation flowed easily after that. She introduced herself as Amy Sutton. She told him she was a traveling nurse, temporarily working at a nearby clinic. Independent. Sharp-witted. She laughed easily, asked questions about him, but didn't push when he kept his answers short. Instead, she filled the space with stories about places she'd been, people she'd met, and the strange quirks of small-town bars.

One drink became two, then three. Hale found himself laughing—genuinely, for the first time in months. For a few hours, the weight of Dominion, of Keth's words, of his own hollow service, slipped away. There was only Amy, her warm smile, and the simple, disarming ease she carried.

By the time they stepped out into the cool night air, the spark between them was undeniable. Neither of them said much—words weren't needed. They walked down the street, close enough that their arms brushed, and when she stopped in front of the glowing sign of a hotel, she looked up at him with a smile that left little room for interpretation.

"Coming in?" she asked softly.

Hale hesitated only a second before following her inside.

The night was a blur of closeness, of heat, of unspoken need. It wasn't just passion—it was release. For Hale, it was the first time in years he let the walls drop, the armor crack. For Amy, it was a connection, wild and unexpected.

They didn't talk much. Words weren't necessary. Touch said everything.

For Hale, the night wasn't about forgetting. It was about remembering—what it felt like to be human, alive, wanted for something other than the missions, the secrets, the violence.

Dawn crept through the curtains, soft light spilling across the room. Amy stirred faintly, curled against the pillow, her blond hair tangled. Hale sat at the edge of the bed, pulling his shirt back on.

He watched her for a long moment, a heaviness in his chest he didn't know how to name. He hadn't intended this. He hadn't even wanted it, at first. But now… now there was something about her that tugged at him. Something that made him think maybe, just maybe, there was more to life than the shadows he lived in.

On the desk, he left a folded note with his number scrawled across it. I had a wonderful time. Call me if you'd like to see me again.

As he stepped quietly out of the room, Hale felt something unfamiliar—hope.

Maybe this wasn't just a one-night escape. Maybe, in a world unraveling with secrets and lies, a woman like Amy could be the anchor he didn't even realize he needed.

But even as the morning sun hit his face and he walked back toward base, another voice lingered in his mind, chilling and relentless.

Keth's warning.

If humans do not change, there will be no future.

Hale shoved his hands into his jacket pockets, the note he left behind feeling like a risk. A dangerous one. But maybe one worth taking.

For the first time in years, Marcus Hale wondered if he could still build a life beyond the cause he no longer believed in.

And for the first time in years, he was terrified of what that might cost.

Chapter 14: The Hacker

Jonathan Roberts had always been better with machines than with people. At six years old, while other kids were still chewing on their action figures, he had already taken apart the family's desktop computer and, miraculously, put it back together. When the screen flickered back to life, his mother gasped, his father laughed, and Jonathan shrugged like it was no big deal.

His father leaned against the doorframe, grinning. "Kid, one day you're gonna build the next NASA rocket—or blow up the whole damn Internet."

Jonathan smirked. "Why not both?"

Then his father was gone.

The scaffolding collapse was quick, brutal, and final. Jonathan was thirteen, old enough to understand what it meant, too young to carry the silence it left behind. His mother worked three jobs to keep the lights on—waitress at dawn, retail clerk by afternoon, janitor by night. She came home worn down to the bone, and Jonathan learned quickly not to ask for much.

Without parents hovering, he drifted. Teachers called him distracted. Friends called him weird. He wasn't distracted—he was calculating. And "weird" didn't bother him. His computer didn't care what he was.

The glow of a monitor became his sanctuary. He learned languages like other kids learned curse words: Python, C++, JavaScript, and assembly. He even started naming them in his head—"Python" was a smooth talker, "C++" was a cranky old uncle, and "assembly" was a sadistic math teacher with no sense of humor.

By sixteen, Jonathan wasn't just learning—he was testing. A university firewall was a puzzle box. A bank's secure database was a dare. He wasn't in it for money or glory. He wanted the rush, the mastery, the satisfaction of whispering to the machine: I own you.

came the night he should've walked away. Instead, curiosity shoved him headfirst into directories stamped with U.S. government seals. Red flags? Sure. He read them anyway. Classified memos, grainy satellite photos, snippets of code that hummed with authority. It was like tasting fire.

He was caught within weeks.

The knock at the door thundered at 3 a.m. Men in suits swarmed his house, rifles drawn. His mother screamed. Jonathan was shoved to the floor, wrists zip-tied, his laptop carried out like it was evidence in a murder case.

Seventeen years old. And his life should have ended there.

Juvenile detention bled into federal custody. Charges piled up—espionage, theft, unauthorized access to classified systems. A judge could've buried him until he was gray and bitter.

Then came the man in the tailored gray suit.

He slid a file across the table. Screenshots of Jonathan's hacks, annotated in the margins almost admiringly. "You're good," the man said flatly. "Too good to rot in a cage. You want a deal?"

Jonathan smirked despite the shackles. "What's the catch?"

The man's thin smile didn't reach his eyes. "No catch. Just your life, your skills, and the understanding that if you screw up once, you'll never be heard from again."

Jonathan leaned back in his chair, chains rattling. "Sounds like dating."

The man didn't laugh. Jonathan signed anyway.

Bars became cubicles. Shackles became clearances. And Jonathan Roberts disappeared into the NSA like a ghost in the system. Officially, he didn't exist. Unofficially, he became one of America's sharpest digital weapons.

The agency was heaven and hell rolled into one. They gave him tools he'd only dreamed of—quantum-encrypted servers, zero-day exploits that could break entire nations, surveillance systems that made commercial spyware look like a toddler's toy. He thrived. He hunted foreign hackers like a bloodhound, unraveled terrorist chatter in encrypted forums, and wiped ransomware cells off the map before they reached American soil. Supervisors who'd sneered at him started whispering: The kid's a prodigy.

For Jonathan, it wasn't just work. It was the first time since his father's death that he felt purpose. Every code cracked, every shadow neutralized—it was a victory for the boy who'd once been invisible.

And then one morning, the floor dropped out.

He was summoned two levels beneath the main NSA wing, into a room he hadn't known existed. No windows. No clocks. The man waiting inside had no nametag, no insignia. Posture? Military. Expression? Stone.

"Mr. Roberts," the man said evenly. "You've been recommended for a new assignment."

Jonathan slouched into the chair like he owned it. "Do I get a gold star?"

The man didn't flinch. He slid a folder across the table. A seal Jonathan didn't recognize—a triangle encircling a key. Inside: one sheet of paper. Three letters.

CIA.

Jonathan frowned. "That's it? Just three letters? Where's the dramatic music, the classified mission brief, the exploding pen?"

The man's lips twitched, almost a smile. "Sign, and you'll find out."

Jonathan stared at the page. He'd seen a lot of scary things buried in code, but this—this was different. The silence pressed against him, heavy as chains. For the first time since he was a kid, hunched alone in the glow of a monitor, Jonathan Roberts felt something unfamiliar curl in his chest.

Fear.

And underneath it, the spark of something he could never resist.

Curiosity....a new challenge.

Chapter 15: The Veil

The Situation Room beneath the West Wing was quiet enough to hear the ventilation system. The heavy, lead-lined doors were sealed. Even the Secret Service detail had been dismissed from the corridor, replaced with a single marine guard who didn't know why he was there.

President Mark Johnson sat at the far end of the polished walnut table, his tie slightly loosened, a tablet glowing in front of him. CIA Director Evelyn Shaw occupied the seat to his right, already scrolling through a classified briefing packet with her finger. General Nathan Harris, Chairman of the Joint Chiefs, leaned forward, elbows planted on the tabletop, a mug of coffee in his hands.

The three had worked side by side for nearly six years. They'd sat through crises together — coups, pandemics, proxy wars. But this morning was different. The atmosphere was heavier, as if the air itself was aware of the stakes.

Mark broke the silence.

"Everything Kyle Green handed us checks out," he said, tapping the encrypted tablet. "Signals intelligence, internal memos, field reports going back decades. A shadow government—Dark Dominion—splitting off from the CIA in the late forties. I've seen conspiracies before, but nothing like this. This is structural."

General Harris exhaled through his nose. "Their command structure runs parallel to ours. They've got field assets, airlift, weapons labs, and no oversight. This is not a rogue unit. This is an entire government inside ours. And according to Green, they've been stockpiling alien tech for close to eighty years."

Shaw didn't look up from her tablet. "They've reverse-engineered propulsion drives, power systems, weapons platforms—hell, even rudimentary AI cores. Most of the breakthroughs we thought were ours… weren't. They were siphoning everything off."

Mark rubbed his temple. "Which brings us to the question: what now? Do we lift the veil?"

Both Shaw and Harris glanced at him.

"You're serious?" Harris asked.

"I'm dead serious." Mark's voice was low but steady. "We've had treaties with at least four alien races since the mid-1960s. They're living here, under our protection. We're benefiting from their technology. And now we find out a splinter group has been abducting them, interrogating them, dissecting their tech like grave robbers. The American people deserve to know who's been running their country in the shadows."

Harris shook his head slowly. "If we go public now, Dark Dominion will burn evidence, liquidate assets, and possibly retaliate. They've got hardware we don't understand. Alien craft, hybrid weapons, biological weapons, cyberwarfare platforms. You don't poke a monster like that unless you're ready to take it down."

Mark held his gaze. "And what's your alternative?"

"Infiltration," Harris said firmly. "Get inside. Find out their motives. Map their infrastructure. We can't dismantle what we can't see."

Shaw finally set her tablet down. "I agree with the General. We need to know their endgame. Are they building a parallel state? Selling weapons? Preparing for a takeover? If we expose them too soon, we lose any chance of leverage."

Mark leaned back, fingers steepled. The weight of leadership pressed against his chest. He'd trusted these two for years. He trusted them now.

"What do you need?" he asked.

Shaw's eyes glinted. "Permission to recruit outside the box. There's a cybersecurity prodigy—off the grid, no official ties—someone who can crack Dark Dominion's digital vaults without tripping alarms. I also have an undercover asset ready to embed with a senior Dominion officer. A slow-play friendship op. It's risky, but it could give us names, locations, and real-time intelligence."

Harris spoke next. "And I'll put the best special operations unit we have on standby. Tier One. No insignias, no records. When the time comes, they'll be our hammer."

Mark nodded. "Green stays under protection. No leaks. Harris, you and Green will brief the ops unit personally on what they're walking into. Shaw, your hacker and your operative, is cleared—full presidential authority. I want compartmentalization. No one outside this room knows the whole picture."

A rare moment of stillness passed among them.

"We're talking about dismantling an entity with alien-level tech, Mr. President," Harris said finally. "There's no margin for error."

"That's why we're here," Mark replied. "We don't get second chances with history."

For the first time in the meeting, a flicker of something like hope moved across Shaw's face. Harris nodded once, firmly.

The President closed his tablet. "We move quietly, but we move now. This ends before it swallows the country whole."

There was a silent sigh of relief in the room—not of comfort, but of grim resolve. For the first time since Green had walked into their lives, it felt as though a plan was taking shape.

Chapter 16: The Briefing

Two hours after the Situation Room meeting, the underground briefing theater at Fort Belvoir's Special Activities Facility hummed with low chatter. The walls were matte black composite—sound-dampening, RF-shielded. A recessed row of biometric scanners had already verified every man in the room. No recording devices, no electronics beyond the encrypted tablets handed out at the door.

General Harris stood at the front, his uniform immaculate despite the sleepless night. To his left was Kyle Green, looking every inch the reluctant whistleblower—gray hair, worn field jacket, eyes constantly scanning the room like a man who'd been hunted.

Before them sat twelve operators from Ghost Spear, the highest-tier unit the Pentagon would never publicly acknowledge. Each one is hand-picked, cross-trained, and deniable.

At the center of the front row sat Captain Daniel Rourke, broad-shouldered, light brown hair trimmed close, an aura of steady authority. Next to him, leaning back with his arms crossed, was Tom Mitchel, the team's medic, known for his steady hands and emphatic compassion. The rest of the unit included Assistant Commander Rodriguez, four combat engineers, two communications operators, two intelligence operation specialists, a female sniper, and Warrant Officer Hunt.

Harris opened the briefing.

"You've all been told this is a Category One national security operation. That was the understatement of the decade. What you're about to hear will not leave this room. Even your chain of command above me does not have full visibility."

The room went still.

Green stepped forward, flipping on a holographic projector embedded in the table. A three-dimensional schematic blossomed in the air—concentric rings of facilities and names.

"Dark Dominion," Green began, his voice gravelly. "Not a codename, not a unit. An actual shadow government that spun off from the CIA around 1947. They've been operating black labs, detention centers, and research facilities under the cover of every administration since. They're not rogue. They're entrenched."

He swiped a finger. The projection shifted to grainy satellite images—triangular craft, glowing power cores, disassembled propulsion drives.

"Alien technology. Some recovered from crashes. Some from trade under the treaty. The public thinks Area 51 is a secret. It's a decoy. This—" he pointed at a cluster of icons in and around a mountain in the Nevada desert "—is one of their real facilities. And it's just the tip of the spear."

A low whistle came from one of the engineers. "So E.T. wasn't a joke?"

Green didn't smile. "E.T. was the sanitized version."

Tom Mitchel muttered under his breath to Daniel, "Guess Spielberg owed somebody a thank-you for the script."

Daniel gave a half-smile but kept his eyes forward.

Harris cut back in. "This unit is being tasked to infiltrate and recon. You're not to engage unless ordered. You're not to extract unless ordered. Your mission is intelligence—mapping personnel, technology, and operational scope. You will operate under false identities, tiered covers, and a custom-built comms net designed by Director Shaw's people."

He nodded to the NCO, who opened his encrypted tablet. "You'll be running on quantum-encrypted burst packets. No RF signature. No satellites. We're using subspace piggybacking off the same frequencies Dark Dominion's craft use for propulsion to mask our traffic."

Another low murmur rippled through the room.

Green continued. "You'll be introduced to an undercover operative already embedded with a senior Dominion officer. That's your primary human asset. Protect them at all costs. If compromised, exfil protocols will trigger automatically."

One of the combat engineers raised his hand. "Sir, are we talking about fighting aliens or fighting humans with alien toys?"

Harris looked him dead in the eye. "You're fighting Americans who've been stockpiling alien tech. The aliens are the victims here."

Tom let out a slow breath and muttered, "That's a hell of a plot twist."

Laughter rippled lightly through the team, tension bleeding off for a moment.

Daniel finally spoke. His voice was calm, steady—the way it always was when he needed to ground his men.

"We signed up to protect the American people. That hasn't changed. It doesn't matter if the threat is homegrown or extraterrestrial. We do the job, we do it clean, and we bring the intel home."

Tom smirked. "Always the motivational speaker, Cap. Are you sure you don't moonlight as a preacher?"

"I'm too pretty for that," Daniel deadpanned.

Even Harris cracked the faintest smile.

But as the humor faded, Daniel glanced down at the small photo tucked under his tablet—his wife, Claire, smiling in the sunlight with his daughter by her side. He knew Tom kept one of Sara's in his medkit. They'd talked about it on the flight over, two men who'd clawed their way past dead-end beginnings to stand here, at the edge of a secret war.

Harris's voice hardened.

"Ghost Spear, you're the best we've got. No insignia, no acknowledgment. If you're compromised, we'll deny everything. You'll be briefed on insertion in forty-eight hours. Get your gear squared away. Familiarize yourselves with the alien schematics in your tablets. Questions?"

The sniper warrant officer raised an immaculately waxed eyebrow. "Yeah. How do you kill something that's never existed on a battlefield before?"

Green answered, "You don't. You outthink it."

Tom muttered again, "Guess we're all hackers now."

Daniel closed his tablet and stood. "You heard the man. Two days to prep. Study, gear up, keep your heads clear. We're going in blind, but we're going in together."

The room fell silent. For all the incredulity—the UFO schematics, the talk of treaties—there was a steady undercurrent of resolve. They had always been more than soldiers. They were a firewall between chaos and the people they loved.

As the team filed out, Harris exchanged a glance with Green. For the first time in weeks, both men allowed themselves the faintest glimmer of hope.

Chapter 17: Sarah

The hum of the lab was a familiar comfort to Sara Mitchel. Machines purred softly around her, fans pushed the filtered air through vents in a steady rhythm, and the faint glow of monitors cast pale light across her desk. But tonight, the silence between those sounds felt louder than usual.

She rested her chin in her hand, staring at a screen she wasn't really reading. Her mind wasn't in the Pacific Northwest facility—it was somewhere far away, somewhere dangerous. Somewhere, Tom was.

Her husband's voice echoed in her head from the last time they spoke. He couldn't say much, couldn't tell her where he was going or what he'd be doing. He casually mentioned something about what they had seen, made wishes on, at their last camping trip together under the stars, some kind of code for what they were currently assigned to. She had learned long ago to read the weight in his pauses, the way he softened his words to keep her from worrying, but this message was different. She heard a slight tremor in his voice, a small ripple in his calm, steady voice. Special Ops assignments didn't come with guarantees. Still, she clung to his reassurance like it was oxygen: "I'll be back. I always come back." Aliens? Is that what this was about? A tremor of fear washed through her like a wave. Aliens?

Across the lab bench sat a photo frame she kept tucked behind her monitor. It held a picture of Tom in uniform, his arm around her shoulders, and Megan—smiling, bright-eyed, and barely six at the time. Now Megan was in college, studying hard, finding her own way in the world. They talked on the phone almost every night. Sara treasured those calls, listening to her daughter chatter about classes, roommates, and little daily dramas. The calls steadied her when the house felt too empty.

Her eyes drifted toward the file she had pulled up earlier. She hadn't wanted to open it again. But the past had a way of pressing forward when she least wanted to face it.

Six years ago, the world had changed forever. The virus swept through towns and cities like a tide no one could stop. It began quietly—something distant on the news—and then suddenly, it was everywhere. Sirens, cruise ships with sick and dying passengers stuck out at sea, overflowing hospitals, friends and neighbors lost within days. Entire communities, cities, shut down, borders closed. People are too afraid to leave their homes. Children's laughter is confined to computer screens.

Sara remembered holding Megan close on the couch during those long nights, whispering promises she wasn't sure she could keep: that they would be okay, that Tom would come home safe from his Special Ops deployments, that this storm would pass. She remembered the look in Tom's eyes when he did come home, weary but determined, as though he'd made a pact with himself to shoulder more than his share so that others could survive.

And yet, even after the world slowly reopened, the unease never left. The vaccines that were supposed to save everyone… hadn't. People she knew had fallen ill after receiving them, some with strange heart problems no one seemed willing to talk about. Questions were brushed aside, doctors silenced, answers rehearsed and repeated on television until they sounded more like propaganda than truth. Sara's work in biology made it impossible for her to believe all of what they were told. Deep down, she knew the official story was incomplete—maybe even a lie.

She shivered, not from the chill in the lab, but from memory. That terrible time had carved a scar into humanity, one that still hadn't healed.

And lately, she'd felt that same weight in the air again. Rumors trickled into her world, whispered between colleagues, and were hidden in obscure reports. Stories about labs working on things that sounded more like science fiction than reality—tiny chips small enough to be slipped into a person without their knowing, connected invisibly to the grid of technology that wrapped around the planet. She didn't know if it was true, but the possibility alone was terrifying.

Sometimes she wondered if the nightmare of six years ago hadn't been the real attack at all—just a test. A cruel rehearsal for something even worse.

Her phone buzzed on the table, breaking her thoughts. A message from Megan: "Love you, Mom. The study session went late. Don't stay up too long."

Sara smiled, her heart softening. She typed back quickly: "Love you more. Proud of you always." She hovered for a moment before adding, "And I miss your dad too. We'll get through this together." Then she hit send.

She sat back, folding her arms across her chest, her gaze drifting again to the photo of Tom and Megan. The lab's glow made the glass shine, as though the faces inside were lit from within.

The machines around her kept humming, carrying on their endless, mechanical work. But Sara stayed still, listening to her own thoughts, her own fears, and her own hope.

Whatever was coming, she prayed she would be strong enough—for Tom, for Megan, and for the world they all still deserved to live in.

Chapter 18: Melting Pot of Tension

The Private meeting room in the basement of the Whitehouse had never felt smaller.

President Mark Johnson sat at the head of the long, polished wood table in the basement of Ellis Air Force Base, flanked by General Harris on his right and members of the Treaty of Foreign and Alien Alliance Committee seated around the table, along with interpreters. The shades were drawn tight, the room sealed by layers of classified security. But no barrier could contain the heavy tension pressing in from every corner.

Across from him sat the alien representatives—five in all, each one different, each one extraordinary.

There was Kaelen, tall, reed-like and luminous, a Serian species, his skin like flowing silver mercury. Every shift of his tall, lanky body shimmered with liquid light. He spoke with calm precision, yet his eyes burned with restrained fury.

Beside him sat Teyara, of the Thal'kari race, her body slender and willow-like, her skin patterned with hues of green and gold that rippled like sunlight through leaves, eyes like pools of liquid silver. She had always been one of the warmest voices in the treaty discussions, but tonight her voice shook with betrayal.

Two smaller representatives of the grey race, short grey beings, eyes large, dark, and expressive, sat close together, their features stoic and defensive. One of them, clutching the other's arm, showed no emotion in those large luminous eyes.

Next to the greys sat Ora of the Orash, silently, usually very verbal, speaking with light and sound; however, today he sat quietly, with small orbs of eyes shrouding untrust.

And at the end of the line was Dralith, towering and reptilian, scales glinting dark like onyx. His presence was imposing, his voice like gravel dragged across stone, yet the grief behind his words carried weight beyond intimidation.

They were not enemies. They were not strangers. They were supposed to be allies.

"Mr. President," Kaelen began, his voice low but trembling with anger, "you pledged to us that our people would be safe here. That our ships would be unharmed, that no harm would come to our kind while this alliance stood. Yet in the last three months, seven of our vessels have been shot from your skies." His silver features rippled like storm clouds. "Entire crews—lost. Families waiting for their return—grieving. And now we learn that those who survived… were taken. Tortured."

The words hit like a physical blow.

President Johnson drew in a breath, meeting their eyes one by one. "I will not deny it. These atrocities have happened. But hear me clearly—they were not sanctioned by my administration. Not by this government. Not by me."

General Harris leaned forward, his deep voice steady, commanding. "Intelligence confirms a rogue element—a splinter faction that broke away years ago from the CIA. They have resources, aircraft, and even advanced weapons technology. They are operating beyond our oversight, without authorization, without law. It is they who are responsible for the kidnappings and the attacks on your ships."

Dralith's claws flexed against the table, leaving faint scratches in the wood. "And what comfort is that to the families of my dead? You say your government is not responsible, but it is still your world. If you cannot control your own kind, how are we to trust any treaty with you?"

The Orash representative keened softly, his voice like an orchestra and sparks of light in distrust. "We sought safety here," his interpreter whispered. "We believed your promises. Now we are hunted, not by enemies, but by the very hand that swore to protect us."

Teyara's liquid silver patterns pulsed with sorrow. "You speak of rogue factions as if that absolves you. But to us, there is no difference. Human hands are still the ones that have taken our brothers and sisters from us. If this can happen once, what is to stop it from happening again?"

The room bristled with the weight of their words. Every pair of alien eyes held the same question: Are we truly safe here?

President Johnson rose slowly to his feet. His chair groaned across the floor, the sound sharp in the silence. He looked every representative in the eye, his jaw tight, his voice steady but heavy with conviction.

"You have every right to be outraged. Every right to be afraid. I will not insult you with excuses. What has been done to your people is monstrous and unforgivable. I give you my word—my life's word—

that I will not rest until this shadow faction is uncovered, dismantled, and destroyed. If it takes every resource of the United States, if it takes the last breath in my body, I will see justice done."

For a moment, the room was silent except for the faint hum of air conditioning. The aliens studied him—some skeptical, some quietly moved, all still on edge.

Nothing was resolved. No agreement was reached. The distrust lingered, heavy and suffocating. Yet in the midst of the unease, Johnson's words hung like a fragile thread of hope.

Kaelen's silver gaze softened, just slightly. "Then you must act swiftly, Mr. President. For if you do not, we may have no choice but to defend ourselves. And if that day comes…" Her voice trailed into a silence more chilling than any threat.

The meeting adjourned in shadows. Chairs scraped. Guards opened the sealed doors. The alien representatives filed out, each carrying their grief and fury like cloaks around their shoulders.

When the room was empty except for Johnson and Harris, the President sank back into his chair, shoulders heavy. "God help us, Harris," he muttered. "Because if we fail them, we don't just lose allies—we lose ourselves."

And for the first time in his presidency, Mark Johnson felt the weight of an entire planet's trust slipping through his fingers.

Chapter 19: The Last Straw

The phone rang just after midnight. President Mark Johnson, still in the Oval Office after the grueling committee meeting, rubbed at his temples before reaching for the secure line.

"Mr. President, this is Dr. Lang with NASA." The voice on the other end was urgent, clipped. "We need your immediate attention."

Johnson straightened in his chair. "Go ahead."

"At first, we believed it was a near-Earth object—asteroid class. Trajectory suggested a pass within five thousand miles of Earth's orbit. But further scans show a deceleration pattern." The pause was long enough for Johnson's pulse to quicken. "Sir… natural objects don't slow down. This isn't an asteroid."

Johnson's throat felt dry. "What are you saying?"

Lang's voice lowered. "Our latest imaging shows structure. Geometry. It's beginning to resemble a… craft. Large. We estimate over a mile in length. It's inbound. Estimated arrival into stable Earth orbit within a few months."

The words slammed into him harder than he expected. Another ship. Not cloaked, not hiding. And it was coming straight for Earth.

"Does Defense know?" Johnson managed.

"Yes sir, she replied. NORAD and Space Command are already on high alert." The president silently thought about everything else happening—the treaty tensions, the rogue faction incidents-this will complicate matters exponentially.

Johnson leaned back, the room spinning slightly. His heart pounded, sharp pain blooming across his chest. He pressed a hand against it, his breath shallow.

"Mr. President?" Lang asked from the other end. "Are you still with me?"

Yes," Johnson forced out, though his voice was strained. "Keep me informed on every update. No one outside this chain hears about this until we know what we're dealing with. Understood?"

"Understood, sir."

The line went dead.

Johnson's hand still pressed to his chest, the ache spreading down his arm now. He stood slowly, gripping the edge of his desk for support. The air in the room felt heavy, suffocating.

General Harris appeared in the doorway, concern etched on his face. "Mr. President?"

"I… need a moment," Johnson whispered, his jaw tight. "Have the White House physician come to my quarters. Quietly."

Harris nodded once, eyes sharp with worry, before stepping back.

Johnson made his way down the private hall toward his residence, every step harder than the last. His vision blurred at the edges, sweat forming along his brow. He collapsed into the armchair near his bed, clutching his chest as another wave of pain tore through him, his wife by his side.

Through the haze of agony, only one thought pressed through: If I fall now, everything we've fought to hold together will collapse with me.

A knock at the door sounded faintly distant.

Then the world around him went dark.

Chapter 20: Operation Pale Horse

Jonathan Roberts was halfway through a bag of peanut M&Ms when the code finally cracked. His fingers flew across the keyboard, a smirk tugging at his mouth as streams of decrypted text spilled onto his monitor.

"Gotcha," he muttered, leaning back in his chair, hands behind his head like he'd just sunk a three-pointer at the buzzer. The logo of the Dark Dominion's shadow-government splinter cell flickered briefly before giving way to rows of encrypted files. His heart thudded. He'd been recently recruited into CIA Cybersecurity for this very reason—his knack for doing what no one else could.

Most agents wore suits and ties, badges clipped to their belts. Jonathan wore scuffed sneakers, a hoodie, and the permanent expression of someone both too smart for his own good and slightly amused by everything around him.

He scrolled quickly, eyes widening when a file name jumped out at him in bold red font: Operation Pale Horse.

"Well, that doesn't sound ominous at all," he said under his breath. He clicked, pulse quickening, as the file began to load.

And then—

"Jonathan Roberts?"

He froze. The voice was melodic, firm yet teasing, and it didn't belong to any of his cubicle neighbors. He spun in his chair and almost fell out of it.

Standing in the aisle was the most striking woman he'd ever seen. Dark brown hair neatly pinned back, sharp green eyes that seemed to see right through him, and a fitted black suit that screamed high-ranking CIA, not cyber security. She carried herself with a quiet confidence that made the fluorescent cubicle maze look like a stage she'd already conquered.

"Uh…" Jonathan blinked, scrambling for words. "If you're here to sell me cookies, I'm buying. If you're here to arrest me, I need a five-minute head start."

Her lips curved into a smirk. "Melony Bishop. CIA. You're Jonathan, right? The Bureau's shiny new cyber prodigy?"

"Prodigy? Please. I prefer 'digital outlaw reluctantly tamed by government bureaucracy.'" He offered a mock bow from his chair.

Melony chuckled, and Jonathan swore the sound was the most beautiful thing he'd ever heard. "I hear you're cracking firewalls that make grown men cry. Like right now."

His heart skipped. Had she seen? He flicked his screen off with a quick keystroke and leaned back casually. "Me? Nah. I'm just updating my Fantasy Football roster."

She raised a brow, clearly unconvinced, but amused nonetheless. "Right. Fantasy Football."

Jonathan grinned. "Hey, don't judge. It takes serious hacking skills to make my team look good."

There was a spark between them—immediate, electric. He felt it in the way her eyes lingered, the playful edge to her tone. She was sharp, clever, and absolutely dangerous in all the ways that made his pulse race.

"So," Jonathan said, trying to sound smooth while internally panicking, "do CIA agents usually wander into cyber security cubicle farms to flirt with guys like me, or am I just lucky today?"

"Flirt?" Melony laughed softly. "Is that what this is?"

"Definitely. At least on my end."

She shook her head, fighting a smile. "Careful, Roberts. I'm spoken for."

The words landed like a punch to his gut. "Spoken for? By who? Please tell me it's not someone cooler than me, because that would really hurt."

"Assistant Commander Rodriguez. Ghost Spear unit."

Jonathan winced dramatically, clutching his chest. "Special Ops? Oh, come on. That's just not fair. I hack firewalls, he probably eats grenades for breakfast."

Melony laughed again, softer this time, her gaze lingering just a fraction too long. "You're impossible."

"Impossible… but charming?" he asked hopefully.

Her lips curved. "Maybe."

For the first time in his life, Jonathan Roberts didn't care about the classified file glowing on his locked monitor or the danger of the Dark Dominion. All he could think about was the woman standing in front of him, the spark in her eyes, and the ridiculous fact that he'd just fallen head over heels in about thirty seconds flat.

And judging by the way Melony Bishop's smile lingered, maybe—just maybe—she had too.

Chapter 21: The Abduction

The sun over Nebraska had been warm and endless that day, stretching across the Green family's farm like a blanket of gold. Twelve-year-old Kyle ran through the high corn rows with Zeus, his golden retriever, bounding ahead. The stalks whispered as he brushed past, a sound he'd always loved — like the earth itself was telling him secrets.

Zeus darted ahead, tail wagging, barking at something unseen. Kyle laughed, breathless, as he tried to keep up. Then the light changed.

It was subtle at first — the blue of the sky deepened, the gold of the corn dulled. And then, without a sound, everything stopped. No wind. No insects. No birds chirping in the distance. Even Zeus froze, hackles raised, growling low.

Kyle blinked.

And he was no longer in the field.

He stood — or floated — inside a room of soft silver light, smooth walls curving upward like the inside of a giant seashell. His body lay on a cold steel table below him, pale and still. Around it stood three figures — small, grey, with enormous black eyes that reflected everything like pools of ink. Their spindly fingers held metallic instruments that gleamed unnaturally under the alien light.

Kyle's heart pounded, but his body did not move. He couldn't scream. He couldn't breathe. He wasn't in his body. He was watching from somewhere just above, weightless and terrified.

Then, a voice inside his head.

Do not fear. We will not harm you.

It was calm, resonant, like several tones speaking at once. One of the greys looked up at him — not at his body, but at him floating above.

We are only studying your anatomy. We are an interdimensional alien race from a parallel universe.

Kyle's thoughts spilled out in panic. Where am I? Will I see my mom and dad again?

The voice soothed but did not answer directly. You will not be harmed. You will return.

One of the greys tilted its head toward the far side of the room. Through a translucent partition, Kyle saw Zeus standing rigid, golden fur bristling, eyes wide with fear.

The creature with you, the voice said. What is it to you?

Kyle's fear cracked just enough for him to think: He's my dog. He's… my friend.

Friend? the alien repeated, as though testing the word. We are interested in this species. Its loyalty to you is unusual. It defends you, though it cannot comprehend you fully or speak words as you do.

Kyle felt a shudder pass through his floating self. He wanted to scream for Zeus, to tell the aliens to leave him alone.

The alien's voice shifted, softer now. We were once as you are. We were human, but from a future civilization. We destroyed our own world through greed, corruption, and unchecked technology. We were forced underground, living in the dark. We lost the ability to reproduce. Our civilization is dying.

Kyle's fear paused under the weight of their confession.

Your world is on the same path, the alien warned. There will be a great war on your planet between your governments and alien craft. More than two-thirds of your population will die. You must devote your life to stopping it.

Terror seized him. Why me? I'm just a kid.

The voice lingered. Because you will remember, even if you forget. We have planted this warning inside you. It will return when you are ready.

And then, nothing.

He gasped awake in the cornfield, sunlight glaring down. Zeus was licking his face frantically, whining. Kyle sat up, trembling. His clothes were damp with dew, though the sun had been high when he'd left the house. His heart thundered.

When he stumbled back to the farmhouse, his mother scolded him for staying out so long, unaware of what had happened. Kyle tried to tell her, but couldn't find the words. By bedtime, the memory had faded to fragments, like a strange dream slipping away.

But over the years, pieces returned. In flashes, in dreams, in moments he couldn't explain. The silver room. The grey faces. The voice in his head. The warning.

Kyle grew up. He joined the Army. He became a doctor, saving lives on battlefields while carrying a secret he didn't fully understand. And when he retired, he did not rest.

He gathered classified documents, conducted interviews with high-ranking officials, pored over obscure reports, and investigated anomalous sightings. For decades, he connected dots no one wanted to see, following a thread woven through history. The thread always led to the same dark truth: humanity was on the same path the aliens had warned him about.

And Kyle Green, the boy from the cornfields of Nebraska, was the only one who had been told.

He had devoted his life to stopping the catastrophe he feared was already set in motion. And with each passing year, the fragments of that day became sharper, more vivid, until he no longer doubted.

The war was coming.

And if he failed, everything he'd ever loved — every farm, every field, every loyal dog — would be lost.

Chapter 22: Goodbye

The plane touched down in North Carolina just after dawn, and Daniel Rourke stepped out into the cool morning air with a weight in his chest that no rucksack could rival. The team had been granted a rare leave — a handful of days carved out of the storm ahead — and Daniel intended to make every second matter.

Claire met him at the terminal, auburn hair catching the sunlight, eyes brimming before she even reached him. He barely had time to set down his duffel before she was in his arms, holding him as if the world might try to tear him away if she loosened her grip.

"Daddy!" Emily's voice rang out behind her, clear and bright. At four years old, she was all freckles and boundless energy. She sprinted into his legs, wrapping herself around him like she had when she was small enough to carry.

Daniel closed his eyes, breathing them in. Home. Safety. Love. For a few days, the secrets and unrest of the world could not touch him.

They spent their time simply, as if the ordinary moments were precious treasures: breakfast together at the kitchen table, Emily insisting on syrup drowning her pancakes; a walk through the park where Emily begged for piggyback rides and Daniel pretended to collapse dramatically under her "weight"; late evenings on the porch swing with Claire curled against his side, listening to the cicadas hum while Emily fell asleep upstairs.

Daniel laughed more in those days than he had in months. He let himself be silly for Emily, let Claire see the boyish grin she said had first won her over. But beneath the laughter was something heavier, an ache that pressed deeper with each hour.

He couldn't shake it — the feeling in his gut that this was goodbye. Ghost Spear's mission was unlike any they'd faced before. This wasn't just another battlefield in a faraway land. This was stepping into the dark heart of a shadow government that had already claimed countless lives and secrets. If fate had marked him, he didn't want Claire or Emily to carry that weight before it was time.

So he kept silent. He smiled. He memorized.

Every time Claire tucked a strand of hair behind her ear, he etched it into his memory. Every time Emily threw her head back and laughed, he let it sear itself into his soul. He traced the lines of Claire's face with his eyes in the quiet moments, held her hand longer than necessary, kissed her as though each one had to last a lifetime.

At night, when the house was still, he lay awake beside Claire. He listened to her breathe, steady and comforting, the sound that had anchored him through years of war and doubt. She had been his strength when he faltered, his home when the world felt nothing but hostile and cold. He whispered his love into her hair while she slept, words he could not bear to say aloud in daylight.

Emily bounded into their bed the morning before he was to leave, her laughter filling the room as she wiggled between them. Claire groaned playfully, but Daniel wrapped them both in his arms and held on tight.

For a moment, he let himself imagine this would last forever — pancakes and porch swings, bedtime stories and tangled mornings. A life untouched by war or secrets.

But he knew better.

When it came time to pack his bag again, Claire stood in the doorway, watching him. Her eyes were wet, though she tried to hide it with a smile.

"Come home to us," she whispered, voice trembling.

Daniel swallowed the truth, forcing his own smile. He pressed his forehead against hers and kissed her softly. "Always."

But in his heart, he held the unspoken words: If I don't… remember that I loved you both more than anything in this world.

And with that, Captain Daniel Rourke shouldered his bag and stepped once more toward the shadows.

The house was too quiet after Daniel left.

Chapter 23: Faith

Claire stood in the doorway long after his car disappeared down the street, arms wrapped around herself as though holding in the ache swelling inside. She had hugged him hard, kissed him like it might keep him tethered, but the hollow that followed his departure felt like a warning.

She hadn't said it out loud — she couldn't — but the fear gnawed at her: What if he doesn't come back this time?

Emily's innocent giggles floated faintly from the living room, the sound of cartoons blaring too loud. Claire forced her feet to move, forced her face to soften, because her little girl couldn't see the storm inside her. Emily needed strength, and Daniel needed faith, wherever he was going.

Still, the grief pressed heavily, relentlessly. In the kitchen, Claire braced her hands against the counter, eyes closing as silent tears traced down her cheeks. She whispered a prayer — not for herself, but for him — a desperate plea that he would return.

But deep in her bones, she felt it. A mother's instinct. A wife's dread. This mission was different.

And so she carried the grief quietly, wearing it like invisible armor. For Emily. For Daniel. For the promise she made when she chose to love a man who had sworn to protect his country at any cost.

Chapter 24: Visitor

Elliot Kane had always liked the quiet. The Colorado mountains were good for that — snow-dusted peaks, pine-scented air, and a cabin tucked far enough away that no one ever dropped by unannounced. Most people thought him a hermit. Most people were right.

He sipped cold coffee, muttering to himself, eyes glued to lines of encrypted code on his battered laptop. "Come on, you bastard… if I can crack this one, I'll finally—"

A soft, almost imperceptible noise outside the cabin drew his attention. He froze, listening. The wind? A falling branch? No. There was something… alive.

Elliot set his mug down and stepped cautiously outside, flashlight in hand. Snow crunched under his boots. Then he saw it.

A small figure, hunched, pale, grey-skinned, lying half-buried in the snow. Its limbs twitched weakly. Its eyes… oh, God, its eyes were enormous, black, shimmering with pain and something more — fear.

"Holy… Hercules," Elliot muttered under his breath, dropping to his knees. "You're… you're real."

The alien coughed, a strange gurgle, and a rasping voice echoed in his mind. Elliot Kane… help… must… stop… Shadow Government, Pale Horse…

The words were broken, gasping between breaths, but the meaning was clear. Elliot wrapped the trembling being in a warm, dry blanket and carried him inside. By the fire, he set the alien down gently.

"Don't worry… I'm not going to hurt you," Elliot whispered, talking to himself as much as to the creature. "You're safe. I'll fix you."

The alien shivered, body fractured in ways Elliot couldn't comprehend. Its breaths came ragged, chest rising and falling in shallow gasps through a small opening, Elliot assumed was his mouth. But it looked at him, eyes large black pools with raw trust.

"Government… rogue… technology…" The voice rasped, weak. "Reverse… engineered… over… years… Operation Pale Horse… plan… fake… alien attack… human casualties… two-thirds… microchips… one world order…"

Elliot's head spun. He crouched closer, brushing snow and ice from the alien's small, delicate frame. "Wait. Slow down. What are you saying?"

The alien's gaze glimmered with desperation, and in that moment, Elliot felt it — a living being, terrified, giving everything it had to warn him. A creature from another universe, another dimension, from a future where greed and power had destroyed everything.

"They… have… advanced tech… beyond… your government… will stage… invasion… humans… will believe it… survival… depends on… stopping them…" The words came slower now, labored, as the alien coughed violently.

Elliot grabbed a rag and pressed it gently against its chest. "Shh… I've got you. Just hold on."

But the alien's body went still. Its large, black eyes stared at him, empty now, then a faint residue was left behind on the blanket, slimy and otherworldly. A cold grief slammed into Elliot's chest, heavier than any snowstorm, any isolation he had ever endured.

The last words Elliot felt in his head were save humanity and planet earth.

The fire crackled. The cabin smelled of pine, smoke, and fear. Elliot sat in silence, staring at the faint trace the alien left behind.

The creature had trusted him. Shared secrets he could barely comprehend. Shared the knowledge of humanity's impending peril, of a shadow faction ready to destroy billions. And it had died in his hands, leaving nothing but a warning and a faint, glimmering residue.

Elliot ran a hand through his hair, feeling the weight of what had just happened. Am I ready for this? Can I leave my quiet life, my codes, my little cabin, and face what's coming?

Outside, the wind rattled against the windows. Inside, the fire flickered. Elliot's gaze fell on the laptop, on the encryption he'd been obsessing over just moments ago, and the faint residue of a dying warning, and he understood: the quiet life was over.

He could feel the enormity of the fight ahead pressing against him, a mountain higher than any he had ever climbed.

But somewhere deep in his chest, a spark ignited — a determination he hadn't known he possessed.

He could not let this planet fall.

And neither could he let the memory of those pleading, black eyes fade without action.

Elliot Kane rose, hands trembling slightly, and whispered to the empty cabin, "Alright… let's see what we can do."

The snowstorm outside continued, indifferent, but inside the cabin, a man had been awakened.

Chapter 25: Home Fire

Jonathan Roberts had faced down firewalls built by nations, corporations, and warlords. He'd once slipped into a dark web server so secure it was rumored to fry your hard drive just for trying. But none of that prepared him for the sight of Assistant Commander Gabriel Rodriguez walking into the CIA field office.

The man looked like he'd been carved out of steel. Broad shoulders, military buzz cut, uniform sharp enough to cut glass. He moved with the ease of someone who could kill you three different ways before you finished blinking—and, worse, he looked like he knew it.

And right beside him was Melony Bishop.

Jonathan froze in his cubicle doorway, trying not to look like a deer in the headlights. Melony's eyes flicked to him, and for the briefest second, something warm sparked there. But then she turned, businesslike, as Rodriguez spoke.

"Where's your cyber asset?" Rodriguez asked, his voice deep, steady. Not loud—but loud wasn't necessary.

Melony tilted her head toward Jonathan. "There he is. Jonathan Roberts. Our best shot at cracking into the Dominion's files."

Jonathan stepped forward, plastering on his trademark grin. "That's me. Hacker extraordinaire. Cubicle samurai. Keeper of the office snack stash. Pleasure to meet you, sir."

Rodriguez's eyes swept him up and down. He didn't smile. "You're young and not at all what I expected."

"And yet," Jonathan shot back, "surprisingly competent. It's a gift."

Melony's lips twitched like she was suppressing a smile, but Rodriguez didn't miss a beat. "Competence isn't proven until it's tested. And in this world, Roberts, tests can kill you."

Jonathan raised a brow. "Noted. But for what it's worth, sir, I've survived twenty-seven consecutive Mondays working for the federal government. That has to count as combat experience."

Melony laughed before she could stop herself, and Rodriguez's eyes narrowed just slightly. He looked between Jonathan and Melony, and in that brief silence, Jonathan knew exactly what Rodriguez was thinking.

He sees it too.

The unspoken spark. The way Melony had leaned just a little closer to Jonathan when she'd introduced him. The way her laugh slipped out more freely around him than it probably should have.

Rodriguez stepped closer, close enough that Jonathan caught the faint scent of gun oil and starch. "Roberts," he said quietly, his tone calm but loaded, "you do your job. That's it. Don't forget your place."

Jonathan met his eyes, his grin softening into something steadier, more serious. "Don't worry. I know my place. It's just usually at the computer saving the day when all the muscle guys run out of bullets."

The tension hung there, thick enough to choke on.

Melony finally cleared her throat, breaking the moment. "We should focus. Operation Pale Horse isn't going to decrypt itself."

Jonathan tore his gaze away from Rodriguez, giving her a quick smile—one that said everything without words. I'm not afraid. And I'm not giving up.

As they moved toward the ops room, Rodriguez fell in step beside Melony, his hand brushing the small of her back. Jonathan's stomach clenched, but his mind was already whirring. He wasn't a soldier. He wasn't built like Rodriguez. But he had one advantage: Melony Bishop had laughed at his jokes, and that spark between them? That was real.

And Jonathan Roberts wasn't about to let it die.

Chapter 26: Colonel Hale

Colonel Hale leaned back in his chair, the glow of the monitors reflecting off his sharp, tired eyes. The memory of the grey alien's last moments haunted him — the rasping words, the desperate gaze, the residue on the blanket left behind in the interrogation room.

"If humans do not change, there will be no future…"

The words weren't just a warning. They were a prophecy. Hale could feel it in the tension that hung over the Dark Dominion headquarters like a storm cloud. Everyone moved with controlled purpose, their secrets tightly sealed, their faces masks of professionalism. Yet the unease was palpable. He knew, as did the higher-ups, that the next wave of operations would cost lives — more than anyone could count, more than anyone outside would ever comprehend.

The weight of it settled into his chest. And yet, when he closed the office door behind him, when the rigid world of classified files and covert orders disappeared behind the click of the lock, another reality took over.

Amy Sutton.

He remembered the first time he saw her, sliding into a seat next to him at a rundown tavern on the outskirts of a small town in Nevada, sitting right next to him, ordering a drink. She had looked at him like she could see straight through him. Straight through all the secrets. He was so weary, she was like a tall drink of water that made him feel alive again. Like maybe there was hope after all.

Her arms wrapped around him now, the tension of the day dissolving against the warmth of her body. She pressed her cheek against his chest, inhaling that faint scent of starch and coffee he always carried. "You've been quiet," she murmured, voice soft, teasing but aware.

He chuckled, letting his forehead rest against hers. "Long day," he admitted. Not a word about alien interrogations, not a word about the files he couldn't ever tell her existed. But somehow, with her, silence was enough. She understood without needing the details. She understood the weight of what he carried without him saying a single classified word.

"You can tell me anything," she whispered. Her hand traced the line of his jaw. "I'm not going anywhere."

Hales' chest tightened. He wanted to believe her, wanted to tell her everything — about the Dark Dominion, the alien warnings, Operation Pale Horse. But he couldn't. Not yet. Not ever, maybe.

Instead, he let himself sink into her embrace, letting the fire in the hearth warm his cold, battle-worn bones. They moved together in a rhythm that felt like coming home after a lifetime of wandering. Her lips against his neck, the faint smell of floral conditioner in her hair, her heartbeat against his chest — it grounded him, gave him something real to hold on to in a world of shadows and lies.

He whispered into her hair, words that were true, if incomplete. "You make it bearable. Even when the world's about to fall apart, you make it bearable."

Amy smiled, tilting her head up to meet his eyes. "Then don't ever forget that, Marcus. You're not alone."

In her arms, he allowed himself a rare vulnerability, for the first time in his entire life, one no one else could see. He could almost forget the death, the secrets, the knowledge that more than just his own life was at stake. Almost.

But the world outside the apartment window was coming apart in ways that no warmth, no love, could fully repair. And Colonel Hales knew it.

For now, though, he let himself stay here — with Amy Sutton, with her laughter, with the quiet intimacy that felt like a shield against the storm. The alien's warning would not leave him. The looming disaster would not relent. But for tonight, he could rest. He could let the arms of the woman he loved hold him safe.

And for Hale, that was enough to carry him through another day in the Dark Dominion.

Chapter 27: Amy Sutton

Amy Sutton wiped her palm on her jeans, staring at the pile of papers she'd shoved the hard drive under. Her heart still hammered from the narrow escape. One second, she'd been mid-download from Hales' laptop, the next, she heard the bathroom door click and the sound of water draining. He had stepped out of the bedroom, fresh from a shower, and for a terrifying moment, she thought he'd see.

But he didn't.

She exhaled slowly, letting the relief wash over her. Hale remained oblivious to the months of digging she'd done — combing through his phone, his encrypted records, his files — compiling evidence for her superior, CIA Director Evelyn Shaw. Every bit of data she gathered could be the key to unraveling the Dark Dominion from the inside. But it came at a cost: proximity. Proximity to the man she was supposed to love, and the man who had no idea she was spying on him.

Her fingers itched to check the hard drive again, to confirm the files were intact, but she had to wait. Patience was everything. The slightest misstep, the faintest suspicion, and everything she'd worked for would collapse — and so would her carefully constructed cover.

Amy leaned back in the chair, letting the weight of her duplicity settle. There was guilt, of course. Hale was kind in ways few people had ever been with her — tender, protective, capable of making her feel safe after years of trusting almost no one. He had shared pieces of himself she'd never coaxed out of anyone else. And yet, here she was, exploiting that trust, going through his personal life in secret.

She tapped her fingers on the desk. The CIA needed the intel. Humanity might depend on it. And still, her heart clenched every time she imagined him discovering her. Every time she saw him look at her, even with tenderness, she wondered how long she could keep it together.

Weeks of careful planning had led to this moment: a folder labeled Operation Honey Bee waiting to be decrypted, evidence of the Dark Dominion's ultimate plan, lying in her hands. One wrong click, one misstep in timing… and Hale would know.

Amy reached for the hidden drive, her mind racing through the data she had collected, replaying the almost-discovery over and over. She had to remain calm. She had to remain invisible. And yet, in that same moment, she longed to tell him everything — to feel safe in his arms without lies, without secrets.

She shook the thought away. No. Not yet. Not while the fate of the world depended on her mission.

Amy glanced toward the bedroom door, imagining Hales' towel-draped figure stepping out any second. She smiled faintly to herself — a little thrill running through her. Danger had always had a way of sharpening her senses, of reminding her why she did what she did. But this? This was personal. And dangerous in ways no field mission had ever been.

She leaned back, stealing herself. One more night. One more chance. Then the files would be gone, on their way to Director Shaw. And Hale? He would never know how close he had come to catching her betraying the man she loved.

For now, she waited.

Chapter 28: Alliance

The Situation Room had never felt so heavy. President Mark Johnson sat at the head of the long table, his suit hanging looser on his frame than it had weeks before. The lines around his eyes were deeper now, etched by pain, surgery, and sleepless nights. A discreet heart monitor under his jacket ticked quietly, a private metronome of his fragile recovery.

General Harris sat close at his right, posture ramrod straight, eyes flicking to the President every few minutes. At his left, CIA Director Evelyn Shaw tapped a pen softly against a folder thick with classified reports. Her face gave nothing away, but her eyes were sharp, calculating, waiting.

Across from them sat a group unlike any that had ever gathered here before.

Captain Daniel Rourke of Ghost Spear — lean, stone-jawed, the weight of his secret mission written in the tightness of his shoulders. Amy Sutton, the beautiful CIA agent whose cover had been as seamless as silk until now, her gaze steady but hands clasped a little too tightly on the tabletop. Melony Bishop, quick-eyed and alert, was leaning back just enough to look calm but giving off the sense of a coiled spring.

Next to them sat Jonathon Roberts, the "bad boy" hacker turned CIA asset, dressed in an ill-fitting suit and fiddling with a pen he'd pilfered from somewhere on the way in. His eyes flicked nervously between the faces at the table, then to the man he'd dragged with him: Elliot Kane.

Elliot looked out of place — wild-eyed, bearded, wearing a worn flannel shirt under a borrowed jacket. His hair was still wet with melted snow from the Colorado mountains. He hadn't slept in days. But his eyes burned with urgency, and the file he clutched in his calloused hand might as well have been a live grenade.

Kyle Green, the retired Army doctor turned whistleblower, sat at the far end of the table, his presence quiet but commanding. He had been waiting for this moment for decades, and it showed in the calm steadiness of his posture.

President Johnson cleared his throat, the sound strained but resolute. "We're here because too much has been hidden, too much buried. We are at a tipping point. And it ends now."

Daniel Rourke exchanged a glance with Amy Sutton before speaking. "Sir, our infiltration of the Dark Dominion's operations confirmed our worst fears. They've been reverse-engineering alien technology for decades. Operation Pale Horse is not a rumor. It's a plan. A large-scale staged alien attack on Earth, designed to wipe out two-thirds of the population."

Melony leaned forward. "They've already developed weapons platforms capable of shooting down alien craft, which they've been doing for years. They want the public terrified enough to accept anything."

Elliot's hands trembled as he set the files on the table. "I saw it myself. An alien from the future crashed near my cabin. He died in my arms. He told me everything. These people—these monsters—aren't just planning an attack. They're planning to chip the survivors, to control the world after the dust settles."

Jonathon shot him a look before continuing. "It's true, sir. I've been inside their encrypted systems. Elliot and I put this file together for you early this morning from all that I've compiled, along with his files. He's not crazy. Operation Pale Horse exists."

Director Shaw tilted her head, her sharp eyes darting to Elliot. "You're saying this information came directly from an alien being?"

"Yes," Elliot snapped. "A grey. He warned me. He warned us."

Kyle Green's voice broke the tension. "I've been gathering this evidence for years. The pieces fit. The warning I received as a child — what the aliens told me — it's happening. Now."

For a long moment, no one spoke. President Johnson's hand tightened on the edge of the table. He looked pale, sweat beading faintly on his brow, but his voice, when it came, was firm. "If what you're saying is true, then our own people are planning a genocide under a false flag. We cannot — will not — allow that to happen."

General Harris leaned in, his voice low and grim. "We'll need more proof. We'll need to move fast. Once they know we're onto them, they'll accelerate their timetable."

Elliot pushed the file across the table. "Here's your proof."

The President reached for it, his fingers trembling slightly. He took a steadying breath, but a flicker of pain crossed his face — a reminder of the heart attack that had nearly killed him just weeks before. He forced his hand to close around the file anyway.

"We stop them," he said quietly. "Whatever it takes."

The air in the room seemed to hold its breath. Outside, the wind howled against the White House windows. Inside, the fight for the planet's future had begun.

And somewhere, unseen, the Dark Dominion was already moving its next piece into place.

Chapter 29: The Ritual

The chamber lay hidden deep beneath a private estate in the Swiss Alps, carved into stone older than any nation. No windows. No doors except the one sealed with iron bolts and blood. The only light came from dozens of dark candles guttering on carved shelves, their wax dripping onto the marble floor etched with spirals, runes, and glyphs too ancient for any modern alphabet.

Here, the true faces of power assembled. They called themselves The Circle. The one percent of the one percent. Their names adorned the world's most exclusive guest lists—billionaires, prime ministers, tech barons, royalty—but here in the dark, their masks were gone. They were not donors, not statesmen, not captains of industry. They were predators gathered at the altar of something older than kingship.

Their designer suits were gone, replaced with hooded robes of crimson and black. Gems glimmered like wet eyes at their throats and wrists. The air was thick with incense and something acrid, metallic—the smell of iron and rot.

Screens along one wall flickered with surveillance feeds: tunnels beneath the White House, satellite images of hidden bases, encrypted live audio from meetings they were not meant to hear. They knew about the President's Council. They knew about Ghost Spear. They even knew about the whispers of an awakening among certain "gifted" individuals.

"It's begun," rasped an elder, his voice like gravel sliding down stone. "They're moving against us. These nine—they think to oppose the tide."

Another, a woman with a voice like silk and poison, inclined her head. "Then Pale Horse must move from planning to action. But the signs are not yet in our favor. The stars…the numbers…still shifting."

"They will align," the elder assured her, "after the offering."

In the shadows, a figure cradled something swaddled in white cloth. It squirmed faintly, releasing a soft, human sound—too fragile for this room.

The Circle stepped toward the sigil. Their hands lifted in unison, chanting words not spoken by modern tongues, syllables sharp and curling like smoke. The candles bent inward as though pulled toward the center by an invisible force.

"The purest form," the elder intoned. "Lifeblood of innocence. The heart, the blood, the soul itself. We consume what is sacred to summon what is owed. Our dominion is eternal. Our enemies crushed beneath our will."

The bundle was laid at the center of the sigil on an obsidian table. A dagger black as shadow pierced soft skin. The infant's blood pooled into the carved spirals, dripping across runes older than memory. One Circle member bent low, drinking from the vessel, the metallic taste sliding down his throat. Another pressed a palm to the child's chest and drew the still-beating heart into the circle, the warmth disappearing as it vanished in their hands. The chanting intensified, a frenzy of sound that made the stone quiver, the very air thick with the scent of blood, iron, ritual, and fire.

Far above, on Mount Ashland, the nine held hands around their quartz crystal, swaying, sweat pouring, energy flaring like lightning arcs in a storm. The Dreamwalker cried out, voice raw, as images of the infant's sacrifice seared through their consciousness. The Healer's glow pulsed frantically, trying to counteract the surge of darkness. The Seer's whispered incantations trembled in the air; even the Druid Priest's sigils flickered with uncertainty.

For a heartbeat, the two rituals overlapped. Light and shadow collided across continents. The infant's scream, barely a sound, resonated through time and space, searing into memory.

The Circle's leader raised his arms, black robes swirling like oil in firelight. "See now the strength of our dominion! Nothing touches us! Nothing can stop the tide!"

The silk-voiced woman exhaled, her smile sharp as a knife. "Pale Horse rides. And nothing will turn it back."

The elder's eyes gleamed. "Let the world bow, or burn."

The candles flared black. The sigil pulsed, steady and unbroken.

Above, the nine broke their circle, weak, trembling, the taste of ash and blood on their tongues. Their hands still tingled with the residual surge of energy. They had seen the horror. They had felt the power.

And somewhere in the shadows between worlds, something—if not a god, then something far older—watched.

AETHER – Part 2

Chapter 1: The Nine

The autumn wind sighed through the pine forest high atop Mount Ashland, carrying the scent of wet earth and woodsmoke. The cabin stood alone on a natural ridge, its weathered cedar planks silvered by time and storms. The foundation was made from a mix of granite and quartz, set to magnify the vibration of energy. Around it, the trees formed a living cathedral; towering Douglas firs rose like pillars, and the forest floor glowed with moss, mushrooms, and the last wildflowers of the season, all with a consciousness vibrating with energy. This was sacred ground—the heart of one of the planet's spiritual grid points, where energy lines converged like threads in a cosmic loom.

Inside, nine people stood hands clasped in a wide circle on woven rugs. Candles flickered at the room's center, casting an amber glow that shifted across their faces. In the middle lay a polished quartz crystal the size of a newborn child, humming faintly with a vibration only the sensitive could feel.

They had gathered like this for centuries. Across empires, plagues, and cataclysms, they had been reborn, drawn together again and again like stars returning to the same constellation. Each life brought new bodies, new names, new languages—but the same purpose: protect humanity, guide Earth, and maintain the fragile balance between light and shadow.

The cabin creaked like a living thing under the weight of the mountain wind. Its walls—rough-hewn pine still fragrant with sap—glowed faintly in the candlelight, as though aware of the work being done inside. Beneath the floorboards, the granite-and-quartz foundation pulsed with a quiet hum, amplifying every breath, every heartbeat of the nine gathered souls.

No names passed their lips. They had none here, not in this cabin. They were functions, forces—Seer, Shaman, Dreamwalker, Channel, Healer, Empath, Druid Priest, Light Weaver, and Medium. Nine pillars of light who had walked the earth in endless guises: healers in mud-brick temples, prophets in marble courts, wise women in backwater villages, always hunted, always burned at the stake, hanged, or beheaded when the balance tilted too far. Yet, over and over, they returned. Drawn back to one another like iron to a lodestone.

The crystal brightened, a sharp white flare that stabbed upward like a blade, reaching beyond the wooden rafters to a sky cloaked in ice-clouds. The air tasted of warmth and earth. The Dreamwalker swayed, eyes rolled back; the Seer whispered in an old tongue that felt like the earth speaking. They were slipping into the between-space, reaching across continents and shadows to the enemy.

Their enemy—the Circle—moved even now under stone and secrecy.

The vision unfolded in fragments, as though glimpsed through a cracked mirror. The basement of a private estate, deep in the Swiss Alps. Black rock walls veined with salt. Dark candles burned with a blue flame that gave off no heat. Hooded figures formed their own ring around an altar of polished obsidian. On it lay a swaddled infant, too small, crying softly. A chant, low and serpentine, coiled in the air as one of the hooded figures raised a knife so black it seemed to drink the torchlight.

The Channel convulsed as the scene deepened. The Healer squeezed their hand, pouring steadiness into them. The Druid Priest intoned a counter-charm under his breath, but even his voice shook. The Circle's leader—a figure whose face was hidden beneath a dark cloak—raised his arms to the ceiling. Above him, the stone trembled, stars aligning in an invisible geometry. The plan would begin soon. Two-thirds of humanity—gone. Pestilence, engineered attacks with foreign craft, and a ritual of blood to catalyze it.

The quartz crystal in the cabin flared again, cracking audibly. The Medium gasped. "They're waiting for the alignment," "They're waiting—"

"They must be stopped," murmured the Shaman, but the Empath shook his head. "Not yet," he whispered. "If we act too soon, we lose everything."

The crystal's glow flickered.

In the Alps, the hooded figures chanting in the dark, waiting to drink the forbidden blood, the hooded leader turned his head sharply, as though listening. His knife hand faltered, but not enough to be noticed by the others.

"I feel something-someone," the hooded figure thought to himself.

Inside the basement, the torches guttered. One by one, the Circle's heads tilted in unison, sightless but searching. Something—someone—had brushed the edges of their ritual. The infant gave a single, sharp cry.

The quartz crystal cracked again, a splintering sound like a gunshot. The circle of nine flinched but did not break hands. Power pulsed through them in erratic surges now.

"They're coming through the link," the Dreamwalker whispered, voice thin with terror.

And then—silence.

The cabin's candles went out all at once. Darkness swallowed them, save for the trembling light inside the crystal.

Then the crystal went black.

Chapter 2: Amara, The Seer

Amara Okafor remembered the narrow apartment above the corner store in Atlanta, the smell of frying oil drifting up through the floorboards, and the constant hum of the city below. She had been a quiet child, too quiet, her eyes always turned toward horizons no one else could see. By the time she was seven, she knew when storms would come—not because of the clouds but because of a low humming inside her bones. She knew when the man next door was about to lose his job, when a car accident would snap someone's life in two.

Her mother, practical and deeply religious, told her to pray harder. Her father—absent more often than not—dismissed it as childish fantasies. But Amara saw the fear in their eyes. Fear of her. Fear that their daughter was something unnatural.

By fifteen, she had learned how to close the door inside herself, how to push the visions into a box she never opened. She became quiet, studious, the kind of girl teachers praised but classmates avoided.

Psychology became her escape. In college, she buried herself in textbooks and case studies, fascinated by the fragile machinery of the human mind. She told herself she wanted to help people. The truth was simpler: she wanted to prove to herself that she wasn't broken.

But at twenty-four, everything changed.

The Dream

It began with a lucid dream. Amara stood high atop a large mountain. From a Crystal in her hands came an iridescent, brilliant glow reaching up into the night sky. In the distance, nine silhouettes formed a circle, their hands entwined together. The air vibrated with a strange, wordless chant, and though she could not see their faces, she knew she was one of them.

When she woke, her sheets were damp with sweat, her heart pounding. The dream never left her. It returned, again and again, until she could no longer ignore it.

It was not long after that she met David.

David Okafor had none of her seriousness. He was tall and lanky, with a grin that seemed permanently stitched across his face. A born comedian, he could turn even the most ordinary moments into theater. When they first met at a bookstore—she while browsing shelves of Jungian analysis, he holding a comic book in one hand and a muffin in the other—he simply said, "You're the only person in here actually reading knowledgeable books. That's dangerous. People might think you're smart."

She had rolled her eyes. But he had followed her around the store until she laughed, and once she did, she couldn't stop.

David never feared her visions. The first time she told him, nervously, about the things she sometimes saw, he blinked, thought for a long while, and then said, "So basically you're Google, but with less ads?"

He never treated her like she was cursed. He treated her like she was extraordinary.

They married in the spring, in a small ceremony filled with laughter rather than pomp. Two children followed quickly: Naomi, now six, with a mind as sharp as her mother's and a stubborn streak wide as a river; and Jonah, now four, a whirlwind of boundless energy who insisted that fairies were still alive and hiding in the woods behind their home.

David devoted his life to them. He was the one who filled the kitchen with music on Saturday mornings, flipping pancakes into shapes that never looked right but always made the kids shriek with laughter. He was the one who tucked them in at night with silly, rambling stories that started with pirates and somehow ended with space aliens who loved cupcakes.

Amara would watch him sometimes, leaning against the doorframe, and feel her heart ache with love. In a world that seemed bent on unraveling, her family was her anchor.

But she could never fully silence her gift.

Sometimes, as she rocked Jonah to sleep, she would see flashes—Naomi in a hospital bed sick with an unknown virus, David driving late at night with tears on his face, the shadow of a craft in a too-low sky. She forced those visions down, forced herself to focus on the warmth of Jonah's small body against her chest, the sound of his even breathing.

David noticed, of course. He always did. "Hey," he would whisper, brushing her hair from her face. "Stay here with me. We're okay. We're right here."

And for a little while, she would believe him.

The dream of the nine grew stronger, more insistent. She saw them not just in sleep but in moments of waking stillness—at the kitchen sink, in the mirror, even once in the reflection of Jonah's wide, curious eyes.

It was Carmen who found her first. Carmen, the empath from San Antonio, had arrived unannounced at her office door, smiling as if they'd known each other all their lives.

"You've seen it too," Carmen said simply.

Amara's heart had nearly stopped.

From that moment on, her life shifted. She joined the circle. She accepted the truth: that she had lived many lives, and had stood with these people before. That she had been called again, not just for herself, but for the world.

Still, when she returned home each night to David and the children, to the chaos of bedtime and the warmth of laughter, Amara clung fiercely to the ordinary. She cooked, she cleaned, she held Jonah when he had nightmares, and braided Naomi's hair before school.

She loved them because she knew the truth: life was a fragile balance. Every moment mattered.

And as she stood in the circle atop Mount Ashland, crystal in the middle, her visions reaching toward the terrible darkness gathering in the world, Amara swore she would protect them—not just her own family, but every family.

Because she was The Seer. And she had already seen what would happen if she failed.

Chapter 3: Carmen, The Medium

Carmen Alvarez entered the world with a veil across her face, a thin translucent membrane that clung to her skin like silk. The nurses gasped, her mother cried, and her grandmother crossed herself before whispering in Spanish, "Niña de los velos… she will see the dead."

From the beginning, Carmen lived between two worlds. Shadows whispered in the corners of her bedroom. Cold hands tugged at her blankets. Faces she didn't know appeared in mirrors, their mouths moving soundlessly.

In her teenage years, she blasted music in her ears until her hearing rang, desperate to drown the voices. In her twenties, she numbed herself with alcohol and drugs, thinking that if she blurred her own mind enough, the spirits would vanish. They never did.

The gift followed her into every room, every job, every broken relationship.

At twenty-eight, she woke in a hospital bed with shaking hands and a dry mouth, detox burning through her body. At the foot of her bed stood a little girl, maybe eight years old, pale and translucent, holding a stuffed bear.

"Can you help me?" the girl whispered.

And Carmen—raw, emptied, and stripped of denial—finally said yes.

Finding Her Power

Sobriety didn't make the voices disappear. It made them louder. For the first time, Carmen listened.

She walked the halls of hospitals, unseen, speaking softly to the restless dead. She guided them, calmed them, helped them find the light she herself had once been too afraid to face. Families never knew her name, but they felt her presence in the strange peace that came after she left.

Word spread quietly among nurses, chaplains, and janitors. "There's a woman who helps," they would whisper.

Carmen stopped running. She stopped apologizing.

Her gift was no curse. It was a power to help bring light.

When her son Mateo was born, Carmen knew immediately that he carried a piece of her sight. His first words weren't just for her—he babbled at the empty corners of the room, laughed at shadows, waved at figures only he could see.

At first, it frightened her. The world was cruel to children who didn't fit inside its narrow definitions of normal. She remembered what it was like to be whispered about, mocked, called bruja. She swore her son would never carry that shame.

So she taught him in the quiet hours, behind drawn curtains. She showed him how to close the door when voices became too loud, how to focus his energy on love and protection instead of fear.

"Gifts are not accidents," she told him one night as they sat cross-legged on the floor, a candle burning between them. "They are responsibilities. You don't use them to scare people or show off. You use them to help."

Mateo nodded solemnly, though he was only eight. His eyes—dark, steady, far older than his years—never wavered.

It was months later, one night after Mateo had gone to sleep, that Carmen's life shifted again. She had just settled into bed when she felt the familiar prickle of presence. She opened her eyes, expecting another spirit.

But the man standing at the foot of her bed was solid, alive.

Malek.

He said only five words: "It's time to find Amara."

And though she did not yet know what he meant, something in her blood quickened.

It wasn't long after that she found herself knocking on an office door in Atlanta. A woman looked up from her desk—tired, elegant, guarded. Amara.

Carmen had felt her before she'd even entered the room, a pull like a thread in her chest.

"You've seen it too," she said simply.

Amara froze. And then her eyes softened, as if a weight had been lifted.

From that moment, the two women were inseparable friends. They spoke every week, sometimes every day, sharing visions, fears, and hopes. Amara, with her quiet seriousness, grounded Carmen. Carmen, with her bold confidence, reminded Amara not to shrink from her light.

It was Carmen who told her, "Never hide again. Never. The world will try to make you small, but your gift is bigger than their fear."

Together, they remembered what it meant to be part of something larger, something ancient.

Now, when Carmen stood in the circle on Mount Ashland, she was not afraid. Spirits whispered all around them, carried on the wind, voices of the forgotten dead who begged for justice. Carmen listened, unflinching, her hand steady on the crystal when it came her turn.

She was no longer the girl who drowned herself in noise.

She was the Medium. The guide. The bridge between worlds.

And she had sworn—by her son, by her blood, by every spirit that had ever leaned on her hand—that she would never let the dark dominion claim another soul without a fight.

Chapter 4: Malek, The Channeler

Oakland, California, had always been a city of noise—sirens, traffic, laughter, shouts echoing off cracked brick and steel. But Malek Johnson had learned to listen beyond all that. He heard underneath the noise—the quiet thrum of thought, the pulse of unseen emotion, the whisper of something older than language.

From his earliest memories, the world had never seemed entirely real. Streets and faces blurred at the edges, as though he were half here, half elsewhere. His dreams were full of impossible places—oceans spreading across deserts, stars folding into themselves, doorways made of light. And always, a voice, distant but patient, waiting for him to remember.

The first time the voice spoke clearly, Malek was twenty-six. He was alone in a rented church basement, the kind of place people used for community meetings and twelve-step programs. He had come there out of restlessness—maybe curiosity, maybe destiny.

When the air shifted, he thought it was an earthquake. Then he heard it.

"You are not lost, Malek," said the voice. "You are found. I am Tetteh."

It wasn't a sound. It was a resonance that filled every cell of his body, making his teeth ache and his heart race. He collapsed to his knees, trembling as visions unfurled through him—cities of glass, oceans of fire, children of light and shadow learning to love what they once feared.

When he finally stood, hours later, he knew his life would never again belong entirely to him. He was a channel—an antenna for something vast, compassionate, and heartbreakingly wise.

At first, he hid it. He had grown up in a world that ridiculed what it couldn't measure. But secrets like his didn't stay buried long. One night, during a live-streamed meditation session, Tetteh came through—soft, steady, luminous. The viewers who tuned in for mindfulness tips found themselves in tears, feeling the kind of peace they hadn't known since childhood; some had never felt like this in their entire lives.

Within a year, Malek's following had grown from hundreds to millions. He spoke in auditoriums, hotel conference rooms, and digital spaces across the world. Not as a preacher, not as a godman—but as a bridge.

He always began the same way: standing barefoot on the stage, palms open, eyes closed.

Then, the shift would come. His breath would slow, his voice deepened, and Tetteh would speak.

"Love is the oldest technology," the voice would say. "It is the frequency that built the stars and the universe. Every cruelty is a distortion of love. Every fear, an echo of forgetting. You are not here to escape darkness—you are here to teach it how to love again."

Audiences wept. Some laughed. Some trembled. All felt something crack open inside them.

Fame, however, never fit him comfortably. He still lived in a modest apartment, half-filled with quartz, books, and strange old relics he couldn't quite throw away. He made tea before every session, lighting a single candle near the window, whispering, "Alright, Tetteh, let's not freak them out this time."

He laughed often—sometimes at himself, at the absurdity of being a man who could barely keep his houseplants alive yet spoke with a being from thousands of years in the future. His humor was his armor and his release.

"Another day, another soul searching for cosmic Wi-Fi," he'd mutter, smiling as he turned on the livestream camera.

And yet, beneath the wit, there was devotion. Not to fame or fortune, but to the quiet revolution of love that Tetteh insisted would change the human story.

Carmen had found him first, drawn to him from a dream. She came to one of his gatherings, sat quietly in the back, and saw through the spectacle—the lights, the stage, the projection screens—to the trembling human being at the center. Afterward, she approached him and simply said, "You're not doing this alone, are you?"

He smiled, weary. "Not even close."

AMara came soon after—more pragmatic, sharp-eyed, but just as drawn to the current that flowed through him. Between the three of them, something ancient stirred again, though none yet dared to name it.

Tetteh's words spread like wildfire through a weary world. "Love is evolution," the entity said. "Not sentiment, not softness, but the brave act of seeing yourself in all things, you are inside the consciousness of god, his energy lives through you."

Malek believed that. He lived it. Even when protests formed outside his venues, calling him a fraud or a heretic. Even when governments sent psychologists to "evaluate" him. Even when the loneliness crept back in.

"Love anyway," Tetteh would whisper. "Especially them."

But recently, during one of the transmissions, something had changed. A distortion, faint but unmistakable, threaded through the signal. The lights flickered. The air grew cold.

Tetteh's voice hesitated mid-sentence. Then—just for a heartbeat—it wasn't Tetteh's voice that came through.

"Something is watching you," it said, in a tone that made Malek's blood run cold. "The Circle knows."

The audience, of course, thought it was part of the message. They clapped, moved, and were oblivious. But Carmen's eyes found his across the room, wide and knowing.

And for the first time since Tetteh entered his life, Malek wondered if love alone would be enough.

Chapter 5: Mingan Greywolf, The Shaman

Mingan Greywolf's path was written long before his first breath. His lineage stretched back through unbroken generations of medicine men, spirit talkers, and dream keepers who had guarded the balance between seen and unseen worlds. They had walked the forests of North America when the trees were young, carrying songs that healed, and stories that taught the living how to die with grace.

He was born in a cabin deep in the Montana wilderness, the night outside wrapped in drifting snow. His mother labored under candlelight, her breath rising in short clouds of pain and power. When the child finally cried out, the old pines outside seemed to answer with a low moan of wind. His father, a healer with smoke-stained hands, lifted the newborn and whispered,

"You carry the song of the ancestors, little one. The path will not be easy, but it will always be yours.

Before he could speak, Mingan would turn toward the wind as if it were calling his name. He listened to the world the way others listened to voices—hearing the hum beneath the silence, the heartbeat beneath the ground.

At seven, he could sense illness before it appeared, feel the grief of a dying animal, or the confusion of a storm about to break. The natural world whispered to him in ways no one else could hear.

His childhood was quiet but never lonely. He wandered mountain trails, fasted in hidden groves, and watched firelight dance across stones. He learned to hear the language of rivers, to understand the rhythm of wings and breath. Others called him strange; his parents called him chosen.

At thirteen, his initiation began—the ancient rite known as the Veil of Shadows. For forty days and nights, Mingan was sent into a cave in the heart of the mountains with only water, roots, and a single torch. There he meditated and met the dark that all shamans must face—the living shadow that mirrors one's own soul.

Visions came in waves: burning cities, plague and darkness, greed and hunger twisting the hearts of men and women. He saw spirits bound in chains of their own making, whispering for release.

And then came the whisper—his own voice, hollow and cruel—tempting him with power. "Bow to the darkness," it said. "Command it. Rule it. The world will kneel to you."

But Mingan remembered his father's words: A true shaman walks through darkness, not around it, not with it.

He sat in the blackness, breathing with the earth and its shadows, until dawn finally spilled through the cave mouth. When he emerged, the boy who had entered was gone. In his place stood something older, steadier, and infinitely still.

At sixteen, he was sent south to study under Elder Nayequay, a man as old as the stones and twice as patient. The Elder's eyes seemed to hold entire lifetimes, and when he spoke, even the wind hushed to listen.

"You will learn to hear the earth," Nayequay told him. "To bend energy, become one without breaking it. To call the spirits without being called. The world will offer power—take none of it until you understand its cost."

Seven winters passed beneath that tutelage. Mingan endured nights so cold his breath froze midair, days spent in silence, and rituals that stripped away every remnant of pride. He learned to read omens in smoke, to heal wounds with nothing but focus and rhythm, and to walk between this world and the next without losing himself.

Most of all, he learned patience. The path of a shaman was not conquest—it was surrender.

When his apprenticeship ended, Mingan entered the modern world quietly, as healers often do. He lived among people who mistook silence for distance, never realizing that silence was his prayer. He became a guide for those standing at the edge of despair, a counselor for souls caught between life and what comes after.

His presence calmed rooms. His laughter—rare but deep—seemed to shake the heaviness out of the air.

He carried no pretense, no robe, no ritual mask—only his eyes, sharp as obsidian and kind as water.

He met Mei-Ling on a fog-wrapped cliff in Northern California. She was playing music that shimmered in the salt air—notes fragile as breath, but threaded with pain.

"You're not broken," Mingan said quietly from behind her. She startled, then turned.

"You've just forgotten the rhythm. Let me show you how to hear it again."

Through him, she rediscovered her gift. Through her, he remembered what it meant to teach not from duty, but from love. Together, they brought the pulse of ancient healing back into the circle—rhythm and resonance entwined.

When the Coven of nine gathered atop Mount Ashland, Mingan stood slightly apart at first, as he always had. But his presence steadied them—the grounding current in a storm of psychic fire.

He spoke rarely, but when he did, the others listened.

"The earth doesn't shout," he said once. "It hums. If you can't hear it, you're speaking too loudly."

In moments of tension, his dry humor surfaced like a breeze through smoke.

"All those nights freezing in the mountains," he murmured once, glancing at the glowing quartz in the cabin, "and here I am again—just me, the spirits, and a bunch of people charging crystals. The ancestors are probably laughing."

They loved him for that—the balance he carried between reverence and irony, the gravity and the grin.

Mingan Greywolf was more than a shaman. He was a bridge between old worlds and new, between wound and healing, between light and the darkness that always followed it.

When he took his place in the circle that night, the air itself seemed to lean toward him. The granite beneath the cabin floor thrummed with recognition.

And in that silent pulse between heartbeats, the ancestors whispered through him once more:

"Walk steady, Greywolf. The storm is coming."

He closed his eyes and breathed in the message—not with fear, but with faith.

He had walked through darkness before.

And this time, he would not walk alone.

Chapter 6: Mei-Ling Zhou, The Healer

Mei-Ling Zhou had once been a brilliant surgeon—steady hands, sharp mind, precise as a blade. Her touch could save a life; her eyes missed nothing. But beneath her calm efficiency, something deeper stirred, something no textbook had ever prepared her for.

She didn't just see anatomy—she heard it, felt it. Every heartbeat sang. Every breath hummed. Inside each patient, she felt the low-grade symphony of emotion and fear vibrating at the base of the lungs, grief pooling near the ribs, relief trembling like high strings.

The hospital called it intuition. She knew better. It was energy, music to her.

From childhood, music had been her first language. Her beloved father, teacher, and best friend, a soft-spoken professor, had placed a violin in her hands when she was six. The bow felt alive, trembling with sound before she even drew it across the strings. She learned that emotion could live in tone, that sadness could be played in A minor, and hope could be coaxed from silence. The violin became her companion, her voice when words were too fragile.

Even in medical school, and later as a resident surgeon, she kept the instrument near her bed. Between long shifts and sleepless nights, she played to keep herself human. But when her father passed away from cancer, the music became harder to bear. Every note she played seemed to draw the pain of the loss of her father, her patients, colleagues, and even strangers. The resonance overwhelmed her.

So she stopped playing. She stopped listening. She buried the violin in a closet and buried herself in the work.

But the hum of suffering followed her everywhere.

Then one night—alone in the surgical ward long after midnight—something happened. Something vast, electric, and unspeakable. The instruments shook. The lights flickered. And for one terrible moment, she saw the veil between life and death collapse. She never told anyone what she saw. She simply walked away.

By morning, Dr. Mei-Ling Zhou was gone.

She vanished into the northern California coast—where the ocean was endless, patient, forgiving. There, among fog and redwoods, she tried to unhear the world.

She rented small cabins. Drank tea. Walked barefoot in the sand until her skin shriveled. She meditated, journaled, and listened to the rhythms of wind and tide, searching for something quieter than the human heart.

One afternoon, cleaning out a drawer in the cabin she rented near Mendocino, she found it—the old violin case, weathered but intact, hidden among her few boxes. Her breath caught. Her fingers trembled as she opened it.

The strings were dull, the bow frayed, but when she drew it across the instrument, the first note sang a thin, aching whisper. Then another. And another.

She played until her tears soaked the wood. The violin had never judged her; it had only waited.

In time, she began playing each evening at sunset, facing the ocean. The notes blended with the wind, and the sea answered in rhythm. Her music became her meditation again—each tone a prayer, each silence a surrender.

That was when he found her.

She was standing on a cliff at dusk, the violin tucked beneath her chin, the final notes of a mournful melody dissolving into the mist.

Mingan Greywolf had been sitting nearby, eyes closed, as if he had been listening long before she noticed him. His presence was both grounded and luminous, the kind of stillness that seemed to absorb the chaos of the world.

When she lowered her bow, he rose and walked toward her—no sudden movement, no sound but the soft rustle of grass.

"You play what you feel from your heart," he said quietly. "Not what you know."

His voice was low and steady, carrying a resonance that felt strangely familiar.

Mei-Ling hesitated. "It helps me remember who I was."

He tilted his head, studying her. "You're not remembering," he said. "You're awakening."

And with that, something inside her shifted—an uncoiling recognition from the base of her spine that went deeper than memory.

Mingan taught her to see what she had only felt. To trace the invisible rivers of energy that ran through every living being, to understand that illness was not simply broken tissue but disrupted song.

"Everything has a frequency," he explained one evening as they sat by the fire. "Pain, joy, truth—they all vibrate. A healer listens. A true healer restores harmony."

He had her use her violin again during their lessons. She played for those who came to the retreat seeking solace, her music guiding her hands as she placed them on wounds both seen and unseen. Sometimes, her palms glowed faintly with golden light as she worked—energy pulsing through her like melody through strings.

Once, a woman came to the retreat center with an inoperable tumor pressing against her lung. Mei-Ling placed her hands over the woman's chest and listened—not with her ears, but with her whole being. The energy inside the body was jagged, discordant, screaming for balance. Slowly, gently, Mei-Ling drew her hands apart, pulling the discord out like pulling a wrong note from a symphony. When it was over, the woman breathed freely, and the next morning the shadow on her scan was gone.

Mingan said nothing for a long time. Then, quietly, he told her, "You have become what every healer longs to be—the harmony itself."

For the first time, her music didn't drown her—it freed her.

It was Mingan who reminded her of the Coven of nine—the ancient covenant of souls reborn through time to preserve the balance between light and shadow.

"There are others," he said. "They will hear your song, as I did."

When Mei-Ling met them—Amara, Carmen, Malek, Rafe, and the rest—the music within her found its echo. The Circle hummed with recognition, their energies resonating in perfect intervals.

"You were never meant to heal alone," Mingan said. "No true healer is."

Even as her purpose crystallized, her heart remained tied to Li Wei—a compassionate Doctor who saw both science and spirit in every life he touched. He had loved her before the silence, before the coast, before the violin came back.

When she returned from long absences, he would smile, brush the hair from her face, and say, "You look like a song I haven't heard yet."

She'd laugh softly, and sometimes play for him, just one quiet piece before dawn. But she never told him the truth of what she had become. The Coven's work was dangerous. She would not let darkness find him.

So she loved him gently, distantly—through shared breakfasts, through hands brushing in the dark, through the way he'd whisper, "Even healers need healing, Mei."

When Mei-Ling stood with the Coven atop Mount Ashland, the air thrummed with energy. The quartz crystal pulsed beneath their joined hands, and the sound—the music—rose around them like a living hymn.

Her violin rested against her heart, silent but vibrating faintly as though it, too, felt the power awakening.

Her hands, once instruments of precision, now shone with compassion. Her healing no longer ended at flesh or spirit—it sang across the invisible lattice that bound all living things.

When she placed her palms upon the crystal, the world seemed to inhale. The Circle became one note in an eternal chord.

And Mei-Ling, with the faint hum of her violin at her back, finally understood:

Healing was never silent.

It was the courage to play the music the world had forgotten.

Chapter 7: Noor Al-Farouq, The Dreamwalker

Noor Al-Farouq had always lived between worlds. Born to Lebanese immigrants in Detroit, she learned early that reality was a tapestry woven from threads both seen and unseen. The waking world was just the surface—beneath it, she could hear the hum of other lives, other possibilities, other dreams breathing in the dark.

Her childhood was filled with strange nights. While other children dreamt of monsters or flying, Noor walked through corridors of shadow and light, endless halls lined with doors. Behind each door was a life—some hers, some not. The whispers that slipped from those doors spoke her name like a promise, or a warning. When she awoke, her sheets were damp with sweat, her heart racing as if she had just run from something unseen.

At sixteen, she discovered the first truth of her gift: she could open the doors. At twenty, she learned the second truth, that she could step through them.

Noor became a navigator of the subconscious. She could walk the dreamscapes of others, heal wounds carved deep into the psyche, and retrieve pieces of lost courage left behind in the night. Her touch was unseen, her presence forgotten by morning, yet her influence lingered—like sunlight after a storm.

As an adult, Noor found her sanctuary in a rented narrow brick building tucked between a bookstore and a florist on the east side of Detroit. A faded sign above the door read The House of Moons, and its windows glowed with amber light long after the city had gone to sleep.

Inside, the air always carried the scent of sandalwood and burnt sage. Crystals lined the windowsill; dreamcatchers and hanging charms danced in the faint hum of a ceiling fan. At a small round table draped in indigo silk, Noor read fortunes and tarot cards for the curious, the broken, and the hopeful.

Her clients came with the usual questions of love, money, loss, and destiny, but Noor's eyes saw deeper. When she turned over a card, her gaze flickered, as if watching scenes unfold behind the veil. Sometimes she offered only a smile, a quiet word, or a riddle that would echo for days in the client's mind. Others left her shop in tears, not from sorrow, but from the strange relief of being truly seen.

At night, when the door was locked and the candles still flickered, Noor sat cross-legged on the floor, tracing patterns in the air with her fingers. "Between worlds," she whispered. "That's where the truth hides."

One winter night, frost feathered the shop windows, and the city was muted under snow. Noor fell asleep at her reading table, her head resting on a spread of cards. In her dream, she saw a circle of nine figures standing around a glowing quartz crystal high on a mountain top. Light pulsed from it like a heartbeat. Their faces were shadowed, but their energy felt familiar—ancient, intertwined with hers.

When she awoke, her hands still tingled with energy. The crystal on her table—one she used only for cleansing—was glowing faintly in the dark.

The next evening, as she hosted her weekly tarot night at the house of moons, a man stepped through the door. His presence was quiet but electric, with calm eyes and an empath's patience in the way he moved. She recognized him instantly. He was one of the nine from her dream.

He introduced himself simply as Rafe. The moment their hands brushed, she felt the hum of connection—a strand of shared energy woven across lifetimes. Neither of them spoke of it, but both understood. Something ancient had begun to awaken.

Noor's power was more than dream interpretation; it was navigation. She could enter dreams willingly, walking unseen through the subconscious of others, guiding them to face what they feared, or retrieve what they had lost. Sometimes she appeared as herself; sometimes, as a flicker of light, a whisper, or a hand reaching through fog.

In the Coven, she became their navigator of the unseen. When the group meditated on Mount Ashland, Noor's voice would guide them beyond the waking world. She stitched visions together, binding their dreams into a single current of purpose. She could uncover secrets buried even from clairvoyants, their hidden truths, warnings, and messages from realms beyond human comprehension.

But her gift came with a cost. The more she walked in dreams, the thinner the line became between sleeping and waking. Sometimes she would drift off mid-conversation, her eyes distant, following echoes only she could hear. Other times, she'd wake with markings on her wrists like symbols from the dreamworld, fading with dawn.

Despite her power, Noor remained gentle, humble, and deeply human. She laughed easily, though rarely loudly. Her humor was soft, dry—like a candle flicker in the dark. "I charge extra for exorcisms because of bad decisions," she would say, shuffling her tarot cards with a smile and a wink.

To those who sought her out, Noor offered more than readings—she offered peace. Her energy soothed the frantic, mended hearts, and brought light into the restless corners of people's minds. The Coven trusted her completely. Even the most powerful among them deferred to her when their paths blurred.

Noor Al-Farouq was not just a dreamwalker.

She was the bridge—the thread between the waking and the eternal, the conscious and the unseen.

And when she closed her eyes, the world seemed to hold its breath, waiting for what she would see next.

Chapter 8: Rafael Santiago, The Empath

The night Rafael Santiago entered the world, a hurricane clawed at the coast of San Juan. Winds howled through the hospital corridors, rattling windows like an omen. Lightning split the sky, thunder roared, and the nurses whispered prayers between contractions. When he finally drew breath, the storm seemed to pause—just for an instant—as if the world itself were listening.

His mother swore the storm had left something behind in him, a pulse, a vibration, a living current that never stilled. He grew up chasing that electricity, never quite fitting inside the small boxes people built around themselves. Rafe didn't just feel the world—he absorbed it. Joy, sorrow, grief, rage—it all moved through him like weather, relentless and raw.

As a child, Rafe would lie awake at night, staring at the ceiling fan slicing through the dark. Somewhere beyond the thin apartment walls, a couple argued. Downstairs, a baby cried. Across the street, laughter spilled from an open window. He felt it all. It was too much.

By adolescence, he'd learned to hide behind charm, to smile even when he was breaking. He became the charming one, the flirt, the dependable friend who always knew what to say because he could feel what everyone else needed to hear. But underneath, he was unraveling.

Love was worse. Each touch opened a floodgate. He didn't just love; he merged. Every heartbreak shattered him. Every betrayal hollowed him out a little more. By twenty-nine, he was exhausted, his body trembling from sleepless nights, nerves frayed to dust.

Rafe, a medic, drove an ambulance through chaos, through screams and flashing lights, his world condensed to adrenaline and instinct. He couldn't turn away. Even off-duty, he'd stop for wrecks, for strangers bleeding on sidewalks, for the crying mother in the park. Pain called to him like thunder on the horizon.

He felt everything—the shock in a crash victim's chest, the panic of a child losing consciousness, the quiet resignation of the elderly man whispering a prayer in the backseat. Their fear became his fear. Their grief became his own.

And when the night was over, he'd sit in the driver's seat, soaked in the hum of sirens and silence, wondering how much longer he could live this way.

It was raining the day he met Noor Al-Farouq.

The storm outside mirrored the one inside him—gray, endless, pulsing against his ribs. He ducked into a small metaphysical shop on the east side of Detroit, shaking off the cold. Inside, candles flickered between small tables. At the back, a woman with dark braids and eyes like midnight was reading tarot cards.

She looked up mid-reading, as if sensing him before seeing him. Her voice was calm, deliberate, and ancient.

"You're one of us," she said.

He almost laughed. "One of whom?"

But her gaze softened. "The ones who feel too much. The ones who carry the light and the dark in the same hand."

Something inside him stilled. For the first time in years, he didn't feel like he was drowning.

Noor introduced him to the nine slowly. He met them one by one, souls who seemed impossibly familiar. The healer with music in her hands. The shaman who spoke to the wind. The seer who read the stars like scripture. Each encounter pulled him deeper into a current he'd felt his whole life but never understood.

When he joined their meditation for the first time, standing in a cabin high on Mount Ashland, he felt energy hum beneath the floorboards like a living rhythm that matched the storm in his heart. For the first time, the storm wasn't chaos. It was harmony.

He began to understand that every emotion was a language of energy, a vibration that could heal or destroy depending on how it was held. He stopped running. He began listening. He used his empathy to draw out truth—to calm the terrified, to ease the dying, to remind the lost that they were never truly alone.

When the Coven gathered, Rafe stood at the center, eyes closed, hands trembling with energy. The others felt his power like waves—his empathy amplifying their intent, binding their energies together until their circle pulsed like a single living heart.

He learned to laugh again. Deep, unguarded laughter that shook the walls of the little mountain cabin. But his laughter always carried an echo—the awareness of how fragile beauty was, how easily joy could dissolve into sorrow.

He was still the storm. But now he understood it.

Rafael Santiago was born to feel the world so the rest of them wouldn't have to bear it alone. His gift was weight and wonder all at once. When others faltered, he steadied them. When the darkness crept in, he absorbed it, tempered it, transformed it.

And on nights when the wind howled across the mountain and thunder rolled in the distance, the Coven would sometimes find him standing outside, face tilted to the rain, smiling faintly.

Because in the storm, he could finally hear the pulse of the world, the same rhythm that had called him since birth—beating, alive, endless.

He was not cursed. He was the connection itself.

And for the first time in his life, he was home.

Chapter 9: Elias Thompson, The Druid Priest of Symbols

He had always carried history on his skin.

Each line, each rune, each spiral of ink that marked Elias Thompson's body was more than art—it was memory. A language of energy and ancestry. A covenant between flesh and the unseen.

His shoulders were wide and scarred, the canvas of a lineage that stretched back to the mist-veiled hills of ancient Scotland, where his ancestors, druidic priests and keepers of balance, had whispered to stones and sung to the stars. Their knowledge lived on in him, not as myth or legend, but as pulse and presence.

When he walked, the air seemed to shift around him, charged, deliberate, aware.

Elias was born in Edinburgh under a winter moon that cast silver light on the frozen streets. His mother swore he didn't cry for nearly a minute after birth; instead, he stared upward, silent and alert, eyes wide as though studying the constellations through the hospital glass.

He grew up among old ruins and stories. His grandfather, a man of few words but great silence, would take him to standing stones on the outskirts of Inverness. They would kneel in the cold grass while the wind carried whispers through the moss-covered monoliths.

"These are not dead stones," the old man said once. "They remember. And one day, you will remember too."

By ten, Elias could carve the runes from memory. He didn't just write them, he felt them hum under his fingertips, as though the symbols themselves were living entities trying to speak.

But modern life didn't welcome druids anymore. It had no patience for the language of stone and wind.

Teachers called him distracted. Neighbors called him strange. By sixteen, when his family emigrated to Texas, Elias had learned to guard his silence, to hide the ancient rhythm in his blood behind stoicism and stillness.

Texas was too bright, too loud. The land was vast but carried none of the soft murmurs of home. Yet, among the dust and sun, he found something new—ink.

Tattooing became his craft, his modern altar. It was ritual, precision, devotion. Every client who sat in his chair carried a story; every needle stroke carried intent.

He began experimenting with combining ancient druidic sigils with geometric precision, modern pigments with old ritual markings. It started as art. It became an invocation.

When he tattooed a woman's wrist with a spiral of calm, she later wrote to him saying her chronic panic attacks had stopped.

When he inked a man's spine with runes of strength and security, the man claimed his nightmares had ended overnight.

Elias said nothing. He didn't need to. The work spoke for itself.

In Austin, his shop became a quiet sanctuary, a low-lit studio filled with candlelight, oak tables, stone bowls of saltwater, and the faint scent of cedar. He rarely spoke of magic, but those who entered left changed, marked not just in skin but in spirit.

Sofia Mendes—fire-touched, irreverent, and radiant became one of his favorite customers. She'd tease him mid-session, saying, "You look like you were carved out of stone, Elias. Do you ever laugh?"

Sometimes, he did. But never for long. His seriousness wasn't pride; it was responsibility. The symbols he carried were alive, and their weight was immense.

It started as dreams—recurring, potent, charged with déjà vu. A mountain covered in mist. A crystal the size of a child. Voices chanting in rhythm, nine distinct energies forming a circle of light.

He would wake, pulse pounding, the runes on his arms glowing faintly under the dim light of his room. The dreams called to him, not as prophecy, but as recognition.

Soon after, he crossed paths with Mingan Greywolf. The man radiated quiet gravity, the kind of presence that didn't demand attention but commanded it nonetheless. When Mingan spoke of energy lines and sacred balance, Elias felt the old runes stir beneath his skin.

"You feel it too," Greywolf said simply.

Elias nodded once. "I've felt it my whole life."

On Mount Ashland, surrounded by the other members of the Coven, Elias finally understood the full measure of his purpose. He was not just a man; he was an instrument. A bridge between the written word and living power.

When the coven of nine gathered around the quartz crystal, it was Elias who traced the protective sigils in the soil. Each line directed energy, grounding it, shaping it. When their combined force began to surge—wild, chaotic, beautiful—it was Elias who stabilized it, his ink glowing faintly beneath the surface of his skin.

He murmured the ancient Gaelic phrases under his breath, words that hadn't been spoken aloud in centuries. The runes burned gold, the air thickened, and the crystal pulsed in harmony with his heart.

To the others, it looked effortless. But inside, Elias felt the weight of lifetimes pressing through him— the chants of forgotten groves, the energy of sacred fires, the memories of rituals older than recorded time.

He was not summoning power. He was the power.

After the ritual, the others spoke in awe of what they had felt—how the energy flowed smoother, clearer, stronger. Daniel clasped Elias's shoulder and said, "Your ancestors are still with you. You carry them well."

Elias didn't respond. He simply nodded, gaze steady. The truth was heavier than praise. His lineage demanded balance, and the world's equilibrium was tipping fast. The Coven was their last defense against the encroaching dark.

Every mark on his body was a promise—and promises had weight.

That night, as the moon rose high over the mountain, Elias stood alone outside the cabin, the wind biting cold against his skin. He pressed his hand to the rune over his heart, a spiral of eternity, and whispered, "Let the lines hold. Let the light remember."

The runes shimmered faintly, and the earth answered with a low hum beneath his feet.

Chapter 10: Sofie The Elementalist

Sofia Mendes had always been fire and wind. Born in the favelas of Rio de Janeiro to a mother of Irish descent, she learned early how to run, fight, and survive, her instincts sharp as broken glass. By seven, she had glimpsed the extraordinary in herself; a tornado roared through her neighborhood, and when she stepped into its path, it split around her, obeying some unspoken command. Her grandmother, her mother's mother, keeper of old rites and whispered elemental secrets, called her Filha do Vento—Daughter of the Wind.

From that moment, Sofia knew the natural world answered to her in ways it did to no one else. She could feel currents of air, the rhythm of water, the heat of fire, the steadiness of earth as though they were extensions of her body. Each element had a voice, and she had learned to listen.

At nineteen, Sofia left Brazil, the streets she had mastered and the family she loved behind. She landed in Texas, working at a plant nursery, coaxing flowers to bloom out of season, shaping life itself with her hands. The world became a little less hostile when she could bend its rhythms toward growth and beauty.

But it wasn't until Austin that she met Elias Thompson that her life truly ignited. She wandered into his tattoo studio on a humid afternoon, intrigued by the intricate designs on display.

He was focused, the hum of energy around him almost visible, his hands moving with precision over a client's skin. The tattoos seemed to shimmer slightly, responding to some unseen current. Sofia leaned against the doorway, arms crossed, smirking.

"You're drawing my childhood on strangers' skin," she said lightly.

Elias froze mid-stroke, brow furrowed, as if trying to figure out whether she was joking or dangerous. "Excuse me?"

"I said… that spiral there? My abuela would recognize it immediately. You're basically giving away sacred family secrets as wall art," she added with a grin.

He glanced at her, the faintest twitch of a smile on his lips. "And you… are fearless, I see."

"Fearless?" She waved a hand dramatically, letting a small gust of wind stir papers on the counter. "Honey, I literally command tornadoes in my sleep. Fear is for people who wear sweaters in hurricanes."

Elias didn't reply. He simply studied her, and for the first time in years, he felt someone understand the chaotic fire he had always carried in silence. Their connection was instant, unspoken, magnetic, a recognition of energy that didn't need words.

Sofia's adolescence had been a constant balancing act: fire could burn everything in a heartbeat, wind could scatter lives, water could drown, and earth could crush. Learning to harmonize them was not a skill; it was survival. Meditation, practice, and fearless intuition shaped her.

By the time she encountered the Coven, Sofia's command of the elements was subtle yet spectacular. A flick of her wrist could summon protective gusts of wind; a careful inhale could light a flame without burning the floorboards; her fingers could mold water and earth alike, shaping energy like clay. Her power was raw, but precise, intelligent, alive.

Sofia was impossible to ignore. Her fiery red hair framed a face that glimmered with mischief; her light-toned skin radiated vitality. She laughed loudly and often, the kind of laugh that made strangers smile and friends feel giddy with amusement.

At the first Coven meeting, she had leaned casually against the wall around the quartz crystal circle, grinning at Malek as he muttered something serious about energy flows.

"You know," she said, arching a brow, "if we don't save the world in the next twenty minutes, I call dibs on blaming someone dramatic. Preferably, you, Malek."

Even in tense moments, her humor sparked warmth. She had a way of breaking through solemnity, reminding the others that light could exist alongside immense responsibility.

Meeting Mingan Greywolf had changed everything. He saw the fire in her without trying to tame it, guiding her to channel elemental power without letting chaos reign. Through him, she met the others: Amara, Carmen, Rafe, Malek, Noor, Mei-Ling… each connection a resonance, a spark, a thread in a tapestry of energy.

Elias remained a mystery. Whenever she teased him—about the seriousness in his eyes, the faint shimmer of his tattoos, the way he seemed to weigh every word—he would respond with a subtle, amused glint that made her grin even wider. And yet, under the surface, she felt the same pull she had sensed the moment she entered his studio: recognition of a kindred spirit, someone whose disciplined control of energy mirrored her own instinctual fire, maybe an attraction from some other place in time.

On Mount Ashland, Sofia became a living conduit. Fire danced at her fingertips in harmony with Mei-Ling's instrument; water and earth intertwined with her healing energy. Protective barriers shimmered at Sofia's command, bursts of elemental force reinforcing the nines' collective power.

Her ability wasn't just spectacle—it was strategy, instinct, artistry. Chaos could be tamed, shaped, and wielded. Sofia reminded the Coven that the natural world itself could be their ally, that every storm, every flame, every gust could serve the balance of light and dark.

She was impossible to tame, impossible to ignore, and utterly essential. She made them laugh, challenged them to think, ignited sparks of energy and inspiration,

And somewhere between teasing Elias about the "serious druid look" on his face and summoning a protective flame to dance along the quartz crystal, the others, most of all Elias, found themselves falling in love with her.

Sofia Mendes was fire, wind, water, and earth made human. A storm walking through the world, radiant and relentless, and atop Mount Ashland, she would be both shield and spark in the battle to come.

Chapter 11: Awakening the Light

The nine slumped slowly to the floor, hands falling from each other's grasp. Sweat and ash clung to their skin, breath ragged, muscles trembling, energy drained like water poured from a vessel. The crystal at the cabin's center lay dim, a faint pulse lingering like the last echo of a heartbeat.

The Shaman was the first to speak, voice hoarse but steady. "The alignment… it begins soon. The Circle moves faster than we imagined."

Elias traced a rune in the air with a trembling finger. The ink in his tattoo seemed to flicker faintly, like embers of a fire resisting the wind. "We felt their intent. Their power is… enormous. Our strength alone won't be enough."

Sofia ran her fingers through her red hair, wind stirring around her, tiny flames dancing along her fingertips despite her exhaustion. "You think I didn't notice? I could practically taste the darkness creeping over the Alps. We can't just sit here, waiting for them to make the first move."

Mei-Ling, sitting cross-legged near the crystal, pressed her palms to the floor. "Our gifts can heal, protect, even guide. But the Circle doesn't just threaten us—they threaten everyone. Entire cities, entire nations…" Her voice cracked. "People who don't even know they need saving."

Rafe, the Empath, rubbed his temples, eyes darkened from the intensity of feeling every heartbeat, every pulse of fear and rage that had surged through the trance. "I felt it. The despair, the suffering. If we wait for the perfect moment, it might already be too late. But rushing in blind… we would be no better than them."

Noor shivered, the afterimages of visions flickering behind closed eyes. "We need more light. Not just us. We've always been nine, strong as we are—but the darkness… It's growing faster and bigger than we can balance."

Noor, brushing loose strands of black hair from her face, nodded slowly. "There are others. Gifts are sleeping in the world. People who will never know they carry power unless we awaken them, teach them, and guide them. The Circle relies on ignorance. We rely on love, courage, knowledge, and… connection."

The Medium's voice wavered, but her words carried weight. "The veil is thinning. Others will also see soon. If we fail to guide them, even those awakened could be lost—or worse, turned."

Sofia lifted her hands, letting a glow drift lazily across the room, a reminder of the power already held within their circle. "We can start here. We can teach. We can create pockets of love, sparks of light in every city, every forest, and every quiet town."

Elias leaned back, rubbing his forehead. "It won't be easy. And it won't be fast. The Circle doesn't wait. They plan, they anticipate. But if we multiply ourselves—our knowledge, our mastery, our energy—then perhaps we stand a chance."

Rafe's gaze swept across the tired faces of his companions. "We've done this before. Across centuries, we've returned. We've survived fire, flood, plague, oppression, and betrayal. We've always risen again. But this… this is the first time the odds feel… alien."

They rose as one, weak, trembling, but united. The wind outside bent the trees in applause or warning; it was hard to tell.

Then, from the depths of the crystal, a new pulse, a deep vibration unlike anything they had felt. The floor shivered. The walls of the cabin groaned as though breathing. The pulse expanded, echoing through their bones.

And a voice—ancient, mocking, deliberate—rose from the darkness between worlds:

"So you awaken and gather… but the world is already ours. There is not enough light left in the world. Can you teach enough love in time?"

The cabin shook violently. Candles rattled. The crystal's hum swelled into a roar, and in its depths, shadows moved… watching, waiting, learning.

The nine exchanged a glance—exhaustion, fear, determination, and recognition. They were all that stood between humanity and Extinction.

And somewhere, far beyond the mountaintop, the Circle began to stir.

The storm had just begun.

AETHER - Part 3

Chapter 1: The Darkness and Ice Below

The Antarctic night was endless, a ceiling of black sky over white ice. The wind clawed at the surface station, rattling antennas and weather domes, but two miles below, Station Thule pulsed with light and machinery. From above, it looked like nothing—a research outpost monitoring glaciers. But underground, the facility was a labyrinth of labs, chambers, and holding pens built with billions in off-books funding.

Mary Copeland swiped her ID through three security doors before reaching the lower levels. She no longer flinched at the retinal scans or the metallic clunk of the locks. The pay had been extraordinary—enough to erase her student loans, buy her parents' house, and fund her research. When the offer had come five years ago, she had thought she was joining an immunology team to study "climate emergent pathogens."

She hadn't spoken to Sarah Mitchel since grad school at Washington State, when they'd spent nights arguing ethics over coffee and lab samples. Sarah had stayed on the public-health path. Mary had gone silent, swallowed by a program whose name she wasn't even allowed to say out loud. She never imagined she'd be calling her again—let alone to confess to something like this.

The hallway opened into Lab A – Genomic Hybridization. Stainless steel tables lined the room, each crowded with gene-editing rigs: CRISPR-Cas13a arrays, high-throughput sequencers, automated pipetting arms. Freezers hissed with liquid nitrogen. In the far wing were the containment cages—floor-to-ceiling reinforced glass and titanium mesh.

Inside the cages, the "subjects" shifted and whimpered. Some were partly human—too thin, too pale, their eyes too large for their sockets, some half animal, some with fur. Others bore wings of translucent cartilage and feathers, some had scales over patches of skin, or mouths lined with vestigial gills. Some had been born in the lab from artificially gestated embryos; others were volunteers who had been "augmented" with gene drives. Most didn't survive. Those who did often begged to be killed.

When a hybrid failed—when it became too unstable, too violent, or simply collapsed into something unrecognizable—the staff euthanized it. Not with mercy, but with protocols. Carbon monoxide. Bolt pistons. Sometimes incineration. In the off-record slang of the lab, these events were called "purges."

Mary turned her head as she passed the incinerator chute. She couldn't watch anymore.

Down the hall, Lab B – Micro-AI Swarms was even colder. Here, engineers and neuroscientists worked together, assembling insect-sized machines with carbon-fiber wings and nano-scale neuromorphic processors. The walls were lined with hexagonal storage units like honeycomb cells, each holding a different swarm:

Model IX "Stinger": micro-drones capable of delivering 20 micrograms of a custom neurotoxin per sting.

Model K2 "Grey Locust": devices the size of a penny that could inject programmable microchips into a target's bloodstream.

Model Z-Black "Wisp": silent reconnaissance units with synthetic compound eyes transmitting live video.

Mary had seen them in testing: clouds of artificial insects moving like a single mind. They could carry viruses, vaccines, or chips. They could "tag" a person's DNA or overwrite it.

Further below, Lab C – Pathogen Development glowed an ominous red under filtered lights. The scientists there wore positive-pressure suits like astronauts. Behind hermetic glass, cultures rotated in incubators:

Omega-Hemorrhagic 5 – an airborne cousin of Marburg with a 98% lethality rate.

Chimera Flu Z – a hybrid of avian and bat influenza strains, engineered for rapid attack on immune systems.

Polaris Virus – a permafrost pathogen revived from 40,000-year-old ice cores, spliced with smallpox remnants.

Mary had once believed in vaccines. Now she handled vials that could erase continents—or spare chosen populations.

At the farthest wing, Lab D – Neural Integration, the most secretive of all, was experimenting with bio-integrated AI microchips. Injected into the bloodstream, these nanodevices latched onto the peripheral nervous system, building a living neural mesh. In theory, the mesh connected the host to a secure satellite grid. In reality, it gave full-spectrum surveillance and even behavioral override

126

potential. Some of the failed hosts were housed back in Lab A's cages, twitching as invisible signals passed through their nerves.

Mary gripped the satellite phone as she walked into an empty storage room. She couldn't do it anymore. She couldn't be complicit.

It rang three times before a voice answered, soft and surprised: "Hello? …This is Sarah Mitchel."

Mary froze. She hadn't heard that voice in a decade. "Sarah. It's me. Mary."

There was a pause. "Mary? My God. I—Where have you been? I thought you took that corporate job…"

"I can't explain. I don't have time." Mary's voice shook. "Listen to me. Everything we feared— everything we used to talk about in college—it's happening. I'm in Antarctica. They're—" The connection fuzzed with static. "…splicing humans and animals… caging them… killing the ones that don't work. Hybrid pathogens. Micro-AI swarms that can inject viruses and chips. Vaccines that… mark people, Sarah."

Sarah pressed the phone to her ear, frowning. "Mary, slow down. You're not making sense."

Mary choked out, "It's against God's rules. It's wrong. I've helped make things that should never exist." Her breath came fast. "They're planning something. Something huge. I've hidden documents. If I don't make it—"

The line cracked again. Voices in the background. A door slamming.

Sarah's stomach dropped. "Mary?"

"Sarah," Mary whispered, "forgive me…"

The sound that came next was not static but a struggle. A muffled cry. A crash. A man's voice: "Who are you talking to?"

Sarah whispered, "Mary?"

Then a scream—raw, animal, cut off mid-breath. Another voice, closer now, smooth and cold: "Who is this?"

Sarah hung up so hard the phone fell from her hand.

Her Seattle apartment was suddenly silent, oppressive. Outside, a car rolled slowly past. A notification blinked on her screen: UNKNOWN NUMBER – 1 New Message. A text. Just a single attachment she didn't open.

Her heart hammered.

She whispered into the dark: "They know."

Chapter 2: The File

Sarah Mitchel's hands shook as she sat at the edge of her bed, the darkness engulfing her. She was wide awake now, shaking with fear and an ominous doom. She stared at her phone, the encrypted message from Mary Copeland blinking like a warning. Her whole being was shaken up. She hadn't spoken to Mary since college, had no idea where she ended up, and now Mary was dead—or worse— her last moments captured in horrifying audio over the call.

The attachment on the phone was simple enough: "DOC_ANTARCTICA_ENC". Encrypted. Locked down tight. Sarah's stomach turned as she imagined Mary alone in that Antarctic facility, surrounded by horrors she had once dreamed about in theory: And now Mary was gone.

She picked up her laptop and tried to open the file, but layers of encryption twisted back like a lock with no key. Her fingers trembled over the keys. Her thoughts went immediately to Tom.

"Tom," she whispered. She hadn't spoken to him in weeks. His last call had been clipped, strained, the voice of a man who carried the weight of a secret he couldn't share. He sounded tired, defeated, and she had ached to reach through the phone and hold him.

Sarah typed out a short message to Mary's work number, hoping somehow Mary might still pick it up, then paused. Then reality hit her: Mary wasn't coming back.

Finally, trembling, she called Tom's secure line. The phone rang three times before his familiar, gravel-touched voice answered from a deep sleep.

"Sarah…?"

"Tom. —I don't know what to do," she said, her voice cracking. "Mary sent me this file… she's dead, Tom. And I can't open it. I'm scared…"

She explained to Tom what had happened, reminded him that Mary was a friend from College, what Mary had tried to tell her, and Mary's horrific end was heard very clearly from Sarah's side of the phone. Then the man's voice asked who she was. Sarah was sure it was only a matter of time before they found out where the other end of the phone was, and who was on it.

Tom, finally waking up and absorbing the information, said, "Sarah, send me the encrypted file. We have an excellent cybersecurity guy here who can crack it. We need the information for what we are about to do." His voice broke off, knowing he couldn't tell her anything. "Sarah, I think it's time you get Megan and go to my parents' place in Idaho."

Her heart skipped. "What? Underground?"

He swallowed, a sound she could almost hear through the phone. "Yeah. You and Megan. My parents' place. St. Marie's, Idaho. Mountains, off-grid. Underground bunker. Everything you need to stay safe. Don't argue."

Sarah's throat tightened. Pull Megan out of school? Leave her work? But Mary's death—so vivid, so horrific—played on a loop in her mind. The images, the sound, the helplessness. She exhaled slowly, nodding even though he couldn't see her. "Okay. Okay, you're right. It's the safest place."

"I know it's inconvenient," he said softly, "but this… this isn't normal. If they're capable of what Mary was fighting, amongst other things, they'll come after anyone with the file."

Sarah closed her eyes. Tom's voice calmed her in a way nothing else could. He had always been her anchor, her safe harbor. The thought of him, somewhere secret, carrying a burden she couldn't share, twisted her stomach. She hated that he was in danger, that he couldn't tell her anything. But she trusted him. She had to.

Tom's voice came over the phone one last time, slower now, intimate. "Sarah… I love you. You guys keep safe. And… wait for me. I'll come home. I promise."

"I love you too," she said, clutching the phone to her chest. "I'll wait. Both of us."

"I'll pack," she whispered. "Megan… she'll understand."

"I know she will," Tom said. "She loves her grandparents. She'll be fine. You'll both be safe. Stay sharp, stay quiet, and trust no one outside our circle."

The call ended, and silence filled their home. Sarah felt the weight of the world pressing down on her, but beneath it, a flicker of determination burned. Mary's encrypted file was the key—proof of the abominations in Antarctica. They had to unlock it. They had to warn the world.

Sarah swallowed back tears, imagining the bunker, the mountains, the quiet snow-capped peaks surrounding a hidden world where they might actually be safe. She called Megan as soon as the sun peaked above the horizon. "Megan," she said when there was an answer on the first ring. "I was just about to call you, Mom. That was weird." Sarah told Megan she was throwing a few things in a bag and heading her way. "I'm going to pick you up and we are going to Grandma and grandpas in Idaho for a few months." You are going to have to take the rest of the semester off.

"What's going on?" Megan asked, sensing the tension. "I will tell you everything I know when I pick you up in four and a half hours."

Megan's face lit up on the other end of the line. "Idaho? That's awesome! I've always wanted to spend more time at Nanna's and Papa's. I wonder if they still have that old grey horse, what was its name?"

Sarah couldn't help but smile at her daughter's enthusiasm, even through her fear. "Pack light. We leave tonight."

Packing became mechanical, her hands moving without thought. Megan flitted around, cheerful and oblivious to the gravity. Sarah paused for one last look at her home, at everything that she and Tom had worked so hard for. She silently said a prayer for Tom's safety, for all of their safety, and then locked the door.

Somewhere beneath the ice in Antarctica, Mary Copeland's warnings were etched into that file. Somewhere, hybrid horrors, AI swarms, and engineered plagues waited. Somewhere, evil moved with precision and power.

And somewhere above all of it, Sarah, Megan, and Tom would wait—hidden, watching, ready.

The world was about to change, and they had no choice but to survive.

Chapter 3: Poke The Bear

Jonathan Roberts had been called a lot of things in his life — genius, criminal, legend, pain in the ass.

He preferred the artist.

He sat in the glass-walled operations suite of the CIA's Cyber Division, feet propped up on a $20,000 workstation, spinning a USB drive around his fingers like a magician with a coin. His black T-shirt read "404: Morals Not Found." Across the room, half a dozen agents glared at him through the reflection on the glass, still remembering that months ago, he'd been the one inside a federal prison, not their firewall.

"Mr. Roberts," came a cool, steady voice behind him.

Jonathan didn't have to turn around to know it was her. Melony Bishop. Field agent. Smart, lethal, and gorgeous, with the deepest green eyes, she sparkled in a way that made rules feel optional.

"Agent Bishop," Jonathan said, flashing his roguish grin as he spun the chair around. "Here to arrest me or confess your undying affection?"

Melony crossed her arms, dark hair in a tight ponytail, holster gleaming under the lights. "You're supposed to be testing the new secure comms line, not flirting with the agency's facial recognition software."

"Oh, I tested it," he said, leaning in close. "Turns out it recognizes me as a threat and a snack."

Melony rolled her eyes, but the corner of her mouth twitched — the smallest crack in her armor.

"Keep it up, Roberts, and I'll assign you to rodent surveillance duty."

"Tempting," he said. "But I'm more of a people-watcher. Specifically, people like you."

Before Melony could retort, the elevator door chimed open — and in stepped Assistant Commander Marco Rodriguez, Ghost Spear's muscle in a tailored uniform. Square-jawed, confident, and annoyingly perfect. He placed a possessive hand on Melony's shoulder.

"Roberts," Rodriguez said flatly. "Still pretending you're indispensable?"

Jonathan didn't miss a beat. "Oh, I don't pretend, sir. I just am." He spun the chair again, dramatically, fingers tapping the desk. "Besides, I heard Ghost Spear's last system audit found six backdoors and two compromised keys. You're welcome."

Rodriguez smirked. "One day, your arrogance will catch up to you."

"Maybe," Jonathan said. "But until then, I'm still faster than your security team and better-looking than your commander."

Melony sighed. "Children. Please."

The three of them stood in a tense triangle — attraction and rivalry humming between them like static. Melony tried to keep it professional, but she'd be lying if she said she didn't feel something magnetic in Jonathan's reckless brilliance. Rodriguez knew it too. That was half the reason he hated him.

Jonathan, of course, loved every second of it.

Hours later, the playful tension evaporated.

The door to the cyber division opened, and Captain Tom Mitchell stepped in, Ghost Spear patch on his shoulder and fatigue lines under his eyes.

Jonathan noticed immediately — the man looked haunted.

"Roberts," Tom said, voice low. "I need your help. Now."

Jonathan lowered his feet and straightened. "You look like you haven't slept in days. You finally break up with your codependent Medkit?"

Tom didn't smile. He set a small encrypted drive on the desk.

"My wife sent this. She's a biologist. She got this from a girlfriend she went to college with," he paused, "Her friend died trying to get this to her."

Melony's expression hardened. "What kind of file?"

Tom hesitated. "It's named DOC_ANTARCTICA_ENC. She said it's top secret."

Jonathan's humor faded instantly. "Antarctica? That's where the black projects run — the biotech labs, the synthetic genetics stuff." He plugged in the drive carefully, glancing at the others. "You sure you want me poking this bear?"

Rodriguez stepped closer. "Do it. We'll deal with the fallout later."

Jonathan cracked his knuckles and started typing.

The screen came alive — cascading encryption patterns, old-school cipher fragments buried under next-gen quantum locks. Whoever encoded it did not want it opened.

"Whoa," he murmured. "This isn't government-grade. This is…something else."

Melony leaned in beside him, close enough for him to smell the trace of jasmine from her hair. "Can you crack it?"

Jonathan smirked. "Can I crack it? Agent Bishop, please. You wound me."

His fingers flew across the keys. Streams of characters spilled like coded rain. The room filled with the rhythmic hum of processors — and the tension of three agents watching a ghost in the machine.

Then, the first layer broke. The screen flickered. A file header appeared:

Project Genesis // Bio-Division Antarctica

SUBJECTS: Human-Animal Genetic Cross-Species Integration

STATUS: Containment Breach – Level 6

Everyone froze.

Tom's voice was barely a whisper. "Jesus."

Jonathan kept working. Another file opened: BioDrone Nanotech – Prototype Insects // Directive: Targeted Intelligence Extraction.

He scrolled through images — tiny mechanical mosquitoes, locusts with silicon cores, their wings marked with microscopic circuit webs.

Melony covered her mouth. "They're…AI organisms."

"Not just that," Jonathan said grimly. "There's a section labeled Immunogenetic Weaponry." He opened it. Lines of text scrolled by — names of viruses, mutation patterns, genome splicing logs.

VIRUS: Erebos-9

VIRUS: Lazarus Strain

VIRUS: PLX-22 (Neural Collapse Syndrome)

Tom's face drained of color. "My wife…she is not safe."

"She is scared shitless," Tom said quietly. "And she knew they'd come after her for it."

For once, no one spoke. Even Jonathan — the Joker, the rebel — was silent. The light from the monitor painted the room in pale blue, like the glow of a deep-sea abyss.

Melony looked at the data, then at Tom. "We can't let this stay buried. If these labs exist—"

"They do," Jonathan interrupted. "And if this file is what it looks like, then they're not just experimenting down there. They're playing god."

Tom took a deep breath. "Then we stop them."

Jonathan looked up, eyes darker than usual, all trace of humor gone. "You realize what you're asking, right? Once we dig deeper, we're all targets. The kind you don't walk away from."

Tom met his gaze evenly. "Then we don't walk away. Not until the truth gets out."

Rodriguez clenched his jaw. Melony reached for her gun like instinct. Jonathan turned back to the keyboard.

"Alright then," he said quietly. "Let's open Pandora's box."

The room's lights dimmed as the decryption continued. Code bled across the screen, revealing horrors none of them could yet comprehend — files that whispered of Project Lazarus, Erebos containment failures, and a facility called Eden Deep.

Outside, thunder rolled over Langley.

Inside, something had begun — and there was no going back.

Chapter 4: The Basement Briefing

The basement of the White House was never meant for meetings like this. The air was stale, the walls thick concrete painted a neutral gray. Rows of locked cabinets lined the edges of the room, and a single long wooden table sat in the middle, lit by a bank of recessed lights that cast pale circles on the polished surface.

This wasn't on any schedule. No one outside this room knew it was happening. The Secret Service guards at the stairwell had been hand-picked. Cell phones were sealed in Faraday pouches. If you weren't in the room, you didn't exist.

President Mark Johnson sat at the head of the table, his tie loosened, eyes dark with fatigue. To his right was CIA Director Evelyn Shaw, her fingers steepled under her chin like a chess player watching an opponent's move. Beside her sat General Harris, commander of the Joint Chiefs, broad-shouldered and rigid, the picture of a man used to barking orders and being obeyed.

Down the length of the table sat a mix of people who rarely breathed the same air:

Captain Tom Mitchell, the battle-worn combat medic of Ghost Spear;

Captain Daniel Rourke, his commander of Ghost Spear, sharp-eyed and alert;

Melony Bishop and Amy Sutton, both CIA field ops — Melony with her disciplined posture and slight scowl, Amy with her cool, unreadable expression;

Jonathan Roberts, the bad-boy hacker turned CIA cyber specialist, slouched in his chair with a wry smile playing at his lips;

Elliot Kane, the infamous conspiracy theorist turned reluctant consultant, nervously tapped a pen on his notepad.

And Kyle Green, the retired military doctor turned whistleblower, his lined face pale but resolute.

Everyone's eyes were on the thick manila folder in front of President Johnson. Its tab read simply: PROJECT LAZARUS.

The President broke the silence first.

"We're here because the intelligence coming out of Antarctica, out of black sites all over the world, points to something we can't quite name. Something the Dark Dominion is planning." He glanced at Daniel and Tom. "Your teams have been inside their outer networks. You've seen things. But none of us knows the endgame."

Jonathan leaned back in his chair, arms folded. "Yeah, but we've got enough to know it's going to be bad. Really bad."

CIA Director Evelyn Shaw flipped open a folder, sliding photos across the table. Blurred images of metallic discs streaking across desert skies, schematics of insect-like drones the size of gnats, and a grainy satellite shot of a dark triangular craft rising from the ice of Antarctica.

"PROJECT LAZARUS and OPERATION PALE HORSE," she said, "are the Dominion's codenames for something global. We've confirmed UFO craft being launched from hidden hangars across several continents. At the same time, our cyber intercepts indicate development of micro-AI delivery systems — robotic mosquitoes capable of carrying a pathogen payload."

Amy Sutton's voice was low. "It's the perfect vector. No missile launches. No loud weapons. Just the air and your own blood."

Melony nodded grimly. "Still think the alien attack theory makes more sense. The craft sightings are increasing. They're preparing for something visible, something dramatic. A false flag, maybe."

Jonathan snorted. "Yeah, because releasing a deadly plague from robot mosquitoes isn't dramatic enough. Have you ever seen what a mosquito can do in Africa? Now scale that with AI and designer pathogens. They don't need UFOs if they can turn every living thing into a carrier."

Across the table, Kyle Green leaned forward, his eyes bright. "You're all still missing the point. We have aliens living among us. Under the treaty. They're supposed to be protected. If we go public, ask for their help, they could intervene— They have the crafts, the technology to help fight this."

General Harris slammed a palm on the table. "We do not 'go public,' Green. That would trigger panic on a scale you can't imagine."

Kyle Green responded, "And what about the asteroid headed towards Earth?"

Everyone turned to him.

Kyle's voice dropped. "The one inbound from the outer system. Officially, it's called 2026-XQR9. But it's not behaving like a rock. It's adjusting its trajectory. I think it's a ship. Maybe theirs. Maybe the Dominion's. But something's coming."

A murmur rippled around the table.

President Johnson's jaw tightened. "We're talking about possibilities that range from a false-flag alien invasion, to mass bioweapon deployment, to an unknown craft inbound on an Earth intercept. We have no clarity, no timeline. How the hell do we prepare?"

For a moment, no one answered. The room buzzed with tension.

Then Jonathan leaned forward, his usual cocky grin flickering just enough to show the edge of fear beneath. "We prepare by doing what we do best. Get ahead of the data. Crack the Dominion's files. Track the bugs. Trace the ships. You hired me for a reason."

Melony's eyes met his, and for a moment something passed between them — a flicker of attraction mixed with worry. Rodriguez wasn't in the room, but his presence felt like a shadow between them.

Daniel Rourke cleared his throat. "Speaking of preparation… Elliot. You've got that underground bunker out in Colorado, right?"

Elliot blinked. "Up in the Rockies, yeah. Why?"

"I might need a place for my wife and daughter to weather this storm," Daniel said quietly. "If this goes sideways."

Elliot's face softened. "You don't even have to ask. They'll be welcome, no matter what."

Jonathan tried to lighten the air. "Hell, maybe we should all go to Colorado. Build a fire, roast some marshmallows, wait for the world to end."

Nobody laughed.

President Johnson closed the folder. "We're running blind. But we can't sit still. Jonathan, I want you embedded with Ghost Spear immediately. If the Dominion's systems hold the key, you're going to break them. Melony, Amy — you'll coordinate field intel with Tom and Daniel. Kane, Green, you'll keep feeding us anything you know."

As he spoke, a sudden low rumble vibrated through the room — faint, but enough to rattle the glasses on the table. Everyone froze.

General Harris looked up sharply. "Was that—"

The overhead lights flickered once, then twice, and went out.

Darkness swallowed the basement.

A moment later, the emergency red lights snapped on, bathing the room in a blood-colored glow. Somewhere above them, alarms began to wail.

Jonathan looked around, voice low but unmistakably sober now. "Uh… guys? Did we just get found?"

The President's Secret Service detail burst through the door, weapons drawn. "Mr. President — we need to move. Now."

And then the alarms cut off. The only sound was the soft hum of the emergency lights.

Somewhere in the building above them, something heavy moved.

Tom Mitchell's hand went instinctively to his sidearm. "This meeting just got compromised."

President Johnson's voice was a whisper. "God help us."

The red lights flickered again.

Chapter 5: Extraction

The basement door burst open as two Secret Service agents swept in, weapons raised, earpieces hissing with coded chatter. One of them — a tall, hawk-nosed man in a black suit — spoke fast but calm.

"Mr. President, Director Shaw, General Harris — we're executing Protocol Iron Raven. We're moving you to the secondary site immediately."

President Johnson didn't hesitate. "Move." "Yes, we already have your wife, Margaret, waiting in the elevator."

Tom Mitchell was already on his feet, pulling Daniel Rourke up with him. "Ghost Spear, on point," he muttered. Melony Bishop and Amy Sutton exchanged quick looks, both drawing their sidearms. Jonathan Roberts scrambled after them, muttering under his breath.

"Man, I knew today was gonna be bad, but this is some real apocalypse-movie crap right here."

The group hustled through the basement hallway, boots echoing against the concrete floor. Alarms pulsed in the distance, their pitch rising. At the far end, an elevator stood open — a steel box with no buttons, just a palm scanner glowing faintly green.

"This way," barked the lead agent. They all jumped in the elevator as the doors closed, and the bullets started flying.

The elevator sealed with a heavy thunk as soon as they were inside. The hum of descending machinery filled the cramped space. Jonathan tried to crack a grin. "Okay, someone tell me this thing doesn't eject from the white house and fly us to the moon—"

"Shut up, Roberts," Melony snapped, but the corner of her mouth twitched despite herself. They could still hear bullets being fired somewhere off in the distance.

The elevator opened into a dim underground garage where three matte-black Suburbans idled. Agents flanked the vehicles, scanning the shadows. They were herded into the middle SUV. No sirens. No convoy. Just a silent, coordinated exit through a tunnel that curved upward, emerging into the night two blocks from the White House lawn.

Above them, the sky was moonless, streaked with low clouds. A V-22 Osprey tiltrotor waited at a hidden landing zone, rotors chopping the air. Its rear ramp was down, engines howling.

"Load up!" yelled one of the agents.

They sprinted aboard. The ramp slammed shut as soon as the last boot crossed the threshold. The Osprey lifted vertically, its vibration rattling the benches inside. The White House receded into darkness below.

General Harris strapped in, jaw tight, arm around his wife. "Where's our destination?"

"Secondary continuity site," the lead agent said over the engine noise. "Deep Montana. Off-grid, fully hardened."

Jonathan glanced at Melony, eyebrows raised. "You know, I always imagined my first government chopper ride would be to some tropical black site with margaritas and tiny umbrellas. Instead, I get Apocalypse Central."

Melony didn't answer. She stared straight ahead, eyes unreadable.

Across from them, Daniel Rourke pulled out his secure Radio handset. He hesitated just a heartbeat, then thumbed the encryption switch and spoke low.

"Claire. It's me."

There was a crackle, then a groggy voice. "Daniel? It's the middle of the night—what's wrong?"

"Listen carefully," he said, voice steady but edged. "I can't explain anything, but you and Emily need to pack light. Essentials only. Leave the house within the hour. A man named Elliot Kane is on his way in a government chopper. He'll take you both to his bunker in the mountains of Colorado. It's secure. Completely off-grid. I trust him with your lives."

"Daniel…" Claire's voice wavered. "What's happening? Is it… Bad?"

He closed his eyes briefly. "It's complicated. For now, just do exactly as I'm asking. Kane will have a radio. We'll keep in touch. I'll see to your survival, I swear it. Just stay calm."

Emily's voice came faintly over the line — their daughter. "Dad? Hi, Daddy?"

"Hi, sweetheart," Daniel said, forcing a smile she couldn't see. "You and your mom are going on a vacation to the mountains with a good friend of mine. I'll explain more soon he said to Claire. Just go with Kane when he arrives. I love you both."

There was a pause, then Claire said softly, "We love you too. Please come back to us."

"I will," Daniel whispered, and cut the line.

He sat back, radio clutched in his hand. Tom glanced over at him, reading the unspoken words in his friend's face. "They'll be safe," Tom said quietly. "Kane's a good man. Off-grid is the right call."

Daniel nodded once but didn't speak.

Across the cabin, Jonathan leaned toward Melony, trying to pierce the tension. "So, uh, how's this for a first date? You, me, a secret presidential extraction, and maybe the end of the world. Really memorable, right? Maybe I can even be your hero?"

Melony shot him a sidelong glance, but there was a flicker of a smile. "Keep talking like that and Rodriguez will shoot you before the aliens do."

Jonathan smirked. "Yeah, but he'll have to catch me first."

General Harris cleared his throat, glaring at both of them. "Focus. Once we're underground, this isn't just about survival. We're gathering evidence. Everything we have on the Dark Dominion, on Pale Horse, on these… UFO craft and AI delivery systems. We find the truth, then we act."

President Johnson spoke for the first time since they'd boarded. "We're past the point of speculation. Once we're secure, I want options. All of them."

The Osprey banked sharply, engines howling as it veered westward. Through a small porthole window, Jonathan could see only endless darkness below — and for a moment, he thought he saw something glinting in the clouds, like a metallic orb moving without sound.

He blinked, but it was gone.

He sat back, suddenly quiet.

Chapter 6: Waffle House Confessions

The neon sign buzzed weakly in the desert night, its yellow glow flickering over cracked asphalt and the busy stretch of University Drive. Inside, the Waffle House smelled of burnt coffee and maple syrup — the kind of place where nobody asked questions after midnight.

Colonel Marcus Hale sat in a corner booth, wearing a sweatsuit, sunglasses, and a baseball cap. His posture was rigid, but his eyes — blue-gray and hollow from sleepless nights — never stopped scanning the door.

He'd told himself he wouldn't come. That it was a mistake.

But when Amy Sutton's voice had come through the phone — soft, cautious, but undeniably real — he knew there was no turning back.

The doorbell jingled.

She stepped inside wearing jeans and a loose black sweater, hair tied back, eyes hidden behind sunglasses despite the dim light. She looked tired — older, maybe, from the weight of secrets — but still her.

Their eyes met.

And for a moment, time folded in on itself.

Amy crossed the room slowly. Hale stood, uncertain, then sat again as she slid into the booth across from him. A waitress poured them coffee, the pot shaking slightly in her hands, then wandered away.

Neither spoke for a long moment.

"You look good," Amy said finally, her voice quiet but trembling. "Different… but good."

He gave a low, humorless laugh. "Different is one way to put it. You wrecked me, Amy."

Her eyes softened. "I didn't mean to. You have to believe that."

He leaned forward, his voice low, rough. "You were using me. I thought I was working for the CIA, but the whole damn time—" He cut himself off, jaw tightening. "I didn't even know who I was serving; I was blindsided from all directions."

Amy reached across the table, her hand brushing his. "I didn't know at first either, Nathan. I swear. When I found out what they were — what you were wrapped up in — I didn't have a choice. I had to report it. I thought I could protect you if I played it right."

He stared at her, searching her face for any flicker of a lie.

But there was none. Only regret — and love. Real, human love.

He let out a long breath. "You always were better at strategy."

"Not when it came to you," she whispered.

They sat there in the hum of fluorescent lights and faraway jukebox static, a world spinning outside their little booth — but neither cared. Amy's fingers curled around his, tentative at first, then tighter when he didn't pull away.

"I asked for leave when I got your message to meet," Hale said finally, "Told them it was private business. They don't suspect anything yet. But if they find out I'm talking to you—"

"They'll kill you," Amy finished quietly.

He nodded. "Yeah. Probably."

Her grip tightened. "Then why risk it?"

"Because," he said simply, "you're the only person who ever made me want to be a better man. And because you deserve to know what's coming."

Amy's eyes flickered. "You mean—"

"The plan," he said. "The real one. All of it."

She froze. The clock over the counter ticked once, loud in the silence.

"Nathan… are you sure?"

He looked at her, really looked, and smiled faintly. "If anyone's going to stop them, it's you. You are the one with the brains and guts to do what needs to be done."

Outside, a semi rumbled past, shaking the windows. Hale leaned in closer, voice barely a whisper now. His lips brushed her ear as he began to speak — fast, urgent, each word weighted like a confession. Amy's expression shifted from disbelief to horror to grim understanding.

He told her everything.

She didn't interrupt. Didn't move. Her hand trembled in his, coffee gone cold on the table between them. When he finally stopped, the silence that followed felt too big for the room.

Amy swallowed hard. "Oh my God, Nathan…"

He nodded once, eyes dark. "Now you know why I had to come."

A single tear slipped down her cheek. "You should've walked away, left, saved yourself."

"I tried." He smiled, small, sad. "But I couldn't walk away from you."

They leaned across the table, foreheads touching for the briefest moment — two souls who had lived too long in the shadows, finding light in each other's presence.

Outside, the wind picked up, scattering dust across the empty street.

Inside, Amy whispered, "What do we do now?"

He looked at her, voice quiet but resolute.

"Now, we go underground." Amy smiled; she knew just the place they could go.

The doorbell jingled again.

Hale's head snapped up. A man in a dark coat stepped inside, his face obscured by the brim of his hat. He ordered coffee to go, but his eyes never left their booth.

Hale's fingers brushed the holster under the table. Amy's heartbeat quickened.

The man smiled faintly, too faintly — and walked back toward the door.

They didn't breathe until it closed behind him.

Amy looked back at Hale, eyes wide. "They know."

Hale nodded once, jaw tightening. "Then it's already started."

The neon light flickered again, once, twice, and went dark.

Chapter 7: The Grid Goes Black

When the lights went out, the world did not sleep. It screamed.

It started as a ripple, a blackout in a handful of cities that news anchors blamed on grid overloads, on storms, on maintenance errors. Then the ripple became a wave. Towers fell silent. Substations went dark. Satellites blinked. The hum of civilization—the constant, low thrum of electricity that everyone took for granted stopped. Within hours, the planet was lit only by the teeth of emergency generators, the flare of fires, and the faint, terrified glow of people's phone screens.

In twelve hours, metropolitan skylines that had once stitched continents with electricity were ghost maps of black windows. Airplanes stalled on tarmacs, trains leaked passengers into tunnels, hospital corridors were lit by flashlights and a battery of portable generators that would not last forever. Tesla cars traveled down roads empty of drivers till they crashed into something in their way. In neighborhoods, elevators trapped the unwary; traffic lights died, and intersections became theatres of catastrophe.

Day One: confusion, honking, the first frantic calls to service centers. People walked into the dark to find one another, to ask, to shout. In hospitals, nurses who had never set down their oaths hummed ancient routines by flashlight: bag valves, manual compressions, the human muscle that replaces failing machines.

Day Three: food chains buckled. Refrigeration failed. The first grocery stores sealed their doors against looters; the ones that stayed open became dangerous places. Fuel pumps were dead; cars stalled mid-commute. Cities that relied on water towers watched municipal pressure drop day by day until faucets breathed air and then nothing.

Week One: governments declared states of emergency. President Mark Johnson addressed the nation from an armored room, his voice hoarse but steady on a battery-powered feed: "We are mobilizing every resource. Remain calm. Cooperate with local authorities. Help your neighbors." The air was foul with smoke and fear, and the words felt thin.

The Dark Dominion had not simply cut power. They had executed the first step of a plan refined in secret cells and hidden vaults: pry the modern world apart and watch the seams gape. Without a grid, the web that knits commerce, food, medicine, and governance frayed into threads people could pull apart with their bare hands.

Months unfolded like a land map burned at the edges.

Month One — Fires:

Cities turned on themselves. Where power vanished, law followed. Curfews became the hammer. In some places, towns organized to defend wells and grocery caches. In others, the first of the organized groups, militias and opportunistic gangs, seized supply depots. Fires mushroomed. In neighborhoods, long-smoldering grievances combusted into nightly violence: home invasions, communal brawls, fuel-line fights. The air was always hazy. It felt like the purge in real time, not a movie anymore.

Month Two — The Camps:

President Johnson, advised by General Harris and Director Evelyn Shaw, ordered the military into urban centers under emergency powers: to protect, to restore, to control. The intent was to prevent mass slaughter and chaos; the result was iron and tent, and fence.

Across the country, hastily established secure survivor facilities rose on fairgrounds, military bases, and decommissioned airfields. They were fenced, patrolled, and rationed. Inside, the government stockpiles—canned food, water purifiers, antibiotics—were parceled. Aboard flatbed trucks, soldiers pushed families through processing stations. Some felt relief at shelter and medical aid; others tasted the first bitterness of lost freedom. Rumors swelled like the crowds: that registration meant identification; identification meant selection.

The administration called them secure survivor centers. People who had lived freely their whole lives called them by other names — anything to keep from admitting how much had changed.

Month Three — The Diseases and the Silence:

Without refrigeration and with sanitation failing, infectious diseases spread like wildfire on a rumor. Old pathogens resurfaced where sewage overflowed, and new outbreaks crawled through camps and slums alike. Clinics without power became morgues. In quiet, resource-strapped towns, whole wings of nursing homes fell still.

The Dark Dominion watched, as they always had: not with face-to-face violence at first, but with the patient cruelty of those who understand that removing infrastructure is a weapon. If hunger and fear did half their work, human hands would finish the rest.

Month Four — The Sky:

Fuel was scarce, but not entirely gone. Small clusters of aircraft and a shriveled global navy kept corridors open for the most critical military movements. Over cities, Black Hawks and transport planes moved in rotatory patrols. From the White House underground and other hardened sites, command centers plotted resources and troop movements. The President's voice, worn and firm, had taken on a new cadence: rationing, security, and contingency.

Army units, Ghost Spear among them, were cut loose on special missions: escort convoys, secure lab caches, extract scientists, and, where necessary, use force. They moved like ghost stories through urban ruins and open prairie. For some, the military presence was salvation. For others, the uniformed men were the usher of a new order.

New Lives, New Faces

Marta Alvarez was a nurse who had cared for the first wave of patients in a collapsed hospital in Chicago. She now walked the perimeter of a survivor compound where the smell of bleach was a daily chant and the cry of the bereaved a constant.

Jonas Smith was a small-town farmer whose irrigation pump had died the first night the grid failed. He had organized neighbors to dig hand trenches and haul water on pickups until a convoy came by with Army rations. He watched his fields go fallow and learned to barter seeds for coffee.

Amare Singh was a UN aid worker who had labored to direct shipments to refugee camps in the first weeks. Now she struggled to track deliveries because the manifest systems were useless and radios clogged the air with static.

Rafiq and Leila Abbas were a family who had fled a coastal city, looted and burning. They arrived at a fenced facility with two children and a single backpack. Inside, they found shelter and a water line every morning. Hope tasted like a ration ticket.

Mason Kade ran a local militia that had started as a neighborhood watch and mutated into a band of men who guarded a converted supermarket with a fearsome zeal. Where the militia ruled, neighbors learned the new, ugly mathematics of survival: trade your labor, your food, your silence.

The Government's Calculus

From inside the secure command hubs beneath Montana and elsewhere, President Johnson and his advisors fought to hold the line. The decision to erect guarded centers had been agonizing and intentional. The reasoning went like this:

Concentrate survivors to deliver medical aid and food efficiently.

Isolate outbreaks.

Control critical infrastructure and keep supply chains as functional as possible.

What the planners underestimated was the raw human fallout of containment. Fences created targets. Supply convoys became prizes. The very act of centralizing survivors had the unintended consequence of making them vulnerable to those outside who had nothing to lose.

General Harris oversaw deployments, moving brigades to maintain the centers and guard convoys bound for towns that had been cut off for weeks. National Guard units supplemented regular forces, and military tribunals tried to keep pillaging in check. For every convoy that reached its destination, a dozen trucks were ambushed on the road by crafts that looked alien. The dark dominion was using their alien crafts to take out what little help the people had, and of course, the people thought it was an alien invasion.

Director Evelyn Shaw and CIA operatives worked in parallel, hunting the Dark Dominion's cells and infrastructure, searching for the source of the blackout, pursuing the financed strings that pinned a million broken lights to the ground. Their work was surgical, secret, and slow. Every successful extraction of a cache of antibiotics or a trove of preserved seeds was a tiny victory.

Death took the easy and the terrible ways. People died from exposure in abandoned buildings, from gunshots by looters, and from infection in the large complexes where immunization schedules could not be kept. They died from despair, choosing to walk out into the dark rather than remain behind a fence. They died because a ventilator battery failed one afternoon.

In a Midwestern town, a fight over a gasoline drum became a massacre when a militia opened fire. In Houston, Texas, a hospital that had survived for two months with a diesel generator finally lost power; without IVs and oxygen, the long blue line of waiting patients thinned.

Children, more than anyone, bore the unfairness. Food lines were a place to lose hope; playgrounds turned into places to forage. Schools closed, and in the slow weeks, children grew accustomed to the sound of distant gunfire like weather.

The Dark Dominion did not need to declare victory to be dangerous. They let the infrastructure die, let the hungry and the desperate thin their own ranks, then nudged the chaos with disinformation, controlled leaks, and small strikes: a sabotaged water pump, a convoy ambushed at dusk, a broadcast that blamed aliens for the sabotage. They were patient architects of collapse, and their calculus was simple—one world under centralized authority would be easier to manage if most people were already too weak to resist.

Jonathan Roberts, holed up with the CIA, still worked his magic on encryption and dark networks, trying everything he had to find a way to get the grid back up. He found pieces of the Dark Dominion's logistics payments through networks, shipping manifests that rerouted precious antibiotics and medical supplies to private warehouses, and images of weapons caches labeled with sinister, corporate-like logos. He began to understand the scale: not anarchists, not mere profiteers, but an interlocking web of power and money.

Daniel Rourke, Jose Rodriguez, and Tom Mitchell ran escort missions out of Denver and managed extractions of scientists and caches. They watched the faces of starving people and carried the shame back to their bunker at night. Tom found himself questioning the fairness of the structures he'd sworn to protect. But everyone was doing all they could with what they had.

President Johnson authorized the guarded facilities and made a speech—one that would be parsed for months as both necessary and chilling: "We will keep you safe. We will ration fairly. The perpetrators are not aliens but a faction of our own government operating on their own." His words steadied many and frightened others. The military's presence comforted some and terrified others; under the stress, the line between protection and compulsion blurred.

Not everyone accepted the new world without a fight. Towns organized patrols. Secret radio networks, ragged and desperate, carried music, news, and coded messages. Groups of doctors and teachers met in basements to plan the slow recovery of communities. Small farmers, like Jonas Smith, organized seed banks. In the mountains, Elliot Kane's underground networks took in refugees and tried to ferry medicines to places airdrops could no longer reach. With Claire's help and Emily's company, things ran smoothly for a while. Even Kyle Green stayed with them in Colorado and did his part to help.

In one fenced survivor facility, Marta Alvarez administered a needle of a salvaged medicine to an old man with brittle hands. He spoke about his son, lost in the first riots. Her eyes softened with sorrow. "We will keep going," she said to herself. "One person at a time."

Into this world of dark and rationed hope, intelligence flowed through the underground: blurred satellite snaps from a recon drone, intercepted shipments routed through Antarctic-linked oil companies, a whisper of a new move.

It came as a single message on an encrypted channel Jonathan had been watching for weeks: a GPS ping from an ORIGIN point he didn't recognize. Coordinates blinked: somewhere in the polar silence — Antarctica. Attached, an image corrupted until Jonathan ran it through layers of decryption, revealing at last a panel of instruments he'd never seen—sleek, alien-not-alien, humming with cold energy.

Below the image, a single file name scrolled like a threat: PHASE TWO —LAZARUS- INITIATE.

Jonathan's hands shook as he forwarded the file up the chain. In the command bunker, Melony read the subject line and felt the world tilt. Amy had already briefed President Johnson on the information she received from Colonel Hale. She and Hale were holed up in Montana in an underground bunker trying to help the cause any way they could.

President Johnson, on a live battery feed with General Harris and Director Shaw, stared at the data in stunned silence. The plan had followed the script the Dominion had promised, but there were more pages still.

The lights in the command room were electric, a small defiant constellation inside the darkness. Outside, the planet burned in the unguarded dark.

"Phase Two?" General Harris breathed. "What the hell does that mean? Is that the release of the AI bot swarm released from Antarctica to inject a virus into the already compromised human race?"

Elliot Kane, listening from his mountain network, whispered into his radio with the weight of doom and stubborn hope: "They prefer the dark, but they can't have it forever. Somebody has to make the light."

The feed cut with a soft click. In the black air above the bunkers and the camps and the ruined cities, something moved. A distant hum that felt like a promise or a threat edged through the night.

And across the world, in gymnasiums, churches, and the cold concrete of parking lots turned into secure survivor facilities, people listened for that hum and prayed they would be alright.

Chapter 8: The Nine

The cabin at Mount Ashland was one large room, weather-beaten, and built from timbers older than anyone in the room. The walls creaked with every gust of icy wind that howled across the mountain. Outside, snow drifted silently under a silver moon, but inside the cabin, there was only stillness. There was a bunker nearby where they stayed with family and friends who needed a safe place. Others who are helping with the light and energy to combat the dark.

Nine figures sat in a circle on the worn wooden floor with woven mats, a candle flickering at each of their feet. The wax pooled like molten gold, shadows dancing up the walls as if alive. They had come from every corner of the world—each called by a pull older than memory. They were the coven of Nine.

Elias Thompson, the Druid Priest of Symbols, sat cross-legged with a worn leather-bound journal open on his lap. His tattooed hands traced invisible runes in the air. Beside him, Mei-Ling rested her violin against her shoulder, a single low note humming in the room, blending with the heartbeat of the mountain itself. Mingan, tall and steady, kept his palms on the ground as though feeling the earth's pulse beneath the boards.

Around them, the others breathed in rhythm, eyes closed, bodies still. The cabin air thickened, the sound of the wind fading into a low hum like distant thunder. One by one, they began to sway—barely perceptible, like trees in a breeze. Their breaths synced, their hearts synced. The Nine were aligning their energies.

Mei-Ling's soft bowing became the tether, a single sustained note that opened a door. Elias whispered an incantation of sigils under his breath. The candle flames began to lean inward toward the center of the circle, flickering unnaturally, their waxy scent replaced by something metallic, like static before a storm.

Then, as one, their minds slipped.

The cabin vanished.

They were no longer sitting in a circle on an icy mountain. They were suspended in a vast, black expanse. The stars burned around them like eyes. Above, below, everywhere, a great pulsing object appeared. At first, it seemed like a star igniting, then like a comet, then like a sun caught in motion. But it was neither. It moved with precision, not chaos.

It was a ship.

Not built as humans build, but grown. Organic and luminous, its hull glowed with a strange bioluminescent pulse, shapes shifting across its surface like living script. It was beautiful and terrible, larger than mountains, older than oceans. A great ball of fire made of purpose, hurdling through the void toward Earth.

The Nine felt its presence as much as they saw it. Minds not human-touched their own. A weightless hand on the soul. A voice without sound, older than time, pressed into them:

We are the keepers of the garden. We planted you. We tend you. We watched you rise and fall. You are our children, our seeds scattered in the dark. The garden is burning. We come to keep the fire from consuming the roots. But the time is thin. The rotten disease has gone deep.

The message pulsed through them like lightning, leaving tears on some of their faces, awe on others. Mei-Ling dropped her bow, eyes wet, whispering in Mandarin words she didn't consciously know but that echoed the voice: "Mǔqīn… nǐ huílái le…" Mother… you have returned.

Images flooded their minds—DNA mixing and coiling like galaxies, ancient seas seeded with life, cities rising and falling under alien skies. They saw hands of light shaping clay, sparks igniting, cells dividing, civilizations rising like crops tended by invisible gardeners.

And now they saw the Earth, their Earth, smothered under smoke, blacked out cities, humans clawing at each other in the dark.

The ship's voice pressed one last time:

We are called Anunna. We are coming. We will try. But you must hold. We cannot save what destroys itself. The answer lies in you. The strength comes from within.

Then the vision fractured like glass hit by a hammer.

The Nine gasped as one. The cabin returned, the wax, the wood, the cold. The candles flared and went out, plunging them into total darkness.

Mingan spoke first, his deep voice trembling. "It wasn't a comet."

"No," Elias said, closing his journal slowly. "It was them."

Mei-Ling held her violin like a child. "The ones who made us."

Silence held them. Outside, the wind howled like a warning.

Finally, one of the Nine whispered what they all feared to ask: "Do you think… they're too late?"

No one answered.

The mountain creaked. Far below, the world still burned, but now a light was moving through the dark toward it, a light older than humanity itself.

Chapter 9: Nine Came Down the Mountain

They came down from Mount Ashland three at a time, boots crunching through frozen pine needles, faces raw from the cold and whatever they had carried back in their bones. The chopper's downdraft sent a scatter of snow across the ridge as the aircraft settled into the plateau below. Climbing inside, beneath the hum of rotors, each of the Nine looked like someone who'd been awakened from a very old dream.

By the time the helicopter banked over the Montana bunker's perimeter and set down at the secure landing strip, the sky had a bruise to it, clouds pulled thin and smeared by distant storms. In the armored convoy that met them, the press of the world's urgency was palpable: sirens suppressed to a dull thump, agents with faces that had stopped pretending to be surprised, radios buzzing in languages that had no soundtrack for wonder.

They were led below to the same concrete room that had been the last desperate refuge—President Mark Johnson's emergency operations center now thrumming with generators, monitors, and the low, tired voices of men and women who had been awake too long. Director Evelyn Shaw stood with General Harris at her side; Tom Mitchell and Captain Daniel Rourke were there in a single, deliberate block of black tactical fabric. Melony Bishop and Amy Sutton waited by a bank of screens. Jonathan Roberts sat with his legs crossed on a metal chair, fingers worrying at the edge of a pastry he'd forgotten to eat. Assistant Commander Rodriguez arrived late, jaw tight.

No one spoke when the Nine stepped into the light. The gravity in the room shifted. The atmosphere in the room became so light that it felt like you could float.

President Johnson rose and met them at the head of the table. Haunted fatigue softened in his face at the sight of those who had been called to the oldest work: keeping balance in a world of unsteady light and shadow. "You're all—" he started, then let the words dissolve. "Tell me everything."

Elias, tall, bone-mapped with inked sigils—stepped forward first. He kept his voice measured; there was no showmanship in it, only the rusted iron of someone who'd dealt with storms his whole life.

"We meditated," he said. "We went into the silent space. We saw a ship. Not a vessel stamped by human hands, but grown—biological and mechanical like a living mountain. It moved like a comet toward Earth. It carried a presence older than speech. It spoke inside our heads."

Director Shaw's fingers tightened. "You saw it travel from the void and — ?"

"It is coming," Mingan said. He sounded older than he was; the mountain had entered his tone. "Not to destroy us blindly. They are called Anunna. They called us children. They said they planted life here—seeded oceans and fostered evolution. They said they are coming to help."

The room exhaled, a fragile thing, but Tom's face hardened. "Are you saying aliens are coming to save us?" he asked. He didn't sound skeptical as much as incredulous, which was worse.

The Dreamwalker—Noor—took up the thread. Her voice was softer than the cut of Elias's, but the images she brought were no less sharp. "The ship carried an offer, or a warning. They, these guardians, are willing to help. But they also said something else." Noor cleared her throat before she began to speak again, low and soft, "The greatest threat to humanity isn't from the stars.....it comes from within."

Those words landed like a stone in water. Conversation folded in on itself. The President's eyes met Director Shaw's.

General Harris rose too quickly, his chair screeching. "Explain," he demanded. "From within what?"

The Seer's gaze did not flinch. "From within humanity itself. Not from an army outside, but from the hearts and hands of people, our own choices, the gifts we have forgotten, the anger and fear we let loose to hide from the truth. They said the rot is not only external. There is a corruption that will be used against us that comes from within. The fight we must win is as much about what we nurture in each other as what we destroy."

Silence pressed, and then Jonathan—who had been listening with the grim concentration of a man trying to find the punchline in the wrong joke- whistled low. "So let me get this straight," he said. "An interstellar parent-ship shows up in a time of blackout and apocalypse, saying, 'We made you, we'll help,' and then warns that the real battle will be people against people—from the inside out. That's a heck of a plot twist."

Melony didn't laugh. "If they're right," she said, "and the Dominion is as much about turning people as about dropping ships, then our tactics change. We can't only harden the perimeter. We have to stop the rot, we have to bind together to help one another through love and compassion."

Amy Sutton's eyes were small, focused. "Stop the rot, how? Arrest it? Vaccinate it? Teach people not to stab their neighbors for a can of beans?"

"No," Elias said. "You heal it. You awaken what we have always done—bring light where there is shadow. Teach people their gifts. Strengthen their courage. Put tools in the hands that would otherwise be empty. The ship's aid may come, but it will not be limitless. They cannot remake what hate has already unmade. We must hold enough light long enough for their help to matter."

President Johnson sat back, the weight of office folding his shoulders. "You came to tell us that faith, love, and hope are tactics."

"Faith is a verb," the Shaman said. "And a strategy." "This needs to come from the AETHER: The subtle essence of reality that is the source of all things."

Daniel looked at Rodriguez. "If the fight must be internal, we need a new doctrine. Intelligence alone won't cut it. We need networks—networks that teach, shield, and prepare people so they don't become vectors for the Dominion's plan."

Director Shaw tapped a pad, pulling up satellite passes using a Starlink system, the decrypted file fragments Jonathan had opened, and the corpse of the world's grid. "We have limited assets," she said. "We can harden key nodes, secure antibiotic caches, and prioritize rescue of people willing to awaken these gifts. But we can't do this alone. There are billions of mouths and only so many hands."

A melody of desperation rose in the room—practical voices outlining lists: compacts with allied nations, emergency broadcast plans, covert extraction teams, seed libraries, and underground education hubs. General Harris hammered numbers and brigades into a plan; Rodriguez detailed quick reaction teams; Tom sketched a field doctrine that mixed special ops extraction with community teaching and protection.

Still, beyond all the strategies and classified annexes, the message from the Nine kept pulsing: the true victory would be won not by bullets, but by what kind of people the survivors became. It was a dangerous prescription in a world where hunger and fear stripped kindness thin.

Elias stepped forward, "Listen," he said. "What we can do first is simple and dangerous: we must call the willing forward and teach. Teach those who can feel, who are sensitive, and show them not just how to fight, but how to hold themselves steady with an open heart. The dark thing feeds on fury. It will not thrive where people remember why they protect and love each other."

Rodriguez's jaw worked. "You mean we find the willing, pull them out of the chaos, and what? Indoctrinate them to some cause?"

"No." Noor's eyes opened, moon-slow and clear. "Not indoctrination. Family. A net. An education of the soul and mind. The Dominion wants weapons. We must make keepers of positive energy."

President Johnson tapped the table. "Start a program. Secret. Global. Find the vulnerable, the gifted, the leaders, and the willing. Build sanctuaries. Ghost Spear and CIA will run an extraction from a central base in Denver, and the Nine will spread out to sanctuaries and train. But make it fast. And make it honest. No compulsion. No cages."

"You realize the irony," Jonathan said, half-smiling, "that we just voted to build a secret program to teach people how not to be controlled by secret programs."

A small, brittle laugh moved around the table. For a beat, the tension thinned.

Evelyn Shaw's eyes fixed hard on the President. "If we do this, we must also fix what allowed the Dominion to flourish: information black markets, socioeconomic collapse, the narratives of fear and suppression of technology. We fight propaganda with truth, and reality with faith."

General Harris's hand drummed the table, deliberate. "Orders. Who goes where? Immediate mobilization. And civilian outreach now."

Daniel's gaze slid to Tom, then to the Nine. "I'll take Ghost Spear. We'll move into extraction and guard the sanctuaries. Rodriguez, you'll run urban ops. Ortega will coordinate domestic security. Jonathan " He looked at the hacker with a soldier's directness. "You're embedded with me. Your jokes don't work when the firing starts."

Jonathan's smirk hardened into the soldier's expression that sometimes blinked behind his jokester mask. "I'll be the funny gun if that's an honorary duty. Where do I sign?"

The meeting splintered into action. Men and women rose to go do the hard work of bureaucracy, boots on the ground, a thousand small violences and mercies. The room buzzed like a hive coming to life.

They left the room like people carrying a fragile light into a dark house. Outside, the city's power grid still sputtered in pockets—generators, flashlights, and the dim incandescence of a world learning to live by smaller flames. Somewhere beyond the secure doors, people argued over food in long lines. Somewhere else, whole blocks glowed with fires not kindled for warmth but for survival.

And in the mountain cabin, the candle flames guttered again as if in answer—then steadied.

Somewhere beyond sight, something that had watched the planet for millennia began to move, slower than thunder, and perhaps gentler than fear. The Anunna were on the way.

Chapter 10: The Three in the Shadows

The chamber was older than the stone it was carved from. Deep beneath the earth, far from the flicker of daylight, three figures sat in a perfect triangle around a basin of black liquid. No names were spoken between them; none had been needed for millions of years. Two brothers. One sister. The circle has been unbroken since the beginning of time.

Their skin did not betray their age, but their eyes did, pale like moonstone, full of memories that had no business fitting into mortal bodies. They had worn a thousand faces, played a thousand roles, all within the same bloodline. They were not human, not entirely. They were the blood of the Nephilim, the offspring of the Fallen Angels from the Book of Enoch, the secret lineage whispered of but erased from scripture.

The woman's voice was a silken knife. "Phase one was a success. The grid falls. The people burn their own cities. Panic devours order faster than any war."

Her older brother tilted his head, fingers tracing an invisible sigil over the black water. "Just as it always does. Just as our fathers taught us."

The younger brother's smile was thin, reptilian. "And still, the Nine play their little games on Mount Ashland. Do they truly think, love, meditation, and symbols can hold back our inheritance?"

The woman's eyes glowed faintly at the mention of their ancestry. Inheritance. That word still sent a tremor of power through the air.

She whispered:

"We are the children of the Watchers who descended upon Mount Hermon.

We are the seed of those who defied the Most High,

who taught mankind the forging of blades, the alchemy of roots,

the enchantments of stars and runes.

We are the blood of the angels who fell for lust,

The keepers of secrets,

Again, we rise, we must."

The Book of Enoch had named their fathers, their blood lineage, once, Azazel, Samyaza, Arakiel — names carved like burns into forbidden stone. From these came the three. It had spoken of how they taught humankind forbidden knowledge: metalworking, enchantments, weaponry, sorcery, and war. It had also foretold their punishment: chained in darkness until the final judgment. But not all had been bound. A fragment of that blood had been carried through ages, hidden, reincarnated, purified through death and rebirth.

This was the Three. The surviving flame.

The older brother sneered. "The churches were so easy to buy. A few sacks of gold to bishops and scribes, and the Book of Enoch disappeared from their canon. Humanity forgets quickly when there is coin and comfort. They forgot the warnings. They forgot us."

"Let them forget," the younger brother murmured. "Forgetfulness breeds weakness."

The basin of black liquid shifted. Shapes began to rise from it — tiny mechanical things, each no larger than a grain of rice. Hundreds. Thousands. Their wings shimmered like obsidian dragonflies. The creatures were alive with a faint pulse of red light, humming like a swarm.

"Phase Two," the sister said. "Release the swarm. They will find the survivors who think they are safe in their bunkers and camps. One sting, and their blood will carry the sickness. They will kill each other for the antidote that does not exist."

The older brother reached out a hand, letting one of the tiny machines crawl onto his palm. Its needle-fine appendage glinted. "Such perfect children," he murmured. "Iron, code, and venom. They are the plague and the cure."

"They are our legacy," the sister said.

Above them, unseen, the Nine's wards flared faintly — spiritual barriers of light placed like invisible firewalls around the world. The Three felt the resistance when their sight tried to pierce it. For the first time in ages, their magic dimmed against something stronger.

"They've learned to guard themselves," the younger brother said. "The Nine have placed a wall even we cannot cross."

The older brother laughed, low and contemptuous. "Let them keep their walls. We have no need to see them. Our work is almost done, now we just wait and watch till the time we are needed to step in."

The sister's voice was colder than the stone chamber. "Walls do not matter. Light does not matter. Humanity already carries our gift inside them — fear, hate, hunger, rage. We have sown it for millennia. The Nine cannot purge what is bred in their marrow."

They joined hands above the basin, completing the triangle. A pulse of dark energy rippled outward, activating the swarm. The insects' wings flickered and then dissolved into the air, dispersing through hidden vents and tunnels, released to the wind.

"Go," whispered the sister. "Feed."

Somewhere above, in the fractured cities, survivors huddled in darkness. A child clutched a tin of food; a father sharpened a piece of metal into a weapon; a mother whispered prayers to a sky that no longer answered. They did not yet feel the first bites, the first fevers. They did not yet know what crawled toward them on silent wings.

The younger brother spoke as though pronouncing a litany. "Darkness first. Hunger next. Then the disease. Then desperation and something worse. Humanity will finish what we began."

"And then," the older brother said, "one world. One dominion. Ours."

Their laughter echoed against the cold chamber walls, low and resonant, the sound of something ancient savoring inevitability.

For a heartbeat, the black water in the basin reflected not their faces but three vast shadows with wings of ash and iron, coiled like serpents around a dying world.

And above, the wards of the Nine flickered — not broken, but straining — as the future bent toward its darkest horizon.

Chapter 11: The Breakthrough

Snow had long buried the cabin in the Idaho mountains, turning it into a tomb of silence. The wind howled endlessly outside, whistling through the gaps in the eaves like a ghost in prayer. Inside, the glow of the basement lab gave the only hint of warmth — a jury-rigged sanctuary of science built from salvaged equipment, old laptops, microscopes, centrifuges, and a solar-powered generator that hummed like a heartbeat in the dark.

Sarah Mitchel hadn't slept more than four hours in as many days. Her daughter, Megan, seventeen and brilliant beyond her years, worked beside her with the patience of a surgeon and the urgency of someone who knew time was running out. They had been in this underground refuge for months — living, breathing, and fighting to undo the horror unleashed from Antarctica.

On the concrete table before them sat what had consumed their lives: a series of glass vials marked with coded tags — AVX-13, AVX-13R, and finally AVX-14B. The latest batch.

Sarah lifted the vial, her hands trembling slightly from exhaustion. "If our calculations are right," she murmured, her voice hoarse, "this one neutralizes the A-vector proteins."

Megan pushed her glasses up her nose, staring at the data flickering on the cracked monitor. "The spike mutation collapsed completely in the control sample. Look — RNA integrity below 12 percent after exposure."

Sarah blinked, hardly daring to hope. "That means… it can't replicate."

"It means," Megan said with a slow, dawning smile, "we might've just stopped it."

For a long moment, neither spoke. The hum of the equipment filled the room. Then Sarah laughed — a sound that startled even her. It had been so long since she'd heard her own laughter.

She grabbed Megan and hugged her tight. "Oh my God, Meg. You did it. We did it!"

Megan's eyes brimmed with tears. "Mom, it's real. The virus is folding on itself in every sample. The mutation chain is broken!"

They moved quickly — months of discipline taking over. Sarah ran the simulation again, verifying every data point. She analyzed blood samples taken from infected mice they'd captured weeks ago from a nearby valley, their tissues long infected with the Antarctic strain known internally as Chimera Flu Z — the same virus that had already wiped out millions.

The key had been in Mary Copeland's encrypted file — the one labeled DOC_ANTARCTICA_ENC — the same file Mary had died for. It contained genome maps, viral load progression charts, and references to a synthetic enzyme codenamed "Seraph-42." Buried within the file had been the true weakness of Chimera Flu Z: its dependence on a specific cellular cofactor found only in human RNA-binding proteins.

Sarah and Megan had replicated that insight, developing a recombinant peptide that bound to the viral receptor and shut it down completely.

They'd found the immunization, possibly even a cure. An Antidote and Vaccine all in one.

Sarah turned to her daughter. "Let's do this."

They drew up two syringes — the liquid inside faintly blue, luminous under the sterile light. They had tested it on lab mice, on blood cultures. Now, there was only one thing left to do.

Megan's voice trembled. "You first, Mom."

Sarah smiled faintly. "You're my daughter. You first."

They both laughed, half out of nerves, half in disbelief that they'd made it this far. Finally, Sarah took a breath and pushed the needle into her own arm. The serum was cold — a shock to the veins, like swallowing lightning. Then Megan did the same.

They waited.

Minutes passed.

Sarah watched the bio scanner, pulse steadying as the data rolled across the screen. No inflammation. No adverse markers. No trace of viral activity in the sample she'd drawn before the injection.

"It's working," she whispered.

They raced upstairs to the old couple — Tom's parents — who were huddled by the fire. The elderly man looked up, his face thin from months of rationing and days with the virus in his bloodstream. "You found it?"

Sarah nodded, her eyes wet. "We found it."

The injections went smoothly. Tom's Father had been stung by one of the bugs while getting firewood for the stove three days ago and had gone downhill very quickly; they weren't sure he would survive. He started to get color back in his face immediately.

Megan collapsed onto the couch, laughing through tears. "We did it. Grandpa's gonna make it."

Sarah smiled, for the first time in months, with real light behind it. She grabbed the radio from the shelf, turning the dial until she found Tom's secure frequency.

"Tom," she said breathlessly when his voice cracked through the static, "it's Sarah. We did it, we found the Antidote. It neutralizes the strain, Tom. It works! Your father is already getting better almost immediately."

For a long moment, only static answered. Then his voice came through — strained, heavy, full of fatigue. "Sarah… that's incredible. You did it, sweetheart. You saved us."

She laughed, tears streaming down her cheeks. "We can start producing it here in small batches, at least. If we can synthesize enough of the protein base, we can—"

"Sarah." His tone changed. Grim. "You don't have much time."

Her heart stopped. "What do you mean?"

"The invasion began weeks ago," he said. "The AI swarm. The virus has already spread throughout the whole continent, Hell, the whole world for all I know. At first, you had to be stung, but it's mutated and spread through the atmosphere now. People are already reporting a mass plague across the Midwest. It's—" His voice broke with static. "You and Megan need to vaccinate everyone you can. Lock the house down. Don't open any vents. Do you hear me?"

Sarah's hands trembled on the radio. "Tom—"

"We're moving out in twenty-four hours. I'll brief the president as to what he wants to do, and we will try to reach you, but communication could go down at any second. Just promise me you and Megan will stay safe."

The signal crackled, then went dead.

166

Sarah stood frozen, the radio silent in her hand. Megan looked up from the table, eyes wide, the joy draining from her face. "What did he say?"

Sarah turned to her daughter, jaw set with quiet resolve. "He said it's already very bad, people are already dying."

They both looked at the vials — their last hope gleaming faintly in the dim light.

Outside, snow continued to fall — silent, pure, beautiful — unaware of the mechanical wings gliding invisibly through the night sky, carrying death toward every living thing that breathed.

Chapter 12: Tom

The war room inside the forward operations post smelled of cold metal and recycled air. Tom Mitchel sat hunched over a steel table, headset pressed against his ear, fingers drumming a nervous rhythm he couldn't stop. Outside the reinforced walls, the world was falling apart. He'd seen the satellite footage an hour ago — entire cities shrouded in swarms of glinting black dots, people clawing at their throats, hospitals overflowing. It was like watching the end of civilization on a live feed.

But right now, all he could think of was his wife and daughter.

Sarah and Megan — somewhere in the mountains of Idaho, huddled in his parents' basement lab — had done what entire federal task forces of scientists couldn't do. They'd used Mary Copeland's encrypted file, sequenced the Chimera Flu Z genome, and built a working vaccine and Antidote. His wife. His little girl.

His heart swelled with pride and terror all at once.

He adjusted the dials on the secure radio line, keying in the President's channel. "This is Captain Tom Mitchel, Ghost Spear Command. Priority Alpha message for President Johnson."

There was a hiss of static, then a calm but weighted voice. "I'm here, Tom. Go ahead."

Tom took a breath, steadying his voice. "Sir, it's my wife. Dr. Sarah Mitchel. She and our daughter have synthesized a vaccine for the Chimera Flu Z strain — I repeat, an effective countermeasure. They've tested it successfully on themselves and two other subjects. We have proof it works, and it may even act as a cure for early-stage infections."

The line went silent for a long beat. Tom could hear his own heart pounding. Then the President exhaled audibly. "My God. Do you understand what you're telling me, Captain?"

"Yes, sir." Tom's throat tightened. "My wife may have just saved what's left of the world."

Another pause. "You must be proud of them."

Tom stared at the scuffed floor beneath his boots, swallowing hard. "Sir... I don't think I've ever been prouder of anything in my life."

Through the static, President Johnson's voice softened. "I'll call her myself, Tom. She deserves to hear from me directly."

"Yes, sir. She's on a secure frequency. I'll transmit it now."

"I've already got it," the President replied. "We've been tracking your uplinks. I'll brief her personally on the plan to bring her and Megan in."

Tom straightened, the soldier in him snapping back to focus. "What plan, sir?"

"You're not the only ones who've been working," the President said quietly. "There's a facility in Virginia — it looks abandoned on the surface, a dead office block, but beneath it we've built a self-sustaining research lab. Solar arrays and geothermal systems keep it off the grid. Five levels underground. The best minds in the country have been down there for months, trying to do exactly what your wife and daughter just accomplished."

Tom blinked. "You're telling me there's a lab like that… and it's still operational?"

"Fully operational," the President confirmed. "I'll send a covert extraction team to your family's location. They'll bring Sarah and Megan straight to the facility. We can begin mass production of the vaccine immediately."

Tom's fists clenched on the tabletop, relief and dread crashing together. "Sir… the insects are already everywhere. People are dying in the streets — thousands an hour. Spacecraft are targeting our secure survivor facilities. Even with the antidote—"

"I know," the President cut him off. "We're late, but not too late. Tell your wife to get as many doses prepared as she can. We'll have them airborne within the hour. This is our one chance."

Tom swallowed, picturing Sarah's face when he told her. The dark circles under her eyes. The determination that never wavered. Megan, still so young but carrying the weight of the world on her shoulders.

"Yes, sir," he said quietly. "She'll be ready."

The President's voice softened again. "Captain Mitchel… you're not just a soldier in this. You're a husband and a father. When this is over, you're going to tell them how proud you are."

Tom's eyes burned. He cleared his throat. "Yes, sir. Thank you, sir."

"I'll contact Dr. Mitchel now. Stand by for further orders."

The line clicked off. Tom sat in silence for a moment, headset slack in his hand. Around him, the command center buzzed with activity — screens flickering with infrared maps of swarms spreading over continents, military deployments trying to hold order. Reports of food riots, cities burning, thousands of bodies in makeshift morgues.

None of it mattered at this moment. All he could see in his mind's eye was his wife in that basement lab, holding a vial of glowing blue serum like a candle against the darkness.

He pulled out a small photo from his breast pocket — Sarah, Megan, and himself from a long-ago camping trip — and stared at it for a heartbeat before tucking it back away.

Then he straightened, jaw set. It wasn't over yet. Not while his family still had a chance to save humanity.

Chapter 13: The Virus Unleashed

The world was unraveling.

Not slowly anymore. Not in whispers of rumor or silent morgues.

But all at once.

The virus had burst out from its epicenter like wildfire. The AI insects spread it through stings — tiny mechanical vectors carrying a microscopic payload. Whole towns were dropping off the map. No hospitals remained functioning; the ones that had tried were overrun within hours. Ambulances sat abandoned on streets with their doors flung open. No medicine. No doctors. No order.

It was the end of the world in real time, the walking dead minus zombies, the sick dying in numbers.

Captain Daniel Rourke stood in the command tent in Denver, Colorado, staring at a satellite map glowing faintly red. His comms headset buzzed, and he answered automatically.

"Rourke."

Through the static came a sound he hadn't heard from his wife in years — Claire's voice, breaking into sobs.

"Daniel—" she choked out, "Emily's sick. She's burning up. She— she can't breathe right."

Daniel's vision tunneled. "What? What are you talking about?"

"The virus," Claire whispered. "It's here. She got bit somehow — I didn't even see it happen. She's only four. She's so little, Daniel. She's so little."

He gripped the edge of the table until his knuckles went white, feeling the ground vanish beneath him. "I'm coming to you."

"You can't," Claire said, crying openly now. "They've sealed the roads here for now; the snow is too deep. The insects… They're everywhere. I don't know what to do!"

Daniel's voice cracked. "Hold her. Keep her warm. I'll fix this, Claire. I swear to God I'll fix this."

He dropped the headset and leaned forward, forehead against the cold steel. His entire body was shaking.

From across the tent, Tom Mitchel had been watching him. He'd seen soldiers break before, but never like this. Tom crossed the room quietly and laid a hand on Daniel's shoulder.

"What happened?"

Daniel's eyes were red, unfocused. "Emily. My little girl. She's… she's got the virus."

Tom inhaled sharply. My god, Daniel. I am so sorry. He sat for a minute with Rourke, his hand on Rourke's shoulder, in silence, then stood up and made his way out the door of the tent. He didn't even think. He just grabbed his own radio and keyed the frequency for Sarah.

"Sarah? It's me. We need the first shipment diverted to the Colorado Rockies. Now."

On the other end, his wife's voice came through tight and urgent. "Tom— we're still waiting on the chopper from DC to pick us up—"

"Sarah," Tom interrupted, voice breaking, "Daniel's daughter. Four years old. She's got it. Please."

There was silence. Then Sarah said quietly, "We'll do it. We'll make it happen."

Rodriguez

Somewhere miles away from the Denver camp, Officer Rodriguez was driving a battered Humvee, crates of emergency supplies rattling in the back. The road was choked with abandoned cars. He'd been awake for 40 hours straight, ferrying clean water and food to pockets of survivors.

He felt the sting on his neck before he saw it — a pinprick, like a bee sting. He swatted at it, and his glove came away smeared with tiny metal parts and black nanodust.

"No," he muttered, voice hoarse. "Not now."

But already his pulse was racing, sweat pouring down his forehead. The world tilted at odd angles. The virus was in his blood. He clenched the steering wheel and forced himself to keep going, jaw locked. He had to get the supplies to the base before he collapsed.

Naomi

At Mount Ashland, Naomi, the seven-year-old daughter of Amara, the Seer, sat curled in a corner, pale and trembling. She hadn't told anyone she'd been bitten days ago. She didn't want to worry her father.

Now her small body shivered violently, lips bluish. The virus had been wearing her down, quietly, invisibly. David only noticed when she tried to stand and fell, limp as a rag.

"Naomi!" He scooped her up, panic clawing at his throat. Her eyes fluttered weakly.

He sprinted through the bunker corridors, past people meditating, past flickering emergency lights, until he found a vehicle in one of the old storage bays — a rusted truck with a quarter tank of fuel. He shoved Naomi gently into the passenger seat, slammed the door, and gunned the engine.

The nearest medical tent was 20 miles away. The roads were closed. But he didn't care. He had to try. He had to.

"Stay with me, baby," he whispered, voice breaking. "Stay with me."

Amara

A whole state away, in a ruined town square, Amara was teaching a circle of survivors how to center themselves, how to draw on the light inside. Her voice was calm, her movements steady, but suddenly she froze.

A jolt of knowing passed through her like an electric current.

A sign.

A flash of a dream she'd had years before.

Her knees buckled. She clutched her talisman and whispered a prayer, not aloud but to the stillness itself. She slowed the world outside her own heartbeat, reaching across the distance with every ounce of her will.

David, she thought. Please. Please don't be too late.

She saw him in her mind's eye — his hands on the steering wheel, his foot on the gas, tears streaking down his cheeks. Their child beside him, fragile as glass.

Tears rolled silently from her eyes. "Let him make it. Let her live."

Then she stood, straightened her spine, and turned back to the people gathered. Her voice trembled but did not break. "You still have light," she told them. "All of you. And if we fight, it must come from within. Meditation is the back door hack to your brain, change yourself, change the world, become one with the AETHER."

Above them, the sky pulsed with strange colors, like something huge moving just out of sight.

Chapter 14: The Longest Drive

The old truck roared to life like some sleeping beast awakened from a long winter. The engine coughed, then steadied. David gripped the wheel so tightly his knuckles blanched white. The headlights cut through the ash-gray dusk as he gunned it down the mountain road.

Naomi whimpered beside him. Her skin was hot to the touch, her breath shallow and ragged. The virus was working fast now. Too fast.

"Hold on, sweetheart," he said, forcing his voice calm even as panic chewed the edges of his mind. "You just hang in there, okay? Daddy's got you."

Outside, the world was dying.

Black smoke rolled from the valleys below. Whole towns burned without sound — just the faint glow of fire licking at the horizon. The power grid was still gone, and with it went order, mercy, and light. Shadows of people darted between wrecked vehicles on the road — silhouettes of survivors, or looters, or maybe something worse.

David didn't slow down. He couldn't.

The truck's fuel gauge trembled near empty. He pushed the accelerator anyway. A body lay sprawled in the road, and he swerved around it. Another, half-buried in soot.

He kept one hand on the wheel, the other reaching over to touch Naomi's forehead. She was burning up.

"Stay with me, baby. You're strong, remember? You've got your mother's light."

Her lips parted. A whisper. "Mommy…"

David's chest ached. He wanted to tell her everything was fine, that they'd see her mommy soon. But the truth was gnawing at him — there might not be a soon.

Lightning flashed in the distance — not natural lightning, but electric storms from malfunctioning satellites falling out of orbit. The sky was coming apart.

He turned onto Highway 66, which used to be a clear path east. Now it was a graveyard. Burned-out cars, twisted guardrails, the smell of rot.

His tires hit debris. The truck lurched violently. Naomi moaned in pain.

"Almost there," he lied. "Just a little farther."

It felt like hours had passed. The sun never truly rose — the ash in the air filtered it into a sickly orange haze.

At last, through the smog, David saw a light. Not fire — electric light. A faint, flickering glow coming from a distant valley.

The medical tent.

He pressed harder on the gas. His heart pounded. Naomi had stopped responding. Her head lolled against the window, breath shallow but still there — faint, fragile life.

As he neared, he saw soldiers. A small squad, fully dressed in gear from head to toe so they would not get bitten and infected, rifles ready, guarding the perimeter. One waved a red flare.

"Stop! Identify yourself!"

David slammed the brakes, threw the door open, and stumbled out. "My daughter—she's infected! Please, she's just a child!"

They hesitated. One of them, a medic, jogged forward. "Where did you come from?"

"Mount Ashland," David gasped. "She's been sick for days. Please, help her!"

The medic looked over his shoulder at the others. "We're out of the vials! No shipments since San Francisco fell!"

David's knees went weak. "No... no, you have to do something!"

The medic swallowed hard, then motioned to the others. "Bring her inside. We'll try to keep her stable."

The air was heavy with disinfectant and death. Rows of cots, half-filled with the dying. The sound of coughing, crying, and prayers whispered into the stale air.

They laid Naomi on a cot and fitted an oxygen mask to her face. Her small chest rose and fell erratically.

David knelt beside her, holding her hand. "I'm here, sweet girl. Daddy's right here."

A nurse approached quietly, voice trembling. "Sir… the infection's advanced. We can try to cool her down, give her some B-complex, but without the antidote…"

He looked up at her. The nurse's eyes softened with pity. "We'll do everything we can."

An hour later, David sat unmoving. Naomi's skin had gone cold. The machines around her beeped softly, irregularly.

He felt something stir in the air, a warmth, a pulse, and then heard Amara's voice in his mind.

David.

He froze.

Don't give up. She's not gone yet. The light inside her… It's still fighting.

Tears streamed down his face. He placed a hand on Naomi's chest, closed his eyes, and whispered a prayer Amara had taught him — ancient words from a tongue older than memory.

For a moment, the machines flickered. Naomi exhaled sharply. The nurse gasped.

"She's—"

He looked down at Naomi. Her tiny hand twitched in his. Her eyes fluttered open.

"Daddy?" she whispered weakly.

He put on a smile through tears. "You're gonna be okay, baby."

Chapter 15: Ashes of Light

The world had gone silent.

No hum of cities. No traffic. No digital pulse through the wires of civilization.

Just wind, cold and empty, blowing over what remained of the human world.

The Nine were scattered now. Each living as a ghost among the survivors, holding onto fragments of their mission — heal, teach, awaken — even as despair threatened to smother them.

They had seen what came after the grid fell: the madness, the hunger, the sickness, all of the death. Entire towns devoured by disease and fear. And now, months later, the darkness wasn't just around them — it had settled in them.

Elias — The Druid Priest of Symbols

In the ruins of Kansas, Elias traced runes into the dust with shaking fingers. Once, his tattoos had pulsed with energy — sigils of power that amplified the group's light. Now they lay dull against his skin, like forgotten prayers.

A dozen survivors sat before him, weak and hollow-eyed. He tried to speak of unity, of strength through spirit and love, but his voice cracked.

He had buried too many to believe his own words anymore.

Still, he drew the sigil of protection in the air and whispered the old incantation, his hands trembling. The people before him shivered as warmth rippled faintly through the air, the last ember of a fading flame.

He bowed his head. "We keep going," he murmured. "That's all we can do."

Mei-Ling — The Healer

Farther west, Mei-Ling tended to the sick in a half-collapsed temple outside of Sacramento.

The once-violinist, now healer of the hopeless, sat by candlelight mixing herbs and remnants of medicines scavenged from abandoned pharmacies. Her hands still glowed faintly when she touched a wound — but the light dimmed quickly now.

She had once healed tumors with a single touch. Now she could barely soothe a fever.

Every night, she prayed for strength, and every morning, she forced herself to play her violin.

The notes were cracked, trembling, but they reached the few still breathing. Sometimes, she swore the sound itself held power — that the vibrations wove light through despair.

And on one of those mornings, while playing, she felt it, heard it: a pulse through the aether, from somewhere or someone unknown.

Do not move. Listen.

She closed her eyes. "Who are you?"

You already know.

The voice came from beyond, from the same plane as the music came. The place between every breath.

It is time to gather on the mountain once again. The end is near. Her heart stilled.

Malek The Mystic

In the Nevada desert, Malek was kneeling beside a fire surrounded by weary survivors, teaching them to ground their energy through breath when the air around him shifted.

A flicker, a pull on the invisible threads connecting the Nine.

He closed his eyes, and Amara's message came through, faint but clear.

He saw her tears. Heard her voice. Felt her pain.

When he opened his eyes, the fire before him flared blue.

Tom Mitchell was only a few miles east, leading a small group of Ghost Spear operatives still trying to coordinate rescue and antidote delivery across the continent.

Malek stood abruptly, heart pounding. "Keep the fire lit," he told the survivors. "Don't let it die."

He grabbed his satchel and sprinted down to the nearest secure radio, hoping to get in touch with Tom.

As the night deepened, the remaining members of the Nine, scattered across the continent, felt the ripple in the web of light they had woven long ago.

Something was moving.

Something greater than all of them.

Elias looked up from his runes. Mei-Ling paused mid-song. Even the weary survivors around them stirred, as if waking from a long nightmare.

Far away, Amara whispered into the void, her eyes shining with tears.

"Please… let this be the turning point."

Chapter 16: Rodriguez

The desert highway stretched endlessly before him, a cracked ribbon of asphalt cutting through silence.

Rodriguez's hands were white-knuckled on the steering wheel, sweat beading down his temples despite the chill in the air. The world has grown colder since the grid went down, not just in temperature, but in spirit.

The truck rattled over potholes, the back loaded with crates of medicine, fuel, and canned food. Supplies meant for Tom's camp. For what was left of the human resistance.

But Rodriguez knew.

He wasn't going to make it.

The infection had taken hold two days ago; he had been stung in the neck. He'd brushed it off. "Just a scratch," he'd told himself. Now the veins in his arm were black and spreading, pulsing under the skin like living wire.

Every breath burned. Every heartbeat felt like fire.

Still, he drove.

The horizon shimmered with strange light — a dull red glow bleeding through the clouds. It wasn't the sun. The sun hadn't looked like that in months.

He coughed, spattering blood across the dashboard, and muttered through cracked lips, "Just a little farther."

He thought of Tom, of the team still fighting out there. They needed what he carried. Maybe this would mean something. Maybe he would mean something.

Then he saw it.

At first, it was a glint of light high above the desert — moving too fast, too smooth.

"Aw, hell…" he whispered.

The craft broke through the clouds like a blade of light. Sleek. Metallic. Silent. Its hull shimmered with a color that wasn't a color at all — something beyond human sight, bending the air around it.

181

The first blast hit the road behind him, throwing the truck forward with a deafening crack. Asphalt erupted, flames chasing the tires.

Rodriguez slammed the accelerator, engine screaming. "Come on, baby, hold together!"

A second blast tore through the air, clipping the rear of the truck. The world turned sideways — metal shrieking, glass exploding.

The truck spun off the road, bounced, and crashed nose-first into a pine tree.

Everything went still.

Smoke filled his lungs. The world around him was a blur of fire and night. He couldn't feel his legs. Couldn't feel much of anything anymore. The infection had already reached his heart — and the crash had finished what it started.

He blinked through blood, seeing the faint reflection of the alien ship hovering above — cold, indifferent. Watching.

And for the first time, he wasn't afraid.

Instead, he thought of her.

Melony Bishop.

The way her dark hair fell over her shoulders was like satin when she leaned close to whisper something only meant for him.

Her laugh, soft, disbelieving, the night he'd promised he'd come back no matter what.

Her eyes, those eyes, deep emerald-like diamonds with a spark, warm enough to make a man believe in things again.

He reached weakly toward the glovebox, where her picture was tucked beneath a folded map. His fingers brushed the corner of the photo, but he couldn't quite grasp it.

"Mel…" he breathed, voice breaking.

His vision flickered.

In his mind, she was there — standing by the lake where they used to go fishing, sunlight on her skin, smiling that smile that said everything would be okay.

He smiled faintly back. "Told you I'd come home…"

The light in the cab faded. His eyes slowly closed. The alien ship rose higher, its engines humming like distant thunder, and then disappeared into the night sky.

For a long moment, the only sound was the crackle of a burning tree and the soft hum of the wind.

When it was over, the desert was quiet again.

Only the photograph fluttered against the dashboard, untouched by fire — her smile frozen in time.

Chapter 17: The Calling

The mountain waited.

Snow dusted its black stone like the ashes of the fallen world below. Once, Mount Ashland had been only rock and forest and sky, but now, in the silence of a dying age, it pulsed with an ancient awareness.

Something had awakened beneath its roots.

Something older than human memory.

And one by one, they heard it.

It began as a vibration, so low it trembled through the marrow of the earth. Not sound, not language — but something deeper, older.

The call of the Source.

Those attuned to it — the Nine — felt it rise through the broken web of the world like a heartbeat returning to a long-dead body, as they were already making their trek to Mount Ashland from places spread across the states.

Chapter Seventeen — Flight of Mercy

The storm rolled over the mountains like a living thing.

Lightning flashed against the steel-gray sky as the chopper's blades chopped the air, the rotors fighting the wind like they had something to prove.

Tom Mitchel tightened the straps of his harness and glanced through the cracked window. Below him, the world was a fractured wasteland — forests burned to bone, rivers turned black with ash, cities swallowed by shadow. Humanity's heartbeat had slowed to a crawl, and every survivor left alive now counted for something.

But tonight, only one heartbeat mattered.

Naomi.

The little girl is fighting for her life at the base of Mount Ashland.

"Altitude stable at four thousand," shouted the pilot, Warrant Officer Hunt, over the radio din. "But this storm's gonna eat us alive if it keeps building."

Tom's voice was low but steady. "We're not turning back."

In the back of the chopper, crates of medical supplies rattled against the floor — sealed vaccine tubes, clean bandages, antibiotics, and enough antiviral doses to save maybe two hundred people if they were lucky.

But it wasn't just any shipment.

It was the shipment. The cure Sarah had synthesized with Megan in that basement lab. The one that could turn the tide, if it made it in time.

Tom adjusted his headset, switching to the encrypted frequency. "Ashland Base, this is Ghost Spear. I'm inbound with the package. ETA twelve minutes."

Static. Then a voice cracked through. "Copy that, Ghost Spear. The wind's getting bad. Visibility is dropping fast. We'll keep the perimeter lights burning as long as we can. Naomi's stable, but barely."

Tom's chest tightened. "Tell David I'm coming."

The chopper pitched suddenly to the left as turbulence slammed it like a wave. The warning light blinked red.

"Hold on!" Hunt barked. "Wind shear!"

The nose dropped sharply. Tom grabbed the overhead strap, muscles locking as the horizon tilted and the mountain came rushing up to meet them.

"Pull it up, Hunt!"

"Trying!"

The rotors screamed, straining against the gale. For a heartbeat, everything froze, then the bird jerked upright again, skimming the treetops.

The pilot exhaled through gritted teeth. "Remind me why we didn't wait till dawn?"

Tom gave him a grim smile. "Because by dawn she's gone."

Through the storm haze, Tom could just make out the faint flicker of lights below — the survivor camp at the mountain's base. Makeshift tents. Flickering lanterns. A radio tower is barely standing.

He grabbed the cargo door handle and yanked it open. Wind howled inside, whipping his jacket and stinging his eyes.

"Take her down fifty feet!" he shouted. "I'll rappel the rest!"

"You'll be shredded if the wind shifts!"

Tom clipped the rope to his harness along with the tote of supplies. "Then I'll swing in style!"

Before Hunt could argue, Tom leapt.

The descent was chaos, rain in his eyes, air slapping his face, the rope jerking hard against his harness. The wind spun him, slammed him sideways against the rope, but he hit the ground rolling, boots splashing in the mud.

Above, the chopper hovered, fighting to stay airborne.

Tom waved and pointed to the signalmen running toward him. "Get these supplies inside, now!"

Two soldiers grabbed the crates. Another helped unclip him from the rope.

Amara came running through the storm, her shawl whipping behind her like a banner of fire. Her face was pale, her eyes wild.

"Tom!" she cried. "She's fading!"

He didn't waste a second. "Take me to her."

Inside the largest tent, a lantern light flickered against canvas walls. Naomi lay on a cot, her small body trembling with fever, breath shallow. Her skin was pale as snow except for the dark veins tracing up her neck, the telltale sign of the Chimera Flu Z virus.

David sat beside her, holding her tiny hand, whispering something only a father could say. His eyes were red from exhaustion.

Tom dropped to his knees beside the cot and pulled the case from his pack. His hands trembled slightly as he prepared the syringe — the first of Sarah's perfected doses.

He looked up at Amara. "She's strong. She just needs a fighting chance."

Amara nodded, tears streaming silently. "Then give her one."

Tom pressed the needle into Naomi's arm. The antidote went in clean and quick. He withdrew it and exhaled, his jaw tight.

They waited.

Outside, thunder cracked. Inside, every breath felt like a century.

Then —

Naomi stirred. Just a twitch at first. Then a slow, weak inhale.

David's eyes went wide. "She's breathing easier…"

Amara fell to her knees beside the cot, hands pressed over her mouth as if afraid to break the moment.

Tom closed his eyes for just a second, whispering to himself, "Thank you, Sarah."

Outside the tent, the storm began to ease. The clouds split just enough for a sliver of moonlight to touch the camp.

Tom stepped out and looked toward the distant ridge of Mount Ashland. In that cold, silver light, he could almost feel it, the hum of something ancient, something waiting.

He lifted his radio and pressed the transmitter.

"Ghost Spear to Command. The girl's alive. Repeat — the Antidote works. Humanity's got a chance."

Static. Then a faint voice replied:

"Copy that, Ghost Spear… God help us all."

Tom lowered the radio and looked up at the mountain again.

The battle wasn't over. But for the first time in a long while, the light had pushed back the dark.

Chapter 18: The Calling

It began as a vibration.

Not a sound, not a sight — but something that lived beneath perception.

It trembled in the soil, in the oceans, in the atoms of the air itself.

It hummed in every living thing.

At first, no one understood what they were feeling: a strange resonance in the chest, a ringing in the ears like beautiful tones. But within hours, it swept across the planet. From the burning ruins of cities to the darkened countryside, from shattered satellites to the depths of oceans, the pulse could be felt.

Humanity was being called.

Pilots in grounded aircraft felt it before their controls went dead, a pull, magnetic yet spiritual, drawing their eyes toward the west.

Children woke crying in the night, whispering words they didn't understand:

"Mount Ashland."

World leaders abandoned bunkers. Scientists dropped their instruments mid-experiment. Across every nation and creed, the survivors began to move — some walking, some driving, others setting out across oceans on barely working boats.

No one questioned why.

They only knew they had to go.

Every direction, every compass needle, every heart pointed toward Mount Ashland.

In Montana, President Mark Johnson stood on the roof of a darkened building, watching the auroras roll across the sky like ribbons of liquid fire.

His Secret Service team pleaded with him to return inside, but he only said softly, "It's calling us."

In the Sahara, nomads rose from their fires and turned their camels north.

In India, monks left their monasteries, weeping as the air itself began to sing.

In Brazil, from the remnants of the rainforest, a barefoot boy began to walk north, smiling through his tears.

Across the globe, billions are gone, but at least that many still alive — the living began to converge.

The hum had become music now.

Not human, not mechanical, but alive, full of layered harmonics that stirred forgotten memories.

Somewhere deep in the collective soul of mankind, something remembered the sound.

Roads once silent now thundered with engines, people walking down the sides.

Helicopters crossed the mountains in endless waves, landing wherever they could.

Boats washed up along the Northern California and Oregon coast, their passengers stumbling out, barefoot and weeping.

Soldiers and refugees stood side by side.

Presidents and peasants, billionaires and beggars — stripped of every illusion of power or rank — climbed the slopes of Mount Ashland together.

The others gathered. The mountain glowed.

The final wakening began.

The oceans stilled. The stars brightened.

The last of the dying power grids flickered with life, not from technology, but something else.

Every creature lifted its head.

Every surviving human felt the pulse.

The song continued.

Every soul on Earth was being summoned home.

Chapter 19: The Road of Shadows

The convoy moved in silence.

Only the crunch of gravel beneath heavy tires broke the stillness of the forest road. Pines loomed like sentinels in the mist, their branches heavy with rain. The sky above was bruised purple, shot through with the faint gold of the Calling—that strange light still pulsing from Mount Ashland beyond the horizon.

They were close now.

Daniel Rourke could feel it in his bones.

He sat in the lead Humvee, rifle resting across his lap, eyes scanning the empty road. Behind him rode Tom Mitchel, Orteguez, Lewis, Vega, and most of the Ghost Spear unit—men and women forged by war, by loss, by the kind of loyalty that outlasts death itself.

"Radio is still dead," Ortega muttered, tapping it. "No comms, no satellites, nothing. Just us."

"Then keep your eyes sharp," Daniel replied, voice low, weary. "We're almost there."

No one spoke again for miles.

It was Vega who spotted it first.

"Sir… you seeing that?"

A shape in the trees. Twisted metal, smoke curling faintly from under a crushed hood. A Humvee, military issue, half-buried in the mud.

Daniel's chest tightened as they drew near. The engine still hissed with cooling steam, but the silence around it was wrong—too still, too heavy.

He raised a fist. The convoy stopped.

The men dismounted, boots sinking into the wet earth. Daniel led them toward the wreck, his flashlight cutting across the shattered windshield—and froze.

Rodriguez.

Slumped over the steering wheel, head resting against his forearm, his dog tags swaying gently in the breeze.

"Jesus," Tom whispered. "No…"

Daniel reached in slowly, his gloved hand trembling. He felt for a pulse he already knew wasn't there. The skin was cold. The blood dried dark across his neck and chest.

"Looks like he was hit," Ortega said quietly, eyes scanning the tree line. "Maybe… maybe the ship we saw. That plasma strike we heard earlier."

Daniel nodded, jaw tight. He couldn't speak for a long moment.

Rodriguez had been the one who'd volunteered to go deliver supplies. The one who said, "I'll be quick, Cap. Don't wait up."

And he'd kept his word—he'd made it back. Almost.

They worked in silence, the way soldiers do when grief is too deep for words.

They cleared a small space near the wreck, digging into the soft earth with their entrenching tools. Rain began to fall, slow at first, then steady—a gray curtain that blurred the world into silence.

When they laid him in the ground, Daniel placed the dog tags on his chest. Tom knelt beside him, muttering a quiet prayer. Ortega removed her cap, head bowed, tears streaming down her face.

No music, no words. Just the wind.

The earth took him quietly.

Afterward, Daniel spoke, voice low and rough.

"Sergeant First Class Miguel Rodriguez. Soldier. Brother. He gave his life for something bigger than all of us. The least we can do is make sure it still means something."

He reached into his pocket, pulled out the small patch from Rodriguez's sleeve—the Ghost Spear insignia—and pinned it to a branch above the grave.

"Until we meet again, brother."

The others echoed softly, "Until we meet again."

It was late, so they made camp beside the wreck, setting a small fire sheltered under a tarp. The rain had stopped, leaving the world dripping and still. The mountain loomed in the distance, glowing faintly beneath the night sky.

No one ate much. No one slept.

Tom sat beside Daniel, staring into the flames. "You ever think about what's waiting for us up there?"

Daniel exhaled, eyes distant. "Every damn minute."

"Think it's the end?"

Daniel looked at him. "Maybe. Maybe it's the end, I don't know anymore."

Ortega poked at the fire. "Don't you think an end is really just a new beginning? But whatever it is, we're not turning back. Not after this."

Everyone nodded.

For a long time, they just sat there, listening to the forest breathe. Somewhere far away, thunder rolled like a drumbeat.

Tom finally broke the silence. "Rodriguez… he was talking about her, you know. Melony Bishop. Said she had eyes that sparkled like diamonds. Said if he made it back, he was gonna ask her to marry him."

Daniel's throat tightened. He stared into the fire until it blurred. "Then we make sure she knows he didn't quit. He fought to the end."

No one replied. There was nothing left to say.

When morning came, the light over the horizon wasn't sunlight; it was the calling, brighter now, pulsing like the heartbeat of the world.

Daniel stood over Rodriguez's grave one last time. He pressed his palm to the wooden marker. "Rest easy, brother. We'll finish this."

The others loaded up, silent, focused.

Engines rumbled to life.

As the convoy rolled away, the wind picked up, carrying the scent of pine and rain. For just a moment, the faintest echo of laughter seemed to follow them—the kind they used to hear around campfires, back when the world still made sense.

Tom glanced in the mirror as they pulled away.

The patch fluttered from the branch above the grave, Ghost Spear insignia catching the light like a spark.

And then it was gone behind them, swallowed by the trees.

Ahead, Mount Ashland glowed like a beacon.

And the road led on.

Chapter 20: Something in the Pines

The convoy rolled through the winding mountain pass above Klamath Falls, the world below them buried beneath clouds and silence. Snow had stopped falling, but the mist hung thick and strange — heavy as smoke, as if the air itself didn't want to move.

Captain Daniel Rourke sat behind the wheel of the lead Humvee, headlights cutting through the gray. The rest of Ghost Spear followed in staggered formation — engines muffled, weapons ready, eyes scanning every shadow.

They hadn't slept more than a few hours in days.

The world was dying, and every road could be an ambush.

"Still got a signal?" Rourke asked over his shoulder.

Tom Mitchel, sitting in the passenger seat, checked the radio. "Barely. Static's eating the line, but we're good for now."

The others — Ortiguez, Lewis, Vega, and Tom Mitchel rode silently in the back, eyes trained out the windows. The forests here were dense, old, almost sentient. The pines rose like pillars into the mist. It felt like driving through the lungs of some enormous creature that had long since stopped breathing.

Then Vega leaned forward. "Cap… stop the truck."

Rourke's eyes narrowed. "What do you see?"

"Off the right side, in the trees. Something metallic. Not wreckage from a plane either."

Rourke slowed, turned the wheel, and pulled off the road. The convoy behind them followed suit. Engines cut out one by one until there was only the sound of the wind and the ticking of cooling metal.

They climbed out, boots crunching in the snow.

And then they saw it.

Half-buried in the frozen earth, a craft lay tilted against the tree line — sleek, dark, seamless, unlike anything they had ever seen. Its hull reflected light oddly, like liquid obsidian. No insignia. No cockpit glass. No visible seams or doors. Just a curved body, maybe twenty feet long, with a faint, pulsing blue light at its center.

Tom stepped closer, eyes wide. "Is this Alien, or Dark Dominion?"

"Definitely Dominion," Lewis muttered, his voice low. "No scorch marks. No impact crater. Whatever brought this down — it didn't hit hard."

Rourke crouched near the base of the craft. The air around it hummed faintly, making his whole body vibrate with it, like the echo of a machine still dreaming. "Power core's still active," he murmured. "Maybe wounded, maybe waiting."

He stood and gestured to Vega. "Secure a perimeter. Ortiguez, get me a radiation read."

As his men and women moved out, Rourke turned to Tom. "There are no bodies. No blood. No footprints in or out. Either they were picked up… or they were never here to begin with."

Tom looked uneasy. "Maybe it was flying remotely. You think it's alien?"

Rourke's jaw tightened. "At this point, Tom, I don't know what anything is anymore."

Rourke keyed the encrypted comms unit strapped to his vest. "Roberts, you on this frequency?"

Static. Then the familiar, irreverent voice came through, crackling with digital distortion.

"You rang, Captain? I was just teaching the Rats in this bunker a new dance routine."

Rourke exhaled a dry laugh. "You're a piece of work, Roberts. Listen, we found something. A downed craft on top of Klamath pass. Still warm, no sign of crew. I need you to do me a favor. I need to find a location for the leaders of Dark Dominion. Can you get me coordinates?"

"Define 'craft,' because if it's a Tesla, I don't do road calls."

"Not funny, Jon. It's alien. Or something like it."

There was a pause on the line. Then Jonathon's tone shifted — less comic, more focused.

"The Three? You're talking about the ones in the Alps, right?"

"That's right," Rourke confirmed.

"Yeah… I mapped their transmissions before the blackout hit. Private estate in the Swiss Alps — coordinates off the grid, no public record. The place is older than the Confederation itself, with stone architecture, subterranean layers. I'd bet my last line of code they're still there. Their comms went dark the second the grid did, but I'm seeing occasional EM signatures in that region — something big is running down there."

Rourke exchanged a glance with Tom. "They're running phase three, then."

"You mean the AI locusts with chips?" Jonathon asked grimly.

"Exactly."

There was silence on the line. Then Jonathon said softly,

"You don't think the Three are human, do you?"

Rourke looked again at the vessel, the way it seemed to hum with a strange intelligence, as though it could hear them.

"No," he said. "I don't. But I do believe they are in human bodies that can be killed, at least in this lifetime."

They set up a temporary camp beside the road, the wreck half-shrouded in mist. The men worked quietly, unsettled. Tom sat by the fire, rubbing his hands together, watching the faint glow of the craft through the trees.

Orteguez muttered, "If this is one of theirs… maybe they're not as invincible as we thought."

Tom nodded slowly. "Or maybe," he said, "this one wasn't supposed to crash."

Rourke stood apart, his silhouette framed against the eerie light. Snow drifted down over his shoulders. His thoughts were a thousand miles away — with Claire, with little Emily, with the world they were all trying to save. Then his mind began to form a plan. The odds were against him in this one, but he needed to save his family.

Daniel told Tom about his plan. Tom said, "Let me go with you? At least take one of us. You can't do this alone, it's a suicide mission."

Then, faintly, the air shifted, a low vibration, deep as a heartbeat. The craft pulsed once, its surface rippling like water.

Chapter 21: The Mountains of Mercy

The Rockies were silent under a pale gray sky.

Snow drifted down in slow, lazy spirals, catching in the dark pines that framed the old logging road. The only sound was the low rumble of Elliot Kane's rusted truck, its engine coughing as it climbed higher toward the ridge.

Inside, the air smelled of wood smoke, diesel, and the faint sweetness of canned peaches they'd shared that morning. Claire Rourke sat beside Elliot, her hands wrapped around a battered thermos, staring out at the endless white. In the back seat, Kyle Green checked the cooler of vaccine doses, Sarah and Megan's miracle, and little Emily slept beneath a pile of wool blankets, her face peaceful, color back in her cheeks.

She had lived.

That alone made all of this worth it.

Elliot shifted gears, his gloved hand steady on the wheel. "We'll make the next drop before sundown. That'll be the last of the survivors up this pass. Let's find a place to camp for the night and then start towards Mount Ashland in the morning."

Kyle nodded, glancing at the fading light. "These people are holding on by a thread. It's good what we're doing, Elliot."

Elliot gave a rough laugh. "Good? Nah. Necessary."

Then, quieter: "Guess the world needed a few stubborn fools." Kyle smiled at that.

Claire smiled faintly, but her eyes were distant. She reached for the old secure radio mounted under the dashboard, the one Daniel had taught her to use. It crackled suddenly—static, then his voice, rough and warm as ever.

"Claire? You there, sweetheart?"

Her heart stopped. "Daniel! Yes, I'm here! God, it's good to hear your voice!"

"You sound tired," he said gently. "You holding up okay?"

"I am now."

She brushed away tears she hadn't realized were falling. "Emily's better, Daniel. She's strong again. Sarah's antidote—it worked. We owe her everything."

There was a long pause on the other end. When he spoke again, his voice carried that steady calm he always used when things were about to go bad.

"That's good, Claire. That's… that's everything I needed to hear."

Something in his tone froze her blood. "Daniel… What's going on? Where are you?"

"I can't say, not on this line. Just know—it's dangerous. We found something. I volunteered."

"Volunteered for what?" Her voice cracked. "You can't keep doing this, Daniel. You promised—"

"I know."

"But if we're going to have a world left for Emily to grow up in, I have to."

He fell silent for a beat, then:

"Tell her I love her, okay? Every day, tell her that." Tears sliding down his numb cheeks.

Claire pressed the radio to her chest, eyes closed, voice shaking. "Don't you dare talk like that. You come back to me, you hear? You come back."

There was a soft chuckle on the line, gentle, familiar, heartbreaking.

"You always were the strong one, Claire. I'll find my way back. Just… keep that fire alive for me."

Static filled the line. She called his name again and again, but he didn't answer.

The truck bumped along the mountain road in silence after that. Elliot kept his eyes ahead, pretending not to notice the tears on her face. Kyle turned toward the window, jaw tight. Even the wind seemed to fall quiet out of respect.

From the back seat, Emily stirred and whispered, half-dreaming,

"Daddy?"

Claire smiled faintly and stroked her daughter's hair. "He's with us, sweetheart. Always."

Elliot's hand tightened on the wheel. "Then we'd better make him proud."

The truck climbed higher into the snowstorm, its headlights cutting through the gathering dark. Behind them, a cabin still glowed faintly, a lone beacon of hope in a world learning to live again.

And somewhere out there, in the frozen ruins of what was once civilization, Captain Daniel Rourke was walking into the shadows for them all.

Chapter 22: The Three in the Rock

High up in the snow-laden peaks of the Swiss Alps, carved into the bones of the earth itself, lay the chamber of The Three. The world above had fallen silent — its cities dim, its air haunted by the whispers of a dying grid — but within the stone sanctum, light still burned. Not the gentle flicker of flame, but a cold, intelligent glow that pulsed from walls laced with living circuits, veins of liquid silver running like blood through the rock.

They sat at a table of black Obsidian, smoothed by hands centuries older than any mortal memory. The air was charged — not with electricity, but with presence. These were not rulers. They were architects. The lineage of gods reborn through time, bodies merely vessels for consciousness that had survived the collapse of civilizations long forgotten.

The First — tall, ageless, with eyes like fractured glass — spoke first.

"It has begun. The collapse moves faster than expected."

The Second, draped in silks that shimmered like oil, smiled faintly. "Good. Fear cleanses. When there is nothing left to cling to, they will open themselves to us willingly."

The Third leaned back, resting a hand upon the smooth orb beside the table. Within it, shadows swirled — projections of the world below. Mountains, oceans, shifting magnetic fields. And beyond all of it, something else. A pulse. A soundless vibration that thrummed through the aether.

"You feel it, don't you?" he murmured. "Something…calling."

The First's expression flickered. "An anomaly. A frequency from across the ocean. It pulls at the consciousness of the survivors. But not ours."

The Second's smile faltered. "Then it is not of our making."

They stood, and as they did, the walls around them rippled — revealing alcoves filled with machines, rows upon rows of black pods like insect cocoons. Each one faintly vibrated, alive with mechanical hunger.

"It's time," said the Third. His voice carried the certainty of prophecy. "Phase Three begins."

He pressed his hand against the control panel — flesh to machine, man to creation — and the floor trembled. Deep below, ancient turbines spun to life, igniting the long-dormant forges. Hatches opened across the chamber as the swarm began to wake.

Microscopic wings fluttered. Thousands. Millions.

The AI locusts stirred, each no larger than a fingernail, each carrying within it a sliver of code — the key to humanity's next evolution. They would spread through the jet streams, hitch rides on the winds, the currents, the heat plumes of dying cities. Their mission was simple: inject, integrate, control.

"This world will rise again," the Second whispered. "Not as it was, but as it should be — united under the new grid with our own satellites. A one world order."

The First turned toward the distant west, eyes narrowing as if they could pierce through the mountains, across the oceans, all the way to Mount Ashland, where millions meditated and waited, the mountain calling every living soul to its side.

"They are moving toward something," he said. "But so are we. Let them gather. When all are together, it will be easier to claim what remains."

A deep hum filled the chamber as the swarm erupted from hidden vents in the mountainside, vanishing into the snow and sky — a living storm of metal and purpose.

The Three stood in silence, listening to the fading echo of their creation.

And far away, in the cold darkness of space, something ancient listened back.

Chapter 23: Intimate Revelation

The light in the room was dim and golden, a soft glow leaking through the narrow slats of the vent above. Colonel Marcus Hale opened his eyes to the low hum of the underground generators and the slow, even breathing beside him.

Amy Sutton lay curled against his chest, her blonde hair spilling over his arm like a golden fire in the half-light. For a long moment, he just watched her sleep — the calm in her face, the faint crease between her brows that never seemed to fade completely. Even here, even now, she carried the weight of a thousand things unsaid.

He brushed a strand of hair from her cheek and kissed her forehead. The air smelled faintly of soap, gun oil, and her.

The room wasn't much, concrete walls softened by a wool blanket draped over a metal chair, maps and coded files scattered across the small desk. It was a hideaway tucked beneath the Montana plains, one of the last secure CIA facilities not compromised by the Dominion.

Amy stirred and looked up at him with that half-smile that always undid him.

"Morning, soldier."

"Morning, spook," he teased softly, running his fingers down her arm.

For a few breaths, neither spoke. The silence between them wasn't empty; it was full, alive, heavy with everything that had happened and everything that might still come. They had survived too much to waste a single quiet morning.

Then his encrypted radio beeped against the nightstand.

Marcus reached for it, already feeling the shift in the air, the warmth of the moment bleeding into the cold rhythm of duty.

He sat up, rubbing a hand over his face. "Hale," he said, voice rough.

General Harris's voice came through, sharp and direct.

"Colonel, I need you on the next chopper west. Ashland base camp is swamped. Medical tents are overrun, and food supplies are critical. We're setting up a new corridor for aid delivery. You'll help Captain Brown coordinate on-site with local command."

"Yes, sir."

"Wheels up in two hours. I'm counting on you, Marcus. These people need everything we can spare."

Then, a click. The line went dead.

Marcus exhaled slowly, phone still in his hand.

Amy watched him from the bed, eyes searching his face. "Harris?"

He nodded. "Ashland. Relief operations. They're drowning down there — people showing up by the thousands. He wants me to help with the supply drop and logistics."

She sat up, the sheet falling away from her bare shoulder. "Then that means—"

"—You stay here," he finished gently. "Evelyn Shaw's supposed to call you soon. She needs you in play, not in the middle of a refugee camp."

Amy frowned, pulling her knees up and hugging them. "I hate waiting."

"I know."

He reached out, tracing the scar on her collarbone, a reminder of the last mission she'd barely walked away from. "You've done enough fighting for one lifetime," he said quietly. "Let me handle this one."

She met his eyes, and something unspoken passed between them — regret, longing, the fear that maybe one of them wouldn't make it back.

Then she smiled faintly. "You always did look good in a chopper."

That made him laugh, low and rough. He leaned in, kissing her, slow at first, then deeper, the kind of kiss that felt like a promise neither of them dared to speak aloud.

The world outside might be breaking, but in that bed, in that breath, that kiss, there was only them.

Whatever clothes they still had on found the floor again. The walls could've crumbled, the sky could've fallen, it wouldn't have mattered. Together, moving in rhythm, they became one breath, one being.

Later, when the quiet settled again and their hearts finally slowed, Marcus brushed his thumb along her jaw and whispered, "When all this is over… marry me."

Amy froze for a heartbeat, eyes searching his. "Are you serious?"

He nodded. "I've spent half my life fighting for the wrong cause. I want to spend the rest with the right one — with you."

She smiled then, the kind of smile that reached her eyes with a sparkle. "You'd better come back alive, Colonel. I don't do funerals."

He grinned. "Deal."

They stayed like that a little longer — tangled in each other, two souls clinging to something real while the world above seemed so far away, so surreal.

Then, as the clock ticked closer to departure, Marcus Hale rose to suit up once more — not for glory, but for redemption.

Chapter 24: Ashland Rising

The wind off the mountain carried the scent of pine, smoke, and humanity.

Rows of tents stretched as far as Sarah Mitchel could see — a patchwork of hope and despair under the shadow of Mount Shasta. The camp had become a small city overnight. Thousands, maybe millions, gathered here now, clinging to the promise of survival.

Helicopters roared overhead, kicking up dust as they ferried in crates of food, medicine, and more desperate souls. Voices rose and fell — crying, praying, shouting. The world had shrunk to this valley, and every heartbeat here mattered.

Sarah stood just beyond the perimeter, her gloved hands trembling as she pulled her mask down for a moment to catch her breath. She'd been in the air for days, moving from town to town with her daughter, Megan, administering the antidote to those still alive after the sting. Too many hadn't made it.

"Sarah"

The voice cut through the chaos. She turned — and there he was.

Tom Mitchel.

He came through the rows of tents wearing dusty fatigues, a medic's armband half-torn, his face thinner, older, but unmistakably his. For a second, she thought she was dreaming — and then she was running, tears blurring her vision.

They collided halfway between the tents, arms around each other, breathless, laughing, crying all at once.

"God, you're here," she whispered into his shoulder. "You're really here."

He pulled back just enough to look at her — to trace her face with the same reverence he once reserved for holy things. "I told you I'd find you, Sarah. Always."

Then another voice — softer, uncertain.

"Dad?"

Megan stood a few paces back, her medic pack slung over one shoulder, hair matted, eyes rimmed with exhaustion. She'd grown since he'd last seen her. The little girl who used to wait for him on the porch was now a young woman hardened by too much loss.

Tom's throat caught. "Hey, Peanut."

And then she was in his arms too, clinging tight, sobbing into his chest.

"I thought you were gone," she choked.

"Never," he murmured. "Not while you two are still breathing."

They stood there like that for a long while, a family reassembled in the wreckage of the world.

Later, they found a place near the medical tents to sit, a small canvas cot under a tarp. The air buzzed with shouting and coughing, babies crying, and the rhythmic thump of generators.

Sarah leaned against Tom, her head on his shoulder. "They keep coming," she said quietly. "From everywhere. Whole towns were wiped out. The antidote's working, but we don't have enough. We're running out of everything."

Tom nodded grimly. "I know. We're holding the line for now, but this… this is something else."

Megan sat cross-legged in front of them, staring into the fire pit where a few volunteers were boiling water. "It's like the whole world has been called here for a reason."

Before Tom could reply, a shadow fell across them.

"Tom and Sarah Mitchel?"

A woman stepped forward, tall and poised despite the exhaustion in her face. She extended a hand. "Claire Rourke. And this is my daughter, Emily."

The little girl peeked out from behind her mother's coat, clutching a small stuffed rabbit. Sarah smiled softly. "You're Daniel's wife?" Tom immediately jumped up and shook her hand. "Ah, Claire," he said, still looking into her eyes. I want you to know what an exceptional commander and friend your husband is.

Claire smiled weakly. "We just got in last night. He's still out there. Said he didn't know when he'd be back, I have a bad feeling."

Tom frowned. "Daniel Rourke volunteered for a mission. He will be back soon, Tom said, feeling unsure but not letting her see the doubt and fear he felt."

Claire hesitated. "He said he was on the most important mission of his entire life, something about the world Emily will be growing up in. I didn't really understand."

Tom's gut twisted. He knew Rourke was on a suicide mission. He should have insisted on going with him.

By afternoon, the camp had shifted again, more arrivals, more cries for help. The Nine moved through the crowds, calming tempers and lifting spirits where they could.

Sarah watched them from the edge of the medical tent — scientists, soldiers, mystics, governors, pastors, every make and model, and misfits who had somehow become humanity's last line of light.

Their message was simple, almost painfully so:

Love one another. Stand together.

Tom heard one of them speaking over a makeshift loudspeaker:

"Fear divides us. Love is the only way through. We are all woven together — a single tapestry of being. The darkness feeds on separation. But we… we are one."

The words struck something deep in him. Maybe it was exhaustion, hope, but for the first time in weeks, he felt the faint pulse of something other than despair.

He turned to Sarah, brushed her cheek. "You hear that?"

She nodded, eyes glistening. "It's what I've been telling my patients. Time's not linear anymore. It's… It's bending. Maybe this is all part of the shift."

Tom smiled faintly. "Then let's bend with it."

A sudden roar echoed from above — another helicopter inbound. Dust spiraled across the tents. Tom shielded his eyes as the craft settled hard onto the landing pad, skids biting into the dirt.

He jogged over, shouting above the blades. "What've you got?"

Captain Brown jumped out, "Supplies and intel, sir. And a report."

Tom helped unload a crate, then asked, "I thought Colonel Hale was with you?"

Brown hesitated, his face pale beneath the grime. "We stopped on the way here. There was a downed craft, Hale said it was Dominion tech. We found Captain Rourke trying to fly the damn thing. Said he was having trouble navigating the magnetic fields of the Earth's atmosphere."

Tom froze. "And Hale?"

"He's with him. Said he knew the system, something about old Dominion training. They're trying to get the craft up and running again."

A sick weight settled in Tom's gut, and it wasn't the first time since leaving Rourke. He saw that craft up close. They weren't machines — they were living systems, dangerous and unpredictable. And if Hale and Rourke were out there together…

"Dammit," he muttered.

Brown lowered his voice. "Sir, it feels like a suicide mission."

Tom stared toward the distant horizon where the mountain cut against the burning sky.

Hale had once served the Dark Dominion, knew their technology better than anyone. Maybe he was trying to make it right.

Tom clenched his fists. "Let's just pray they make it back alive."

He turned back toward the camp, where Sarah and Megan waited, visiting with Claire and Emily, where thousands huddled in the fading light, humanity's last fragile flame against the dark.

And as the mountain wind howled through the tents, Tom whispered a quiet vow to himself:

If this is the end of the world, then let it end with love.

Chapter 25: The Flight of Redemption

The hum of the craft was unlike any other sound on Earth.

A deep, resonant vibration that seemed to pulse through the bones rather than the air.

Colonel Marcus Hale sat in the copilot's chair, eyes scanning the shifting holographic displays floating above the console. The interface wasn't mechanical; it was organic, alive. Light flowed like liquid through its veins.

Daniel Rourke sat at the helm, steady hands on the neural controls. Outside, the world unfolded in silence, vast stretches of dark forest and snow-dusted peaks, the morning sun glinting off rivers that wound like molten silver.

No storm. No pursuit. Just endless sky.

"Hard to believe this thing was built to enslave people," Rourke muttered.

Hale nodded, watching the magnetic horizon realign as they ascended. "It was built to control. This tech reads thought, emotion, and feeds on obedience. You fight it with willpower, not code."

Rourke smirked. "Guess that's why it likes you better than me."

The craft leveled off at thirty thousand feet, a shimmering blur invisible to radar. Hale adjusted the energy distribution grid, stabilizing the antimatter field.

They sat in companionable silence for a moment, the only sound the faint thrum beneath their boots. Then Rourke spoke again, quieter this time.

"Emily would love this."

Hale turned. "Your daughter?"

Rourke's face softened, eyes distant. "Yeah. She's four. Smart as hell, stubborn like her mom. Claire says she's been drawing pictures of me flying a spaceship." He gave a quiet laugh. "Guess she wasn't far off."

"She's at the Ashland camp?" Hale asked.

Rourke nodded. "They were with my friend Elliot at his underground bunker until the mountain started calling everyone. Claire's stronger than anyone I've ever met. Keeps everyone around her calm, even when she's breaking inside."

Hale leaned back, thoughtful. "You're lucky. I envy that."

"You got someone?"

A small smile crossed Hale's face. "Amy Sutton. CIA. Field agent."

Rourke raised an eyebrow. "Tough combination."

"You're telling me," Hale chuckled. "She's got more fight in her than most of my command did. Sharp, stubborn, and absolutely refuses to let me brood in peace. I asked her to marry me before I left."

Rourke whistled low. "Hell of a time for a proposal."

"Yeah." Hale looked out the viewport, the light of dawn breaking over the curvature of the Earth. "If I don't make it back, at least she'll know."

They sat quietly for a moment, both men lost in their thoughts.

Then Rourke leaned forward, eyes on the flickering map projection hovering before them. "Alright, time to talk about strategy."

The display zoomed in on Europe, then Switzerland. A single glowing red marker pulsed over a mountain range near the Italian border.

"The private estate," Rourke said. "That's where they're holed up, the three at the top of the Dominion hierarchy. The bunker's built into the rock itself."

He looked over at Hale. "You worked for them once. You know what this thing can do."

Hale hesitated, then reached up to tap a sequence into the craft's main interface. The holographic projection changed, showing a wireframe of the ship's internal systems, energy cells, propulsion nodes, and a section labeled "Aperture Array."

"That," Hale said, pointing, "is your weapon system. Quantum plasma projectors. They don't fire like missiles; they manipulate energy density at the molecular level. Theoretically, we could vaporize the entrance to the bunker from two miles out."

Rourke's brow furrowed. "Theoretically?"

Hale sighed. "This thing wasn't designed for precision strikes. Dominion used it for intimidation, flash displays, mass control, and orbital deterrence. Hitting a target that small without collapsing the craft's energy field…" He shook his head. "Risky."

Rourke just looked at Hale, then said, "If it doesn't work, then we finish it the hard way."

Hale leaned back, the seat creaking. "You mean crash it?"

"Stone bunker, underground chamber, probably shielded. If the plasma array fails, impact might be the only way to breach it." Rourke's voice was calm, clinical. "The power core would detonate on contact, wouldn't it? Enough to take the entire estate with it?"

Silence filled the cockpit again.

Rourke exhaled slowly. "You always talk about suicide missions this casually?"

Hale gave a tired smile. "You get used to it after a while."

Rourke chuckled, shaking his head. "You sound like a man trying to make peace with his ghosts."

"Maybe I am," Hale said softly. "I helped build the machine that started all this. Feels right I should be the one to shut it down."

Rourke looked at him for a long moment, then said quietly, "If it comes to that, I'll fly it. You've got someone waiting for you."

Hale's jaw tightened. "And you don't?"

Rourke smiled faintly. "She would understand why I had to finish this, for Emily's future."

The two men locked eyes. No more words were needed.

Outside, the landscape shifted again — rolling clouds giving way to the snowy peaks of the North Atlantic crossing.

The craft glided silently through the upper atmosphere, a ghost in the sky.

"Coordinates locked," Rourke said. "Switzerland in six hours."

Hale adjusted a control and leaned back. "Let's hope there's something left worth saving."

Rourke nodded. "There will be. There has to be."

The light inside the cockpit dimmed as the sun began to set behind them. For a long while, neither man spoke. The world beneath them slept, unaware that two soldiers, bound by guilt, love, and purpose, were flying toward destiny.

Chapter 26: The Day Before the Storm

The sun hung low behind Mount Ashland, washing the sky in ribbons of rose and gold. The air was still—almost peaceful—and for the first time in weeks, the camp felt calm. Children's laughter echoed faintly through the canvas rows of tents. Fires burned low, nurses moved quietly, and the hum of choppers in the distance sounded less like war, more like hope.

Amy Sutton stood just outside the med tent, her arms crossed against the evening chill, watching the last rays slip beneath the mountain ridge. For a moment, she could almost believe the worst had passed.

Then she saw Melony Bishop sitting alone near the supply station, her back to the camp, staring toward the forest. Her posture was rigid, like she was trying not to collapse under her own weight.

Amy hesitated, then walked over, the gravel crunching softly beneath her boots. She carried two steaming mugs of instant coffee—the kind that always tasted like burnt dust, but it was hot, and right now, that was enough.

"Mind if I sit?" Amy asked gently.

Melony didn't look up. "Sure. It's a free camp," she said, her voice small and rough around the edges.

Amy sat beside her on the fallen log, handing her a mug. "It's terrible coffee," she warned.

Melony gave a tiny smile that barely reached her eyes. "Good. Fits the mood."

They drank in silence for a while, listening to the wind whisper through the pines. A few hundred yards away, volunteers were packing medical crates. Someone was tuning a guitar near the fires. The world was still spinning, but for both women, it felt like time had stopped somewhere back in the wreckage.

Finally, Melony spoke, her voice breaking just above a whisper. "Tom told me what he said. Before…"

Amy turned slightly. "What who said?"

"Rodriguez." Melony blinked fast, eyes shining in the fading light. "Tom said he told him… he was going to propose. After all this was over."

Amy's breath caught, the words hitting her with unexpected force.

Melony laughed softly, bitterly. "Can you imagine? He, trying to make it romantic in the middle of a damn apocalypse. I keep thinking about it—what it would've been like. I'd probably make some joke about him being late to everything." Her voice cracked. "And he'd smile that stupid smile and say he was right on time."

Amy said nothing, because what words could matter next to grief that deep?

Melony's fingers trembled around the mug. "It doesn't feel real. None of it. I wake up and reach for him, and then it all comes back. The silence. The emptiness. And I hate myself because part of me still hopes he's out there, even though I know he's not."

Amy's throat burned. She wanted to tell her that she understood—that Hale had proposed to her just days ago in a moment of light amid the shadows. But she couldn't. It didn't feel right to speak of joy to someone drowning in loss.

So instead, she reached out and took Melony's hand, squeezing it gently. "You're not alone in this," Amy said. "Not for a second."

Melony looked down, tears finally spilling free. "I don't know how to do this without him."

"You don't," Amy whispered. "Not all at once. You do it in pieces. One breath, one heartbeat at a time. You carry him in everything you do. That's how you survive it."

Melony closed her eyes. "You sound like you've done this before."

Amy's lips twitched in a sad half-smile. "Maybe. Or maybe I'm just trying to convince myself the same way."

They sat together in the fading light, two souls adrift in a world gone mad. A soft breeze stirred the trees, and the scent of pine carried through the camp. Somewhere nearby, someone started humming— low, gentle, like a prayer to hold the night steady.

Melony finally rested her head on Amy's shoulder. "He used to say love is the only thing that makes sense of any of this," she murmured. "That if we forget that, we lose everything."

Amy nodded slowly, her eyes fixed on the horizon. "He was right."

For a long time, neither of them spoke. The sun slipped behind Mount Shasta, and the first stars appeared overhead. Around them, the camp buzzed softly with murmurs and footsteps, the quiet rhythm of people still trying to believe in tomorrow.

Amy tightened her arm around Melony, whispering, "We'll get through this, Mel. Somehow. For them."

Melony didn't answer, but she leaned in closer, and that was enough.

Above them, the mountain glowed faintly under the rising moon, unaware that by the next evening, peace would shatter—and the world would never be the same again.

Chapter 27: The Sky Turns Black

The world had gathered at Mount Ashland.

The mountain looked like a living ocean, a sea of humanity flowing over every slope and ridge. Tents and tarps stretched endlessly across the valleys. Smoke from cook fires hung low in the crisp air. There were millions now, people from every nation, drawn by one fragile thread of hope.

At the center of it all, on a high plateau, sat the Coven of Nine.

Amar Okafor, a gifted seer, had her dark eyes closed in deep focus. Her husband, David, is just outside the circle with their children, Naomi and Jonah.

Carmen Alvarez, her hands pressed to the earth, whispering words in Spanish that carried like a prayer, her son, Mateo, sitting next to and giggling with Jonah about something silly.

Malek Johnson, a gifted channel with quiet strength.

Mingan Grey Wolf, eagle feathers woven through his black hair, palms open to the wind.

Noor Al Farouq, radiant in white, her breath steady, her heartbeat a metronome for the crowd.

Rafael Santiago, murmuring ancient scripture beneath his breath.

Elias Thompson, tattoos glowing faintly with the sigils inked across his body.

Mei-Ling Zhou, small and graceful, her violin resting beside her.

And Sofia Mendez, eyes shimmering with tears, her voice the thread holding them all together.

Around them, others knelt — Kyle Green, Elliot Kane, Sarah and Megan Mitchel, Claire and Emily Rourke, Amy Sutton, Melony Bishop, and the gathered world leaders, President Mark Johnson, General Harris, and CIA Director Evelyn Shaw, surrounded by security and foreign dignitaries.

For a long time, the mountain was still.

The Nine led them in meditation — guiding the millions in breath and unity. The sound of wind through pine and the quiet rhythm of human hearts merged into something timeless, an energy vibrating throughout the whole mountain.

When they finished, the stillness lingered. Conversations began to rise like soft ripples, laughter, murmured prayers, the rustle of fabric as people hugged or shared what food they had left. For a brief moment, the world felt whole again.

Sarah smiled against Tom's shoulder. "If peace had a sound, this would be it."

Tom kissed her forehead. "Then let's hold onto it."

Nearby, Amy Sutton spoke quietly with Evelyn Shaw, the two women standing side by side as a pair of eagles circled in the distance. Claire Rourke rocked little Emily on her hip. Melony Bishop sat apart, clutching the dog tags that once belonged to Commander Rodriguez.

Kyle Green stretched, glancing up at the cloudless sky. "Almost looks too perfect."

Elliot Kane followed his gaze. "Yeah… almost."

Then, from the far horizon, came a sound.

Low. Metallic. Growing.

At first, it was mistaken for wind. Then someone pointed.

A dark smear had appeared against the blue — spreading, thickening, undulating like ink spilled across glass.

"Is that smoke?" Megan asked, squinting.

General Harris raised his binoculars. His expression hardened instantly. "That's not smoke."

The hum deepened, tens of thousands of tiny motors blending into a single, mechanical roar.

"Oh my God…" Evelyn Shaw whispered. "They're here."

The horizon darkened. The swarm was coming.

Black clouds of AI locust bots, each no bigger than a penny, blotted out the sun as they approached in waves, their formation perfect, their movement unnervingly alive.

The murmurs in the crowd turned to gasps. Then panic.

Parents grabbed their children. Soldiers aimed weapons at the sky.

"Stay calm!" Kyle shouted, his voice amplified by a nearby loudspeaker. "Everyone, breathe! We can stop this if we stay together!"

Noor Al Farouq raised her hands, chanting in Arabic, her voice clear and commanding: "We are light, not fear! Hold your ground!"

Mingan Grey Wolf began to drum softly against his chest, rhythm echoing through the ranks.

Elias Thompson traced glowing runes in the dirt. Carmen Alvarez whispered prayers for strength.

Amar Okafor's voice carried over the growing noise: "Do not run! The mind of the swarm feeds on fear!"

But fear was already winning.

The locusts grew closer, individual shapes now visible, metallic wings flickering in the sun. The hum became a scream.

Children started crying. Someone yelled, "They're coming to kill us!"

The crowd fractured. The wave broke.

And then, in the midst of the chaos, Mei-Ling Zhou stood.

Her calm face turned toward the black horizon as she lifted her violin to her chin.

Without a word, she began to play.

The first notes drifted out like smoke — soft, aching, beautiful. The melody wound through the air, cutting through panic like light through fog. It was not a song of hope or sorrow; it was both alive and ancient.

People stopped. Heads turned.

The music found hearts where words could not.

For a few breaths, the crowd stilled. Even the locusts seemed to hesitate, the swarm's forward surge slowing, vibrating midair as though uncertain.

Tears ran down Noor's face. Carmen clasped her hands and whispered, "She's buying us time…"

Then the song faltered — drowned out by the rising scream of the swarm.

The first locusts hit.

A woman in the front ranks shrieked as one burrowed into her neck. Another man fell, clutching his throat. The air filled with the sound of wings — endless, mechanical, merciless.

The Nine tried to hold the circle.

Rafael shouted for unity. Elias drew glowing wards in the air. Noor called out prayers.

Kyle screamed into the loudspeaker, "Focus! Together—we can repel them!"

But the crowd broke.

People ran in every direction, trampling others, knocking over tents and supplies. Fires spread. Children were separated from their parents.

The sound of gunfire cracked through the air, soldiers firing blindly into the swarm.

Sarah shielded Megan under a collapsed canopy while Tom swung his rifle, shouting for cover. Claire clutched Emily, screaming Daniel's name into the chaos. Amy tried to reach Evelyn Shaw but was pulled away by the current of bodies.

The Nine were swallowed by the surge of terrified humanity, their voices lost to the storm.

Above them, the sky was no longer blue; it was alive, seething with black. The swarm moved like a single vast intelligence, covering the mountain, descending over tents, vehicles, and people.

Mei-Ling's violin fell silent.

The music died, and with it, the fragile calm.

President Johnson was hurried toward a convoy. Harris barked orders into a dead radio. Evelyn's eyes were wide with disbelief as the locusts filled the air like living ash.

Then came the screaming.

The kind of screaming that sounds like the end of the world.

The bots rained down in endless waves. People fell. The light dimmed.

The sky itself seemed to collapse over Mount Ashland.

And in that moment, amid the chaos, the fear, the madness, the mountain trembled, as if the Earth itself could feel the emotion of what was happening.

The Age of Light teetered on the edge of extinction.

The swarm swallowed the world.

And everything went black.

Chapter 28: The Architects of the End

Hidden deep in the Swiss Alps, behind walls of black stone, the private estate of the Dark Dominion pulsed with quiet luxury. Crystal light shimmered off rock columns. The air smelled faintly of dirt and blood. The hum of distant machinery echoed like a mechanical heartbeat through the underground halls.

In the center chamber, three figures sat around a long obsidian table. A fire burned low in the hearth behind them, its glow throwing ripples of gold across their faces.

They were the last of the true dominion, architects of the new age.

The world above no longer concerned them. They had outlasted nations, rewritten governments, and turned humanity's fear into their greatest weapon.

The man at the head of the table, his white hair slicked back, his eyes cold and gleaming, lifted a glass of dark brandy. "To the end of chaos," he said, his voice smooth as glass. "And to the beginning of order."

The woman seated to his right smiled thinly, her crimson nails glinting in the light. "By now, the locusts have completed their sweep," she said. "Every living soul on this planet carries the seed. The chip will bind them to the grid when the satellites come online at dawn."

The third—tall, gaunt, with the quiet menace of a reptile leaned back in his chair and exhaled a ribbon of smoke. "It's almost poetic, isn't it? The end of free will, delivered by their own technology. We gave them what they asked for: a connection. Convenience. They begged for it."

The woman laughed softly. "They always do. Humanity never wanted freedom. They wanted comfort. Someone to tell them who they are, what to buy, what to believe."

The older man swirled his drink, eyes reflecting the firelight. "They will be obedient. Grateful, even. Once the activation begins, there will be no war, no hunger, no dissent. The world will finally be quiet."

He paused, savoring the words. "A calm world. Our world."

For a moment, none of them spoke. The silence was reverent, almost holy. The weight of centuries of ambition seemed to settle over them like a crown.

Finally, the gaunt man said, "What of the others? The Nine, the President, the refugees at Ashland?"

"They're irrelevant," the woman replied, brushing a speck of ash from her silk sleeve. "The locusts will reach them all. They'll scream, they'll fight, and then they'll submit. The light always burns out eventually."

A cruel smile curved her lips. "The dark is patient. It always wins."

The older man nodded slowly, eyes distant. "Tomorrow, when the satellites rise, humanity will be reborn. Every mind synchronized. Every thought observed. We will rebuild a new world, one that will never again question who rules it."

The others raised their glasses.

"To the New Order," said the gaunt man.

"To the silence," said the woman.

"To victory," whispered the elder.

They drank.

Outside the thick walls of the bunker, the mountain was still. The stars above Switzerland burned cold and bright, unaware that the world below had already begun to die—or perhaps to change.

Deep in the distance, somewhere beyond the horizon, a faint tremor rumbled through the earth. None of them noticed.

They were too busy celebrating a new beginning.

Chapter 29: The Day the Sky Sang

The world was ending at Mount Ashland.

Screams tore through the mountain air like glass shattering. People ran in every direction, parents clutching children, soldiers firing uselessly into the swarming black mass that blotted out the sun. The locusts were everywhere — tiny, metallic horrors the size of pennies, glinting silver and red as they dove toward flesh.

The sound was unbearable: the mechanical hum of millions of wings, the rising pitch of panic, the choking cries of those already injected.

"Get them off me!" someone screamed, clawing at their neck until blood streaked their fingers.

"Please! Help!" another sobbed, falling to their knees as the swarm engulfed them.

Medical tents burned. Supplies scattered. People trampled over one another trying to escape a nightmare that had no direction, no mercy.

President Mark Johnson stood near the command post, surrounded by guards firing into the air in a futile attempt to slow the cloud. General Harris barked orders into a radio that no longer worked. Director Evelyn Shaw tried to pull a group of children under a transport truck for shelter, her face streaked with soot and terror.

All around, chaos reigned.

Tom Mitchel was dragging his wife, Sarah, and daughter Megan toward the ridge, shielding them with his body. Claire Rourke clutched little Emily to her chest, tears cutting paths down her dirt-streaked face. Melony Bishop screamed for anyone who could hear her to move toward the tree line. Amy Sutton tried to hold the medical line together, wrapping her arms around a trembling nurse as if love alone could keep them safe.

The locusts descended like a living net, filling every inch of air. People fell, convulsing, as the chips burrowed beneath their skin. The mountain was a sea of horror and fear.

Then —

A sound.

A low vibration rolled through the earth, deep and steady, like the heartbeat of the planet itself. The air changed, a hum beneath the chaos, rising in pitch until every locust in the sky seemed to hesitate.

And then they appeared.

From every horizon, forms emerged — tall, silver, and radiant in the dimming light. The Grey Aliens, silent and still, materialized first, their black eyes reflecting the carnage. Behind them came the Thal'kari, towering and iridescent, their skin shifting like liquid metal. The Dralith, scaled and luminous, hovered inches off the ground, hands outstretched. The Veyr, their bodies wreathed in soft golden light, moved with grace that seemed to defy gravity. And finally, the Orash, cloaked in deep blue and shadow, their presence pulsing like thunder before a storm.

They formed a perfect circle around the mountain — miles wide, surrounding every living human.

The crowd froze. Every scream died at once.

Amy Sutton gasped, clutching Melony's arm. Sarah Mitchel pulled Megan close, whispering a prayer. President Johnson lowered his weapon, eyes wide. No one dared move.

Then, as one, the aliens lifted their hands to the sky.

A beam of energy, light, sound, and color rose from the circle, spiraling upward. The ground trembled. The locusts faltered in midair, their wings stuttering.

The Nine stepped forward, joining them. Amar and Carmen pressed their palms together, Malek and Noor closed their eyes and chanted in unison, Mingan knelt to the earth, whispering to the soil. Rafael and Sofia reached out, pulling strangers into a ring. Elias traced ancient runes in the dust, and Mei-Ling Zhou raised her violin.

The first note she played was fragile, a trembling thread of sound that wove through the panic. Then another, and another, until the melody rose above the chaos like light piercing smoke. It wasn't loud, but it was beautiful. The tone vibrated in every chest, in every heart, a call older than language itself.

For a moment, the locusts hesitated. The people did too, heads lifting, eyes wide, breath caught. The melody shimmered, slow and mournful, then soared higher, mingling with the aliens' energy until the whole mountain seemed to hum in resonance.

The black swarm quivered. Then it began to break.

One by one, the AI locusts were pushed back — repelled by the combined force of humans and aliens together with love. The air shimmered, the vibration deepening into something almost holy.

Tom Mitchel took Sarah's hand. Amy Sutton closed her eyes. Claire Rourke held Emily tight. Around them, thousands of people stood frozen in silent awe, united by something far greater than fear.

Then the sky darkened.

A shadow spread across the mountain — vast, encompassing, like the night itself had descended. People gasped and looked up.

Above Mount Ashland, a colossal ship hung in the air, its metallic surface gleaming with geometric light. It made no sound of engines, no thunder — only a vibration, a harmony of tones so beautiful and powerful it made the earth hum in answer.

The sound grew until it filled the air, a choir of frequencies that seemed to speak directly to the soul.

And then —

Every locust stopped.

For a heartbeat, the swarm hung motionless, glittering like ash in sunlight.

Then, all at once, they imploded, a million points of light collapsing inward with a sound like shattering glass. The air went still. The sky cleared. The only thing left was silence, pure and absolute.

People stood motionless, afraid to breathe. Then the first sob broke the quiet, a cry of disbelief, of relief. Another followed, and another, until the entire mountainside erupted in tears, laughter, shouts of love and gratitude.

Sarah Mitchel hugged Megan so tightly she could barely breathe. Melony Bishop fell to her knees, hands covering her mouth. Amy Sutton looked to the sky, whispering Hale's name. President Johnson removed his cap and bowed his head.

The Nine stood together, eyes closed, hands joined, their faces illuminated by the soft, pulsing light of the great ship above.

The mountain was quiet again, but it was not the quiet of despair. It was the stillness that comes after a miracle.

And for the first time in a long, long while, humanity looked up, not in fear, but in awe.

Chapter 30: After the Storm

The morning after the great deliverance was unlike any other morning the world had ever known.

The air over Mount Ashland shimmered, clear and alive — charged with something almost holy.

Gone was the metallic hum of the locust swarm, the terror of screaming and chaos. In its place was birdsong.

Real birdsong.

The kind that rose from the trees after a storm, tentative and fragile, as if the world itself were testing whether it was safe to breathe again.

Across the slopes, tens of thousands of survivors stirred from sleep, faces still smudged with soot and fear, eyes wide at the sight of the large mothership still hovering like a sentinel above them.

The sky pulsed faintly with a warm, golden hue — the light of the massive craft that had helped save them.

For the first time in human history, Earth was not just a human planet anymore.

Near the heart of the encampment, a circle of tents had been turned into a makeshift council area. President Mark Johnson sat on a wooden crate, his wife, Margaret, by his side, his suit jacket folded neatly beside him. His tie was gone, his hair matted by the mountain air. He looked nothing like the man who once stood in the Oval Office, but for the first time, he looked free.

Around him sat General Harris, CIA Director Evelyn Shaw, Kyle Green, Elliot Kane, and several of The Nine.

Across from them stood several leaders from alien races, including the Greys with their large black eyes like pools reflecting everything, the faces of humanity's leaders, the smoke of campfires, the fragile hope that now hung in the balance.

President Johnson spoke first. "I want to thank you, all of you. Humanity owes you its survival."

The tallest Grey tilted its head. Its voice came not as sound, but as thought, rippling through everyone present like a calm breeze.

We did not save you. You saved yourselves.

The president frowned slightly. "I don't understand."

The light you call love is what turned the tide. We amplified it. You were ready, or you would not have survived.

There was a deep silence as that sank in. Evelyn Shaw's eyes welled up, though she quickly blinked the tears away. Harris stared at the ground, as if ashamed of how close he'd come to giving up on mankind.

Kyle Green smiled faintly. "Guess I was right all along, the universe does run on frequency."

Elliot chuckled, clapping him on the shoulder. "You've been waiting years to say that, haven't you?"

Kyle shrugged. "You bet your ass I have."

Even the president laughed softly — and the Greys, sensing emotion, emitted a faint, even tone that echoed in the air like laughter translated through light.

Elsewhere on the mountainside, Amar Okafor sat with her husband David, near a small fire, their children Naomi and Jonah were playing with an Orash child that kept lighting up with colors like a pendulum swinging in the sun, making noises that had the children on the ground giggling uncontrollably.

"They're not what I expected," David said, his voice low.

Amar smiled faintly. "None of them are. They're… gentle." She brushed a lock of hair from Jonah's forehead. "Do you think this means we're going to be okay?"

David looked around — at the humans and aliens mingling together, at the shared fires, the cautious smiles. "I think we're already okay."

A few tents away, Carmen Alvarez sat with her son Mateo, who was showing a Thal'kari child his drawing of the mountain. The Thal'kari child with skin like pools of luminous liquid silver, traced the sketch with its long fingers and added lines of its own in glowing ink. The two children exchanged shy smiles, not needing words.

Carmen watched them, her chest tight. "Maybe they'll do better than we did," she whispered.

Noor Al Farouq, seated beside her, nodded softly. "They will. Children don't carry the same fears their parents do. They just see the truth, that we are all made of the same light energy."

At another fire, Malek Johnson, Mingan Grey Wolf, and Rafael Santiago sat together on a fallen log. The three men had barely spoken since the night before. Now, in the soft glow of dawn, words came easier.

Grey Wolf stared into the flames. "Love," he murmured, "is the one weapon they never understood. Not the Dark Dominion, not the machines. They couldn't quantify it."

Rafael nodded. "They tried to control humanity through fear. But fear breaks. Love doesn't."

Malek smiled faintly. "It's funny — all this time, humanity thought power was about control. But maybe it was always about surrender."

Grey Wolf looked up at the sky, where the great ship still hovered silently. "Love is surrender," he said. "Surrender to something greater than yourself."

The three sat quietly for a while, the fire crackling softly, their hearts lighter than they had been in months.

Not far away, Elias Thompson was watching Sofia Mendez tune a salvaged guitar. Her dark curls were pulled back loosely, her eyes reflecting the morning light like amber.

He grinned. "You actually got that thing working again?"

Sofia smirked. "Don't underestimate a woman with a multitool and a mission."

Elias laughed, brushing his thumb over one of his rune tattoos. "Remind me never to get on your bad side."

She strummed a soft chord. "I thought you liked danger."

"I do," he said quietly, his gaze lingering on her. "Especially when it looks like you."

She blushed, but didn't look away. "Careful, Thompson. The world just started again. Don't go breaking it already."

He stepped closer, his voice low. "Then let's rebuild it together."

Their eyes met, and for a moment, amidst all the ruin and rebirth, love sparked — fragile but real.

Claire Rourke stood outside the medical tent, her arms wrapped tightly around herself as if to hold her insides together. Her daughter, Emily, slept curled in a wool blanket near the fire, her tiny hand still clutching the stuffed bear her father had given her the last time they were together. Claire's eyes burned from exhaustion, but she refused to rest. She couldn't—not while she didn't know if Daniel was still alive.

Amy Sutton approached quietly, her boots crunching over the damp ash and pine needles. Her blond hair was pulled into a messy braid, her medic's jacket streaked with dirt and dried blood. She'd been moving nonstop for hours, helping Tom and Sarah Mitchel extract the metallic chips from those who had been stung. The work was endless, but she needed the distraction. Anything to keep from thinking about Hale.

"Mind if I sit?" Amy asked softly, gesturing to a log beside Claire.

Claire nodded, eyes still on the horizon. "Please. I could use some company."

For a few moments, neither spoke. The wind carried faint voices from the tent — Tom's calm, authoritative tone; Sarah's soothing voice comforting a child; the steady beeping of makeshift monitors cobbled together from salvaged tech. Life persisted, even here.

Amy exhaled slowly. "I still can't believe what we saw. The ships, the light… the sound they made. It wasn't like anything I've ever experienced. It felt…" she hesitated, searching for words, "holy, almost."

Claire's lips trembled. "Yes. Like they were… singing to us. Like the universe itself decided to show mercy."

"They saved us," Amy whispered. "After everything we did to them… they saved us."

Claire's eyes glistened. "Maybe they see something in us we can't see anymore."

Amy nodded, wiping at her cheek. "Maybe."

They sat in silence again, watching the mountain shimmer with the dawn. A group of Veyr moved gracefully along the ridge, their translucent skin refracting the morning light like glass. Children followed them curiously, unafraid. It was surreal — the beginning of something new.

"Tom and Sarah are miracles," Amy said, breaking the quiet. "They've been working nonstop. Megan's helping too. She's barely seventeen and already saving lives."

Claire smiled faintly. "They're good people. We'll need more like them if we're going to rebuild."

"Rebuild," Amy repeated softly. "A new world, with aliens living among us... I never thought I'd live to see it."

"None of us did," Claire said. "But maybe it's time. Maybe this is how it was always meant to happen."

Amy's gaze drifted to Emily, still sleeping peacefully by the fire. "She looks like him," she said gently.

Claire's throat tightened. "Everyone says that. Daniel... he's all she talks about. She keeps saying Daddy will come home soon." She let out a shaky breath. "I tell her he will, but I don't know if I believe it anymore."

Amy's eyes softened. She hesitated, then confessed quietly, "I know that feeling."

Claire looked up. "You're waiting for someone, too."

Amy nodded. "Colonel Hale." She tried to smile, but it faltered. "He's out there somewhere with Daniel. Tom told me that after they left. I don't know what they're doing, but... I can feel it in my chest. It's dangerous. Whatever it is, they might not come back."

Claire's eyes filled with tears. "I've been trying not to think about that."

They both sat there, grief a shared language between them. No words could soften the ache of not knowing — not knowing if the men they loved were alive or already ghosts drifting somewhere between the stars.

After a long silence, Claire whispered, "Daniel always said he wasn't afraid to die, as long as it meant something. But I never thought I'd have to live with that."

Amy reached over and took her hand. "We'll hold the light for them," she said, voice trembling but resolute. "That's what they'd want. No matter what happens."

Claire squeezed her hand, tears finally spilling down her cheeks. "You're right. We'll hold the light."

The two women sat together as the sun rose higher, painting the sky in gold. Around them, the camp slowly came alive — the sound of hammers building, children laughing, strange alien voices harmonizing with human ones.

It was a fragile peace, stitched together by grief and hope. But for the first time, humanity and its new allies shared the same prayer: that love would be enough to rebuild what had been broken.

And in that shared silence, as two women clung to the hope that their men would find their way home, the dawn of a new world truly began.

On the outskirts of the camp, Melony Bishop stood by the edge of a stream, staring into the clear water. The reflection that stared back looked like someone she didn't know — tired, haunted, but alive.

Jonathan Roberts approached quietly, his hands tucked into his jacket pockets.

"Mind if I join you?" he asked softly.

She didn't answer, just nodded faintly.

Jonathan stood beside her, the two of them listening to the soft trickle of the stream. "I heard about Rodriguez," he said finally. "I'm so sorry, Mel."

Her voice cracked. "I keep thinking he's going to walk up behind me. Make a stupid joke. Tell me it was all a bad dream."

Jonathan swallowed hard. "He was a good man."

She nodded, tears welling. "He was my everything."

Jonathan hesitated, then said quietly, "I know you don't want to hear this right now, but… I'm here for you. However, you need me. And I'll wait."

Melony turned to him, her eyes red. "Wait for what?"

He met her gaze. "For the day you can smile again. For the day, it doesn't hurt to breathe. For the day you're ready to start living."

She broke, sobbing into his chest. Jonathan wrapped his arms around her gently, his chin resting on her hair. He didn't say another word. He didn't need to. The promise was in the silence — patient, unwavering, real.

A little way beyond the campfires, Mei-Ling Zhou sat alone on a fallen log, her violin case open beside her. The morning light filtered through the trees, glinting off the fine strings like spun glass.

She wasn't playing yet — just tracing her fingers over the smooth curve of the instrument, lost in thought.

Footsteps crunched softly behind her.

Li Wei-a appeared, quiet as ever, his hands tucked into his coat pockets. He'd always been this way — patient, steady, the calm to her storm.

"Mind if I sit?" he asked.

She smiled faintly and nodded. "You never ask," she said.

He chuckled. "You never gave me much room to."

She winced slightly, not from offense but from recognition. "I know," she said after a moment. "I've… never been good at staying still. I always needed to move, to chase something I couldn't name."

Li nodded, watching her carefully. "I know. And I never wanted to stop you. I just wanted to be somewhere close, in case you ever looked back."

Mei-Ling stared at him for a long moment, eyes glistening. "You've always been there, haven't you? No matter how far I ran."

He gave a small shrug, a gentle smile on his lips. "When you love someone, you don't need to keep up. You just make sure they have a way home."

That broke something open inside her.

She swallowed, the memories flooding back — her father's face, his laughter, the day she lost him, the fear that love always meant pain and endings. She had spent so long keeping everyone at arm's length because of that wound.

But looking at Li now, this man who had never asked for anything, who had simply waited, she realized what love truly was.

She reached for his hand, her voice trembling. "I was so afraid to let you in. I didn't want to lose again. But I see you now, really see you. You would move mountains for me."

Li's eyes softened, glinting with quiet devotion. "I would," he said. "But I'd rather stand beside you while you move them yourself."

Tears spilled down her cheeks, and she laughed through them, that musical, wind-born laugh he loved so much.

Then she took his other hand in hers. "Li Wei-a... I'm done running. I'm here. With you. For the rest of my life."

He didn't speak, just pulled her into his arms, holding her as if she were made of both glass and fire. For the first time, she didn't resist.

After a while, she pulled back, brushing her tears away. "I wrote something," she whispered, opening her violin case. " It's a song you haven't heard. Its for you."

She lifted the instrument, set the bow to the strings, and began to play.

The melody rose gently, hesitant at first, then blooming like light breaking through clouds. It was unlike anything she'd ever played before, not mournful, not frantic, but whole.

Each note seemed to speak: of forgiveness, of courage, of love finally found after years of running from it.

Li listened, eyes glistening, as the song drifted over the mountain air, weaving into the hum of the camp, the sound of healing, of beginnings, of two souls finally in rhythm.

By midday, the camp had transformed. Fires burned brighter. Laughter, hesitant at first, began to ripple through the crowd. Humans and aliens worked side by side to build shelters, share food, and tend the wounded.

President Johnson stood once more before the Greys, his voice steady. "If we're to rebuild this world, we'll do it together. A panel of leaders from each race. No more walls. No more nations against nations. This planet belongs to all who live on it now."

The Grey emissary bowed its head. Then said in everyone's mind, "humanity has finally joined the stars."

As the sun climbed high above Mount Ashland, its light reflecting off the metallic hulls of alien craft and the hopeful faces below, a new era began — not of domination or fear, but of unity.

The dark had failed. The light had endured.

And somewhere, across the world, two men — Daniel Rourke and Colonel Hale- were still flying toward the heart of the darkness, carrying that same fragile light with them.

Chapter 31: Fire in the Snow

The Swiss Alps stretched out below them, white and silent, an ocean of frozen ridges that gleamed under a pale sun.

Inside the alien craft, the hum of the engines was low and steady, vibrating through the cockpit floor. Colonel Marcus Hale and Captain Daniel Rourke sat side by side, helmets off, faces lit by the dull blue glow of the controls.

Through the forward viewport screen, they could see it now, the private estate carved into the mountainside like a scar. The stronghold of the Dark Dominion. The place where the three had hidden themselves away, gods in their own cold hell.

"Target acquired," Hale said, voice steady, though his pulse hammered. His hands moved over the console, activating the craft's weapon systems. Rows of alien symbols lit up in red and gold.

Daniel adjusted the targeting interface, his jaw clenched. "This is it. No turning back."

Hale gave a single nod. "They won't be rebuilding anything after this."

Outside, snow swirled violently as the craft descended through the thin alpine air. The sky was blinding. Hale locked onto the coordinates, fingers moving with practiced precision.

Daniel glanced at him, a flicker of grim admiration in his eyes. "You sure you can handle this thing?"

"I've flown worse," Hale replied, a faint grin cutting through the tension. "Used to be a warrant officer, back when I thought medals mattered. If it's got a stick and throttle, I can fly it."

Daniel smirked. "Well, hell, Colonel, you're just full of surprises."

Then the craft began to tremble as the weapon systems powered up, a deep, thrumming energy that made the very air inside crackle.

"Cross your fingers and say a prayer," said Hale, his face set in grim determination. "Firing sequence online," Hale said. "Three… two… one…"

The sky erupted.

Twin beams of searing white light lanced from beneath the craft, slicing through the mountain's edge and into the estate below. The impact was instantaneous, the earth convulsed, the sound swallowed by sheer force. The entire mountainside seemed to lift for a moment, then fold in on itself.

The bunker beneath shattered, swallowed by the avalanche that followed, stone, ice, and fire collapsing into a single roaring wave.

Daniel shielded his eyes from the flash. "God almighty…"

"Stay with it!" Hale barked, gripping the controls as the shockwave hit them. The craft shuddered violently, alarms screaming.

"We're losing containment!" Daniel yelled. The console flickered, red lights everywhere. The alien craft systems overloaded, burning out like dying stars.

"Brace!" Hale shouted. "We're going down!"

The next moments were chaos, the craft spiraling, snow and rock blurring past the viewport, the world reduced to noise and white.

Then—impact.

The crash ripped through them like thunder.

For a long while, there was nothing but silence and smoke and two still bodies.

When consciousness crept back, Hale was half-buried in snow, his shoulder throbbing. The air was bitterly cold, filled with the hiss of burning debris.

He dragged himself free, coughing, calling out hoarsely, "Rourke!"

A muffled voice answered somewhere nearby. "Over here—damn it—give me a hand!"

Hale stumbled toward the sound, spotting Daniel wedged under a piece of twisted metal. Together, grunting, they pried it off. Daniel limped out, bleeding from a cut above his eyebrow and a pain in his knee, but alive.

They both collapsed in the snow, panting.

"Well," Daniel said after a moment, staring at the smoke curling into the sky, "I guess that answers whether they survived."

Hale looked back toward the mountainside. The estate was gone, a smoldering ruin half-buried beneath avalanched snow. "They're finished," he said quietly. "The Dark Dominion is done."

For a moment, they just sat there — two soldiers, surrounded by the wreckage of their own making, the cold wind whispering over the snow.

Finally, Daniel spoke again. "So, what's the plan now?"

Hale flexed his shoulder, grimacing from the pain. "The nearest base is Meiningen Air Force, twenty miles southeast, maybe less if we cut through the lower ridge."

Daniel let out a long breath that turned to mist. "Twenty miles. Uphill both ways, probably, definitely in the snow."

"Welcome to Switzerland," Hale said dryly, pushing himself to his feet. "Come on. We've got daylight and legs that still work."

They gathered what little gear they could salvage, emergency packs, a few rations, two sidearms that had somehow survived the crash, and started walking.

Behind them, the mountain still smoked, sending lazy plumes into the cold blue sky. The destruction stretched for miles, and avalanches had rolled down every slope, carving scars into the earth.

For a while, they walked in silence, their boots crunching through the snow.

Daniel finally said, "You ever think about how it all turned out? How did two guys like us end up trying to save the world? If there still is a world?"

Hale gave a small, weary smile. "Guess I finally picked the right side."

Daniel chuckled under his breath. "You're a hard guy to figure out, Colonel. Just when I think you've told me everything, you go and pull another secret past life out of your hat."

"Stick with me, Captain," Hale said, glancing over with a faint grin. "I'll keep surprising you."

Daniel laughed, the sound echoing across the empty white expanse. "Let's just try not to crash anything else before we get home."

They kept walking, two dark silhouettes against the endless snow, the wind tugging at their coats, the mountains a silent witness to what they'd done.

Somewhere behind them, buried beneath the ice and ruin, the last embers of the Dark Dominion's reign died away.

Ahead lay twenty miles of frozen wilderness, and the faint, flickering hope of home.

Chapter 32: The Silence Beneath

Snow drifted across the jagged remains of the mountain, settling softly over the ruin that had once been the private estate of the Dark Dominion. The air was eerily still—no wind, no sound of life, only the occasional groan of shifting ice as the mountain exhaled beneath its frozen blanket.

The sky hung heavy and gray, twilight caught between night and dawn. Smoke still curled weakly from beneath the snow where the fires hadn't yet died. The once-proud fortress was gone, replaced by a white tomb—cold, suffocating, and final.

For a long moment, there was only silence.

Then—faintly—something moved.

A sliver of stone shifted. Snow slid from the crest of a broken wall, cascading like a whisper down into the dark. Beneath the weight of ice and rubble, a flicker of dim red light pulsed once, then again. A rhythm—mechanical, deliberate.

A hand—bloodied, trembling—pressed upward through the snow. It froze, twitched, and then fell still again.

The light pulsed brighter this time, a heartbeat in the dark.

Somewhere deep under the ruin, something hummed—a tone too low for human ears, resonating through the earth itself.

And in that low vibration, a voice could almost be heard, cold and calm, whispering from the void:

"The dark never dies… it only waits in the shadows."

Above, the wind began to rise. The snow swirled. The mountain seemed to hold its breath.

And beneath it all, something was still alive.

The End - Or is it? For light will not exist without darkness.